Kathy Morgan lives in Wiltshire with her partner who is an antiques dealer, and a variety of animals. Kathy chose to train as a librarian when she left school, she reasoned she could enjoy her love of books and have time to ride horses! She worked in a number of public and school libraries, before joining the antiques trade over fifteen years ago.

The Bronze Lady is Kathy's second book; the first is The Limner's Art.

Readers' comments for The Limner's Art

'Well you made a reader out of me. Not just a reader but someone who had to pick up your book every day to discover who was who, who they were related to or was having a relationship with.
A reader that got excited and smiled or said out loud 'what'!
And a reader that realised she was coming to the end of the book, and who wanted to get to the end to see what happened, but didn't want to get to the end because she didn't want it to end.
OMG well done.'
- Linda H.

'Thoroughly enjoyed it, easy to read and I didn't want to put it down. Well done Kathy.'
- Lydia C-L.

'Within a few pages I was hooked! I loved the flow of the book and all the images of the characters I now have in my head.
I highly recommend this.'
- Jacqui G.

Dear Rachael –
Relax with this book!
love Katherine

The
Bronze Lady

by Kathy Morgan

Kathy Morgan's
Woodford Antiques Mystery series

The Limner's Art
The Bronze Lady

Copyright June 2016 Stormybracken Publishing Kathy Morgan.

Printed by CreateSpace.

1st edition

A CIP catalogue record for this title is available from the British Library.

In loving memory of Storm.

Acknowledgements

Thank you Bob, for allowing me to wake you up in the early hours of the morning (well, seven o'clock onwards usually, Bob doesn't 'do' early) so I can read sections of this book out to you.

My mum and dad who have been generous in their support, thank you.

Special thanks to Fiona, Janet, Jeannette, Kate, Lydia, Nova, Steve and Zaria.

Thank you to all my antiques, equestrian and zumba pals who have been so enthusiastic, and provided me with inspiration and motivation.

All plot errors and typos are my own!

Chapter 1

Thursday 19th November 2015, 9.00pm

The town of Woodford is situated on a hill in the county of Brackenshire in the south west of England, and overlooks a number of villages to the west and the east, but the town was enveloped in freezing fog that November evening so nobody could see further than a few yards in front of them. The weather was even preventing the light of the half-moon from penetrating the darkness of the evening. The exterior lights of the local public house, The Ship Inn at the top of the high street, shone strongly through the gloom, providing a welcoming invitation for locals and visitors alike.

This evening was busy as usual for the landlords Mike and Sarah Handley, who had bought the freehold to the pub ten years earlier and established a comfortable environment with excellent food. By nine o'clock most of the meals had been eaten, and the drinkers were long gone, so there were probably only about a dozen customers left in the pub, scattered throughout its various rooms. The atmosphere in one corner of the bar was at odds with rest of the pub, and was more in harmony with the outside temperature because it had been distinctly chilly all evening, and even the brightly burning log fire could not permeate the heavy pressure of an unresolved disagreement between the friends who were sat around one of the tables. Paul Black and Tony Cookson were barely speaking to each other, but neither would tell the third member of their group, Cliff Williamson, what the discord was all about. Instead they were either morosely looking into their pints, or staring off into the distance; neither one was prepared to make light-hearted chit-chat with the other.

Cliff Williamson was in need of his friends at the moment after a trying few months in which he had come very close to losing his business, had destroyed his marriage and ruptured his comfortable family life. He had lost the respect of many family members, friends and work colleagues. As well as being friends, all three men worked in the local antiques trade, and so Cliff felt that Paul and Tony's support was crucial if he was to climb up to his former position of prominent local business person. In the past week he had begun to venture back out into the local community after a self-enforced period of withdrawal, and tonight he was upset that his friends, who had been such strong providers of help to him, were clearly at odds with each other and not enjoying a pleasant evening of their usual banter over a couple of pints. Cliff was keen to try to return to his familiar social life as quickly as possible, and wanted to give back some of the goodwill and support to them, so decided it was up to him to be the grown-up and make them sort out whatever the problem was between them.

'Right, come on then you two, you are not in the playground now, we all grew out of this kind of behaviour thirty or forty years ago! On the contrary you are meant to be helping me get my life back on track but neither of you has said a word all evening. What is going on?'

'Sorry mate,' said Paul, snapping out of his inner-fury. 'You are right, we should be thinking of you. We have had a disagreement over something, but it's nothing, and it's over. Isn't that right Tony?' Cliff noticed the slight pleading tone in Paul's question.

'Oh, er, yes that's right. Just a silly tiff between us; a stupid mis-understanding. Paul got the wrong idea about something, that's all. I am sure he can see things clearly now and realises the error of his ways.'

Cliff noticed Paul bristle at Tony's choice of words, and sighed. Whatever their problem was it wouldn't be resolved if Tony was going to start baiting Paul.

'Hey, this has nothing to do with me, don't you blame me for all this. I wouldn't call it silly or stupid,' Paul said with a flash of anger. 'It is looking fairly serious from my side of the table.'

'Yes, and from my side,' Tony's temper was rising too and Cliff wondered if they were going to start punching each other. Neither of his friends were inclined to resort to fisticuffs over anything, but the aggression in the air was palpable. He regretted pushing them.

'Everything OK over there lads?' Mike Handley, the landlord of The Ship Inn, called over from behind the bar. He had noticed something was amiss with the group earlier in the evening and was keeping an eye on them. He had seen the look on Paul's face and then Tony's response to it and decided to intervene by making them focus on him, rather than putting himself at risk by walking over and standing between them.

'Alright alright, calm down,' Cliff hissed at them. 'We're fine thanks Mike,' he called over, before turning back to his friends who were now sitting looking slightly shame-faced at being caught posturing like two angry cockerels. He decided to try one last time, now that they knew other people were watching them. 'Just tell me what has happened? I may be able to help.'

'No, Paul's right, it's nothing. Who wants another pint?' said Tony, convincing nobody.

'Oh nothing for me thanks Tony,' said Cliff as he also stood up. 'My body hasn't quite got back into the swing of long sessions in the pub. If you two aren't going to come clean about your tiff then I had better be heading for home or I'll never get up in the morning. Three pints in an evening is plenty and I can already feel the negative effects!'

'Oh, I'll walk back with you,' offered Tony. 'Somebody had better make sure you get back safely now you have turned into a lightweight.' His teasing went a little way to breaking up the tension, as they all laughed at the thought of the tall, fit, well-built Cliff Williamson being unable to hold his drink.

'Oi I'm not that bad! Anyway, I live in the opposite direction to your house, your wife will be waiting for you.'

'No, come on, the walk will do me good, and Lesley isn't expecting me home any time soon. She is working late tonight, and I made a chicken casserole earlier today for her to eat when she came in so she won't be waiting for me. In fact knowing Lesley she will be curled up on the sofa watching some drama, and not missing my 'helpful' comments about the flimsiness of the storyline at all. I'll walk down with you, and then probably make my way home from there. I have been stuck indoors all day, and think I need the exercise. Come on Williamson, get your coat, you've pulled!'

As the two men left the pub laughing, Mike Handley said quietly to Paul 'Are you alright Paul? You have been looking out of sorts all evening.'

Paul sighed and wondered how much to reveal to Mike. He knew Mike could be trusted not to betray a confidence, but after a few seconds of internal debate decided this was too risky to share. 'Yes I'm fine thanks Mike; I just have a complicated situation to sort out. Nothing for anybody else to worry about, but I have let it drag on too long. Time to put an end to this thing once and for all.'

If Paul had known then what it would take to resolve his differences with Tony, he would have confided in Mike Handley while he had the chance.

Chapter 2

Thursday 19th November 2015, 9.15pm

As Mike Handley watched Paul Black leave the pub, his wife, Sarah, nudged him and quietly pointed out another man who was sitting on his own and had been observing the exchanges between the three men. The man wasn't a Regular in the Ship Inn, and neither Mike nor Sarah thought they had seen him in the town before, but it wasn't unusual for lone men, or women, to come to Woodford for business or a holiday and use the pub for their lunchtime or evening meal. Because the man had shown such close interest in the friends' exchanges Mike and Sarah wondered if he was also in the antiques trade and had seen them somewhere before.

Running a business in a town which was so closely involved with the antiques trade, Mike and Sarah Handley had developed a system for describing the various people who came into their pub so they could make provision for when they were likely to be busy with customers attending one of the auctions at Black's, or for when their clientele was predominantly tourists while the antiques season was quieter in the summer. They agreed the man was probably a 'Q'. In their code they divided their customers into the 'Q's who were antiques dealers, and the 'P's who were not. A customer who was a 'Q' was likely to want a quick sandwich washed down with a coffee or an orange juice at lunchtime; a 'P' wanted to savour their lunchtime meal, often using the time to recover from a long walk through the Brackenshire countryside before resuming their route after a pie and a pint. The Ship Inn could be very quiet at lunchtime, but if there was an auction taking place, or during the summer holidays, Mike and Sarah could easily be serving over eighty customers.

Over the years their Regulars had joined in with the game, and further divided the 'Q's group into: antiques dealers they called a divvy; members of the public dabbling in antiques were nicknamed wannabes; and the final group were the profiteers, the people who ran venues for the sale of antiques included auctioneers, market organisers, and shop owners.

Cliff, Tony and Paul were all happy to be classed as 'Q's and put up with the teasing about being called divvys. Antiques Dealers are the Professionals in the business. Tony Cookson was a postcard dealer with an interest in militaria, and he more than the other two lived a typical antiques dealer's life of early morning road trips, driving hundreds if not thousands of miles most weeks, drinking lots of cups of tea or coffee or coca-cola, and he always had a mobile phone very close by. They are usually people who both love antiques and who love to deal. They are generally blinkered to the goings on outside of the antiques world unless it is an international event which somehow affects the gold or silver markets, for example a stock market crash or terrorist attack. Ask an antiques dealer about the Foot and Mouth outbreaks in

Britain fifteen years ago and you will find they are well-informed due to the number of antiques auctions and fairs which were cancelled because the venues, traditionally livestock markets and fields on farmland, were under quarantine restrictions. Similarly the SARS virus outbreak a couple of years later directly affected sales of antiques because of the impact the spread of the infection had on international flights in the days before dealers and auction houses were routinely able to sell their stock via the internet. They rely on each other to stay in business, and it is said that an item of stock will be bought from a member of the public and then pass through at least seven pairs of antiques dealing hands before re-appearing back in public ownership again.

Sarah Handley willingly put herself in the 'Q' group as a wannabe, and wasn't at all offended by the teasing of the Regulars. Sarah had an interest in portrait miniatures, and loved to have a chat over the bar with any of the antiques dealers who had recently bought one, or who wanted to look at an item she had bought. She was knowledgeable about her chosen subject, and if she had been interested in dealing in them rather than purely collecting them, the antiques dealers knew she would be a force to be reckoned with in that field.

Members of the public provide the source for antique items through private sales, house clearances, or auctions, and are also the customers, like Sarah, at the end of the cycle who will buy from antiques shops, fairs or auctions. They will often have gleaned their knowledge of antiques and the antiques trade from television programmes, and it shows, resulting in a sometimes antagonistic relationship with other groups in the antiques trade who resent someone haggling over an extremely well-priced nineteenth century silver spoon as though they were at a car boot sale where everything else is being sold for twenty pence.

This lack of knowledge can also lead to false hope, and one of the hardest jobs in the antiques trade is telling someone that Granny Jones' 'antique sideboard' which has been in the family for generations and everybody can relate fond memories to you about, and from whose sale they are hoping to use the money for a Once in A Lifetime Family Holiday, was actually bought from MFI in the 1980s and is now only fit for firewood. On the other hand one of the most rewarding is being able to reveal that the doorstop which has been in place for as long as Granny Jones' grandson can remember is a Renaissance bronze figure worth more than twenty thousand pounds.

Both Cliff and Paul also fit into the third category, the profiteers, and neither was particularly keen on the occasional teasing from their fellow Regulars about this classification, but both put up with it in the name of good neighbourliness. Cliff Williamson established Williamson Antiques nineteen years ago, and his friend Paul Black worked in the auction house his own father set up before taking over as manager five years earlier. They both lived in the town of Woodford, and Black's Auctions was situated at the other end of Woodford High Street to the antiques centre.

The people who own antiques auction houses, shops and centres usually have a history in antiques dealing but have tried to opt for the relative security and comfort of bricks and mortar in which to run their business, as opposed to the ramshackle arrangements most antiques dealers work within of sheds, garages and market stalls. It is usually this group of people who are only in it to make money out of the antiques trade, as opposed to the antiques dealers who live and breathe antiques; and the public who treasure and are often in awe of the items. Within this group antiques market organisers also fit, although these days they rarely have a background in the antiques trade and forget that it is the antiques dealers who pay them to sell their stock at the event who are their customers, not the members of the public who only come through the turnstiles because of the quantity and quality of goods available inside. Auctioneers and market organisers are commonly mistrusted by antiques dealers and members of the public alike, and tend to find their own job is very similar to herding cats.

It is unusual to have three people from different sections of the antiques trade to form as close a bond as Tony, Cliff and Paul. Antiques dealers, shop owners, and auctioneers do not tend to mix well; they all mistrust each other, and people they regularly deal with may be suspicious of any particularly close friendships which develop between them. The antiques dealers think the auctioneers are ignorant and sneer at their mistakes; the auctioneers believe every antiques dealer is ringing their auction and reducing their commission; and the antiques centre owners and the antiques dealers who rent shop space from them are often in direct competition with each other.

Tony, Cliff and Paul put aside their differences many years before, and managed to go about their daily business comfortably without stepping on each other's toes. The three of them often worked and socialised together, and could regularly be found drinking tea in the Woodford Tearooms or pints in their local pub. Mike and Sarah Handley had a lot of time for the three men, and not just because they were very good customers in their pub. All three were both hard-working and friendly members of the local community. As people began to head home, and the couple started their routine of cleaning up and wiping down prior to closing for the night, they entertained themselves by trying to guess what the cause for the disagreement between Paul and Tony could be.

By the time the pub was empty of customers, the last embers in the fireplace were safely enclosed by the pub's ornate fireguard, and the glasses, cups, plates and cutlery had all been stacked in the dishwasher which was now noisily whirring and splashing, they were no closer to an answer, but agreed that they hoped whatever had caused the obvious discord this evening would be easily and quickly resolved.

Chapter 3

Friday 20th November 2015, 10.00am

'Good morning Boss!' Rebecca Williamson, Cliff's estranged wife, looked up as Paul Black walked into the auction house and loudly greeted his employee. She had been concentrating on checking for new payments into the online bank account from a previous sale and took the opportunity of Paul's arrival to push her chair slightly away from the desk and sit up straighter, rolling her shoulders as she did.

'Morning Paul,' she laughed. 'Does that mean you are making the tea, if I am The Boss?'

'Oh alright then!' he faked a moody stance, hunching his shoulders and swinging his arms as he stomped over to the kettle, turning to look at her with his bottom lip pushed out.

Rebecca laughed again 'My grandmother used to say she could fry bacon on a lip like that!'

She had known Paul for a long time, and viewed him to be like a younger brother, even though he was older than her. Nevertheless, she had been concerned about returning to work at Black's Auctions after an eighteen year 'maternity break' for several different reasons. When she gave birth to her first child, Nicholas, she was fortunate to be in a situation which enabled her to stay at home with her baby, and as the years went by and two more children completed their family neither she nor Cliff felt there was a need for her to return to paid employment. But eighteen years later circumstances had changed and she and Cliff were separated; their children were becoming increasingly independent of their parents; and Rebecca now found herself in the position of delving deep into her reserves of inner-strength to step back into the world of employment.

Her reservations about returning to work at Black's Auctions were not just because she had self-doubts about her own workplace abilities, but also because she knew Paul was likely to make life awkward by trying to sleep with her despite, or maybe because, her soon-to-be-ex-husband was his best friend. Within her first week back at work he had made a subtle attempt to seduce her, which if she hadn't known him for over eighteen years and been friends with one of his ex-wives probably would have been successful. It had been years since anyone had made her feel so desirable and the revelations a few weeks before about her husband's behaviour throughout their marriage had thoroughly shaken her, but Rebecca still had enough self-respect and perspective on the situation to kick Paul into touch on that first attempt. Since then he had adopted a lightly flirtatious attitude, which she enjoyed, and the pair of them had very quickly found a healthy workplace rhythm which suited them both.

Paul thought the world of Rebecca. He always had a soft spot for her since they first met when she was nineteen years old, and had been mildly envious of his friend's successful marriage and home life. His own, he freely admitted, had been a disaster with two divorces and a string of affairs and failed relationships. Although originally his intentions had been less than honourable when he offered Rebecca a job, within the first week he had the good sense to see what a fantastic asset she was to his business and altered his personal expectations accordingly.

Black's Auctions was established by Paul's father in the 1980s. He successfully steered the company through the changing times of the antiques trade, his main attribute being willing to move with the times to maintain a profitable business. Although Mr Paul Senior, as he was familiarly known throughout the Trade, officially retired five years ago, in reality Paul had been running the company for the last eight years. He was a hard worker, dedicated to the auction business, and expected his employees to have the same attitude. In Rebecca he saw those attributes he admired, and he appreciated the organisational and diplomatic skills she brought to Black's Auctions which had been lacking in the years since he had been in sole charge. But if she ever gave him the slightest sign that she was interested in him then he would pounce.

'Anything I need to know?' asked Paul, gesturing towards Rebecca's computer where she was sorting through the morning's emails.

'Um, the first one is from Mrs Wheeler, and as always she wants to know when she will be paid from the last sale, so I could send back the usual reply?; Brian Askham wants to know if you can go round and price up his mother's house clearance, you know, the big

Georgian house on the left as you go out towards Brackendon, because she is moving into the nursing home as soon as a place becomes available; and Sarah Handley was asking about the portrait miniature in the job lot due to be in next week's sale, do you have any more information on it? Oh, and there is a voicemail from the Antiques For All film crew. They are coming to film next Friday's sale. That is, two weeks' today.'

'Oh are they? Alright then. Ummh, yes, you can answer Mrs Wheeler, you could probably cut and paste from the last five times she has asked. Oh I know Mrs Askham's house; I should think I will need about three hours there so please sort out a time and date with Brian and put it in my diary. Oh, and tell Sarah she knows more about portrait miniatures than I do!'

'Here you are,' he said as he placed the Best Mum in the World mug Rebecca's children had bought her as a Back To Work present, now full of tea, carefully on her desk. 'I'll be in my office for a while. There is something bothering me about one of the items in next Friday's sale. I need to do some research on it confidentially, so if you can prevent anyone from disturbing me I'd appreciate it. I'll tell you about it when I know something for sure, but just at the moment it is too damaging to someone's reputation to start any unfounded rumours. Don't worry!' he said quickly when he saw the look on her face, recent events involving her estranged husband's affair with a fellow antiques dealer were still too raw for her not to jump to conclusions. 'It is nothing which involves any members of your family! But just tell anyone who asks I am wrestling with the Accounts and do not want to be disturbed.'

'Sure thing tea-boy,' grinned Rebecca with relief, her imagination had started to run away, just as Paul suspected. 'I'll be here all morning, sorting out paperwork, so can act as your doorman and prevent anyone from disturbing you as you count your fingers and your toes.'

Chapter 4

Saturday 21st November 2015, 5.00pm

Rebecca Williamson's mother, Jackie Martin, qualified as a veterinary surgeon, married, and gave birth to two daughters before she was twenty eight years old. By the time she was forty she was a single mum, and had established her own equine veterinary practice. Jackie was rapidly heading towards her sixtieth birthday, and for the past few years had been trying to take a step away from her career so she could spend more time holidaying in Portugal, but the pull to work proved stronger than her desire to relax.

The Woodford Equine Veterinary Practice was a small business, which up until the previous year had worked successfully with a number of veterinary nurses and a solid team of administration staff, and only Jackie Martin and her business partner Alastair Wilkinson in the role of vets. Jackie had officially been a part-time member of the team for the last five years, although her idea of part-time hours would be many people's full-time work. But everything changed when Alastair's wife, Hazel, retired from her teaching career and he decided to follow her lead and retire too, so Jackie had employed a new full-time vet, Peter Isaac. Alastair had a similar work-ethic to Jackie's, and although officially he was retired from the

Practice, he had been happy to keep up his professional qualifications so if ever Jackie needed him to help out, he could. Peter was proving to be a useful asset to the team, and Jackie was again thinking about having another attempt at working part-time.

Her last visit of the day was to a smart-looking yard, but behind the facade was a catalogue of cut corners and sloppy attention to welfare of both horses and staff. The yard owner was a lovely lady who had been a very successful eventer and dressage competitor thirty years ago, but was more likely to be found Happy Hacking her Connemara ponies around the Cornish countryside than over-seeing the competition yard in Brackenshire her husband had left to her in his will when he died two years previously. It was a place Jackie dreaded attending, the issues she witnessed were never serious enough to involve the welfare authorities, and the horses always looked clean and tidy and well fed, but she disliked the constant shouting at staff and horses, the way the horses flinched whenever she went close, and general air of chaos, fear and misery which pervaded the atmosphere.

When the owner's husband was alive the environment was a wonderful combination of relaxed anticipation. The staff appeared to enjoy their work and love the horses, and the horses seemed to respond calmly and willingly. But when he died the owner could not bear to live there any longer so she employed a new member of staff to take over the management of the yard, and moved to Cornwall.

The yard manager, a bulky woman with short brown hair, was waiting for Jackie to get out of her car, and impatiently fidgeted from one foot to another as Jackie opened the boot and took out her ancient vet bag. Jackie's only patient at the yard that day was a 16.3hh dark brown German Warmblood named Mikey, who was an Advanced dressage horse and heading for the Area finals in a couple of months' time. He had been to a competition the previous weekend but his performance there was poor, and, as the two women walked towards the barn housing the internal stables where the horse was kept, the yard manager was telling Jackie that he had seemed disinterested in everything all week and was standing at the back of his stable every day. So why didn't you call me four days ago, thought Jackie. As they entered the building and turned towards the patient the yard manager revealed his owner was coming up for a lesson on him the following day, which answered her unasked question.

As she began her assessment of Mikey, Jackie was thinking evil thoughts about the yard manager and her decision to leave a clearly unhappy horse for seven days without veterinary assistance. It wasn't as though she, or even the yard, would be paying the vet bills as those were always paid for by the horse's owner. Why on earth do people like this choose to work in an industry they clearly don't enjoy, with the mental and physical welfare of living, breathing, feeling beings within their power, she chuntered to herself. Jackie continued her assessment by warming up the digital thermometer, carefully lifting the horse's tail slightly, and gently inserting the thermometer into his rectum.

The next second she felt the most incredible pains shooting all over her body. It was all happening so fast and seemed to be never-ending, bang bang bang, every inch of her felt as though it was being ferociously battered.

'Ow ow ow ow, ooooohhhh, ow ow ow ow!' finally the onslaught came to an end and Jackie was able to draw enough breath to scream. The pain was incredible, and as she tried to gather her thoughts she realised she was lying on the deep litter bed of a stable floor, headfirst in the corner where she had been kicked repeatedly by the terrified horse.

The yard manager was in shock, and for a few seconds stood stock still as she stared at the figure of the tall slim blond haired vet crumpled in a heap on the floor of the stable. The sound of Jackie's screams snapped the woman out of her frozen state and she immediately reverted to type, and began to shout.

'Oh my god, are you OK? I couldn't hold the twitch when he flung his head up. What can I do? Shall I phone for an ambulance? Where do you hurt?' The yard manager could see lawsuits in her mind's eye and was desperate to make sure Jackie was taken care of as quickly and efficiently as possible, preferably away from the premises. Without waiting for a response she turned her attention elsewhere and continued to shout as she strode towards the opening of the stable which was blocked by the body of a second horse, leaving Jackie injured and vulnerable and still on the floor in the corner of the stable, and the horse who had kicked out at her cowering against the opposite wall.

28

'What the hell are you doing, get that horse out of here!' This last question and instruction was hurled with as much venom as the yard manager could muster at the poor girl groom who had been trying to bring another horse into the stable block.

The girl who was being shouted at had been overwhelmed by the sheer size and power of the beast now filling the yard manager's exit from the stable. The girl had been bringing him in from the field, and he was eager to reach the supper he knew would be waiting for him as soon as possible. As they had been passing the stable containing the horse Jackie was treating, the incomer had seen the invalid's feed bucket and lunged through the open doorway leaving no room for his handler to follow, so she was still outside with only his hind legs, tail, and powerful backside to grab hold of.

Meanwhile the yard manager was stuck inside the stable with the two horses and injured vet. By now the cowering horse had realised he wasn't going to be beaten, and had resumed his furious stance to defend his dinner from being scoffed by another horse, even though he hadn't wanted to eat it a few minutes earlier. The yard manager knew she should have closed the stable door while Jackie was treating the horse inside, and was desperately casting around for someone else to blame. Meanwhile Jackie was still lying on the floor, by now in so much pain she could do no more than moan quietly, and was in extreme danger of being further trampled by eight metal-clad hooves.

Eventually the yard manager managed to push the trespassing horse out and pull the sick horse after her, all the time shouting and swearing at the girl who was clearly out of her depth and did not have the necessary horsemanship skills to manage the situation. Hearing all the noise and commotion, two other grooms appeared and between them the three girls removed both horses from the corridor and secured them safely in stables in another block, before returning to see what they could do to help their employer.

By the time the air ambulance arrived the three grooms had done their best to make Jackie as comfortable as possible by gently lifting and then resting her head on a stable rug, while the yard manager continually berated the unfortunate one who had lost control of her charge. It was clear that Jackie was in a tremendous amount of pain, she couldn't tolerate the weight of a blanket being placed over her to warm her and try to alleviate the shaking of her shocked body, and she seemed to be unable to move herself so the girls left her in the crumpled position she landed in while one of them gently stroked her hand and kept up a running conversation with her.

The paramedics were fantastic, and from the time the yard manager dialled 999 to the time Jackie was safely installed on a trolley in Swanwick Hospital's Accident & Emergency Department a total of thirty seven excruciatingly painful minutes had passed by. It would have taken over fifty minutes just to drive to the hospital, let alone all the time it would have taken the road ambulance to reach the livery yard, and the minutes the paramedics needed to take to assess her condition and compose an emergency treatment plan, before loading her into the ambulance and unloading her at the other end to be taken into the treatment room.

As anyone who has ever been in a hospital on a Saturday night will know the waiting rooms are full of people with alcohol- and conflict-related injuries, but as she had been in an accident with a horse Jackie was fast-tracked through the waiting room and into triage.

Jackie's daughter Rebecca Williamson arrived almost two hours after a nurse telephoned to let her know about her mother's condition, with quite a significant amount of that time had been spent trying to find somewhere to park and being rather shocked at the high parking charges required. By that time Jackie had been x-rayed and was waiting in a curtained cubicle for the Consultant to come and give her the bad news.

'Oh Mum, are you OK? What on earth happened?' At the sound of Rebecca's voice Jackie looked up into her daughter's face, and thought how very beautiful she was.

'First time in thirty six years of Practice I have been hospitalised,' she said.

The Consultant was a smiley friendly chap who informed Jackie in a gentle manner that she had several broken bones including ribs, arm and leg, but no concussion, and nothing which couldn't be mended given rest and time.

After he had gone Rebecca was upset to see that her mum was quietly weeping. Her mum who was always so stoic and practical and vibrant was lying in the hospital bed like a little old lady, looking twenty years older than her fifty nine years.

'Oh Mum,' she said, leaning in to cuddle her and realising she couldn't without hurting her. 'Please don't cry, you'll set me off too. You heard what the doctor said, in another few months all of these breaks will have healed and you will be up and about again doing exactly what you were doing before.'

'I know he said that darling, but I am in so much pain I don't believe him. What am I going to do for the next few months? I can't even brush my teeth!'

'Yes you can, you only have one broken arm. You are resilient, a fighter, and I know you will work out how to handle a toothbrush with your other hand. Once they discharge you I will bring you home with me and we will work out what you need to get better as quickly as possible. What are you going to do about work?'

'Oh I don't know!' she wailed. Her mind was too full of pain to think about anything else.

'Does Peter know what has happened and where you are?'

'I doubt it; I haven't told him have I?' Realising she was being unnecessarily rude to her daughter, who was only trying to help, Jackie took a moment to compose herself and then said, 'please could you ring him and tell him darling? I am meant to be On Call this weekend too, I do hope no one has been trying to get in contact about a horse emergency. If you can't get hold of him, phone Alastair and see if he can help.'

Chapter 5

Saturday 21st November, 8.45pm

When Rebecca telephoned Peter Isaac, Jackie's junior colleague, to pass on her mother's instructions, Peter and his fiancé, Gemma Bartlett, had just finished their evening meal, and Peter was settling down on the sofa to mindlessly watch television. As soon as Rebecca told him where she was phoning from and why he stood up and began to pace, continually running his free hand through his hair in time with his footfalls.

'Right, right, yes, OK, thanks for letting me know. I'll switch the phones over now, no need to disturb Alastair. Tell Jackie not to worry about anything here, I'll sort it all out. Oh, wait, Rebecca which ward is she in and is she going to be welcoming visitors tomorrow?' Peter was trying to absorb Rebecca's news whilst simultaneously wondering what he was going to do about filling her vacancy within the next day or so, all the time planning his own short-notice wedding.

'What's happened? Is it Jackie? Is she alright?' Gemma came in with two cups of tea, only catching the tail-end of Peter's conversation with Rebecca.

'Yes and no. Poor Jackie has been flattened by a horse and is in hospital. She's going to be OK, but has several fractures, luckily all below the neck so no head injury, and she isn't paralysed, but she is going to be recovering for several months.'

'Oh no, poor Jackie! She'll go stir-crazy; she is such an energetic woman. I'll give Lisa a ring and see if she can cover for me at the tearooms so I can come with you when you go to see her tomorrow.' Gemma and her sister, Lisa Bartlett, owned the Woodford Tearooms, a popular local business located further down the High Street from The Ship Inn. 'So what does that mean for the Practice? You can't run it on your own.'

'I'm not sure. I'll just give Alastair a ring tomorrow and see if he can help out for a bit.'

'Don't wait until tomorrow; I am sure Alastair would want to know about Jackie's accident tonight.'

Peter then telephoned Alastair Wilkinson, whose retirement earlier in the year had provided the opportunity for Peter to take up his vacated position. Alastair's wife, Hazel, answered the telephone and Alastair was also at home, and happy to step in if Peter needed him to for emergency support until he could find a locum. The two men had a quick planning meeting over the phone, fortunately both were able to access the Practice's appointments system from their home computers, and Alastair also offered to take over all of those allocated to Jackie the following week.

'Oh that is such a relief, what a lovely man.' Peter rubbed his hands over his face as he sank back down onto the sofa and leant back into the cushions. 'I do not know what we would have done if he wasn't able to help out.'

'Why don't you give Jennifer a call?' asked Gemma.

'Jennifer? Yes she may know of someone.'

'Well, I was thinking more of offering your daughter a job. Jackie is going to be out for most of next year isn't she? Jennifer may welcome the opportunity of a change of scene. Go on, ask her!' Peter had two daughters, and Jennifer was the elder at twenty six years old. Peter and their mother, Diana, were now divorced. Peter had moved from Shropshire to Brackenshire the previous year, and met Gemma on the day he came for his interview with Jackie. Jennifer and her sister Alison still lived in Shropshire near their mother, and Jennifer chose a career in veterinary science, while her younger sister trained as a riding instructor.

'Oh I don't know, doesn't sound like the sort of thing my daughter would go for. It would be a big deal for Jennifer to hand in her notice for a temporary position. This Practice is very small compared to what she is used to working in. We don't have the fantastic diagnostic facilities she uses up in Shropshire. And it isn't something I can organise unilaterally, Jackie is the senior partner and she may not approve.'

'I don't think Jackie is going to argue about who you choose to help you to keep her business going for the next few months do you? Why wouldn't she approve of Jennifer?'

'Well, she is still very young, not long qualified. There is no way she could take on Jackie's clients.'

'Maybe, maybe not, but you certainly can. And as you said, Alastair is more than happy to help out if things get tough. Have more faith in your daughter Peter!'

'Hmmh, I'm not sure about me taking on Jackie's clients either. She and I have very different approaches to equine health. I don't think her customers would be too happy about me as her replacement.'

'Oh for goodness sake Peter, who else is there? Some unknown locum or Jennifer? Come on, ask her! She might say no anyway, and then what are your options?'

Chapter 6

Saturday 21st November, 10.00pm

'Uh oh, there goes another poor female heading for heartbreak' commented Mike Handley, as Paul Black and his latest date, a petite red head, walked hand-in-hand out of the door of The Ship Inn.

'Where does he keep finding them? Surely his reputation precedes him throughout the County!' laughed his wife, Sarah.

'Well he is a good looking chap. He oozes charm and constantly pays them attention when he brings them in here. He doesn't stint on the food and drink either. I'd date him,' teased Mike.

'He oozes something, not my idea of a potential partner. I prefer the reliable, cuddly, poverty-stricken type of man,' Sarah said as she gave her husband a big kiss on the cheek.

'Hey, are you saying I am not good looking and charming?' asked Mike.

'No, no not at all! You are the handsomest and most charming man in here!'

'Well that's not saying much' laughed Mike as they looked around at the last few customers, mostly old men hunched over their pints in silence, and one table of about twenty women of various ages who had spent the whole evening talking and laughing from the moment they arrived.

'Those Zumba girls know how to celebrate don't they! Whose birthday is it this time?'

'The one in the middle on the right of the table, it is her fortieth. I think I might give it a go in the New Year,' mused Sarah. 'I need to do something to get motivated to be fit enough to start horse riding again. Nicola and I have been inspired by old Mrs Barker's stories and are going to start riding lessons next Easter, when the weather is warmer and drier.' Nicola Stacey was Sarah's best friend. They had known each other from their school days, and whereas Sarah had moved away from Woodford when she left school and only returned ten years' previously, Nicola moved straight into a job working for Cliff Williamson at Williamson Antiques, and had stayed in the town. Nicola and Sarah had recently been visiting a lady, Mrs Margaret Barker, who used to be a big name in the local hunting scene, and they had enjoyed several afternoons listening to her reminisce while they drank tea out of china cups and saucers instead of their usual chunky mugs, and ate cake. When they were at school Nicola and Sarah used to spend every spare hour at the local riding stables, and Mrs Barker's enthusiasm for the horses she bred and rode was re-awakening that love of horses in Sarah. She continued 'I was going to ask Jackie Martin about where is the best place to book; I'll ask her about Zumba too, she's keen and goes at least twice a week. I am surprised she is not here with this Party.'

'She is probably working,' said Mike. 'For a part-timer she doesn't seem to have much time off. Good to see Lisa Bartlett dating again, I didn't think she would risk it after her previous attempt.'

Mike and Sarah stood quietly for a few moments watching the couple who were deep in conversation over a cafetiere of coffee. Lisa had finally taken the plunge into the world of dating earlier in the year after several years of deliberate singledom following the heart-wrenching collapse of her first marriage. Unfortunately the man she chose to navigate the murky waters, a local antiques dealer named Andrew Dover, proved to be a shark and after weeks of stringing her along was forced to admit he had been focusing his affections elsewhere. Lisa would never have known anything about Andrew's 'other' woman if it hadn't been for Cliff Williamson and Paul Black's intervention one evening in The Ship Inn.

'Who is that chap Lisa is with?' Sarah asked her husband. Mike could usually be relied upon to know a detailed history of most of the people who came into his pub.

'I don't know, I am not sure if I have seen him before. Let's hope he isn't two-timing her like the last one did. That day when she found out in here what he had been doing was one of the most upsetting in my history as a landlord. I can still remember the look on her face when Cliff and Paul told her, and it brings tears to my eyes.'

'Aw you are a soppy old thing,' said Sarah as she gave her husband a hug. 'But Andrew wasn't the first man to cheat on her. I think Andrew was the first man she had dated since her marriage broke up, and that ended because her husband had another woman. In fact, I believe he had another family she was unaware of until the truth finally came out. I am amazed she is back on the dating scene so quickly; good for her. Poor girl could do with some good luck in the romance department for a change. At least her sister has found someone decent. Their forthcoming nuptials are going to provide a much-needed boost to this town after all the scandal of recent months.'

'Yes, Peter Isaac is a lovely man isn't he. Works hard though; well, they both do.'

'Like us, we work hard Mike. I'd love to go away in January, somewhere hot. Thailand or somewhere like that. What do you think? We could renew our wedding vows.'

'Oh I'm not sure about going abroad, I like it here. Just the thought of a long plane journey makes me feel anxious so what's the point of spending thousands of pounds on a luxury holiday only to have it all undone on the journey on the way back? We'd be better off spending our money on refurbishing the pub, don't you think? It is well overdue; we haven't done anything since we moved here ten years ago other than re-painting it every other year. Those carpets could do with being ripped out, and the floorboards are in need of stripping back and re-polishing properly instead of the quick once over we've been giving them. And why do we need to renew our vows? It was nerve-wracking enough the first time!'

'It would be romantic!' Sarah sighed. 'Oh well, if you won't go somewhere warm and relaxing with me then maybe Nicola will. I really need a break from this place.'

Chapter 7

Monday 23rd November, 11.30am

'Hi Gemma,' called Nicola Stacey as she came in through the front door of the Woodford Tearooms.

'Morning Nicola!' replied Gemma. 'Or should I say 'Afternoon'. I have made some of your favourite veggie chilli wraps if you fancy one for lunch today?'

'Oh perfect, yes please Gemma. I expect these tables have been buzzing with this morning's gossip have they?' she asked.

The Woodford Tearooms were situated next to Williamson Antiques where Nicola worked, and the tearooms were a regular haunt for antiques dealers on their way to or from the antiques centre.

'Not really,' said Gemma. 'All the horsey people are too busy working or exercising their horses to come in here and talk about Jackie's accident.'

'Yes, poor Jackie, Cliff went to visit her in Swanwick Hospital yesterday afternoon, he was telling me about it this morning. He said she was feeling very depressed and miserable, poor lady, she is such an active person I should think enforced bed rest for the next few days is going to drive her mad!'

'Yes, Peter and I went yesterday morning. I think it will be several months before she can return to work, judging by the state of her. Veterinary practice is physical work, particularly when horses are involved.'

'Yes I can imagine. Such a shame, she is a super fit lady for her age.'

Gemma laughed 'She is fitter than either of us and she's at least ten if not nearer twenty years older than we are!'

'True. So what is going to happen to the vet practice? Surely Peter can't run the place on his own?'

'Oh no, that wouldn't be possible. Good old Alastair Wilkinson will help out in the short term, and then in the medium term Jackie has offered Peter's daughter Jennifer a temporary full-time position at the Practice, with the promise of a permanent part-time position once Jackie returns to work. If Jackie returns to work I should say, because the way she was talking yesterday I think she has had enough of the whole thing.'

'Oh that's interesting. I should think that would be shock, pain and depression talking, wouldn't you? I can't see Jackie giving up the business she has worked so hard to establish after all these years just like that. Look at Alastair Wilkinson! He was meant to retire a few months ago and yet he is always helping them out when they need him.' Nicola took the plate of food Gemma had prepared for her and moved over to a table near the large open window which separated the kitchen from the eating area. 'Does Jennifer want to move down here and work with her father? Although I suppose she will be working for Peter rather than with him won't she. Not sure I could do that with my father!'

'Once a vet always a vet, I suppose,' said Gemma as she walked past carrying used crockery and cutlery from another table. They were the only two in the tearooms, but she knew the lunchtime rush was just about to start so went into the kitchen to check everything was ready. Her niece Caroline should join her any minute now. Once she was satisfied everything was in place she leaned over the wide shelf in the window so they could continue their conversation. 'I don't know about the whole father-daughter dynamic. I certainly couldn't have worked with my father. Peter took a bit of persuading, but now he is all for it. He is very proud of Jennifer and likes the way she is with horses. Jennifer is keen to come and help out for a couple of weeks, but as you say it would be a big shift in her life so she is sensibly going to take some time to consider her options.'

'Hmmh so could be some major changes for all of you in the up-coming months. There is a little matter of your wedding, too. But no, that wasn't the gossip I meant.'

'Ah, you mean Lisa's date on Saturday night? Yes, one or two people have mentioned it.' Gemma then proceeded to list, ticking off her fingers as she talked with a wry smile. 'She met him through an online dating site, and they have been exchanging emails for three weeks. Saturday was the first time they met, and although they had planned just to have drinks she enjoyed his company so much they stayed for a meal. And yes, she does plan to see him again; they have another date booked for tomorrow night.'

'Well that sounded rehearsed!' laughed Nicola.

Gemma grinned, 'I think every other person who came in here yesterday quizzed her about him, and you are now the fourth person this morning to ask me. The food really is good in The Ship, Peter and I often pop across the road for a bar meal in the evenings when we are both too tired to cook or neither of us has done any food shopping.'

'Are you really telling me that you spend all day preparing and serving delicious food in here, and then go home to an empty larder! They do takeaway food here too you know,' Nicola winked conspiratorially.

'Not exactly an empty larder,' Gemma chuckled. 'But seriously, after prepping and serving and washing up the last thing I want to do when I go home is start all over again. Besides when I do cook at home I am usually experimenting with dishes to put on the menu here, so every now and then it is very nice for someone else to do the cooking and the washing-up, and then the most taxing thing I have to do with my brain is choose something off the menu.'

'I hadn't thought of it like that before. I suppose because the food in here is so delicious I imagined you ate the same at home. But no, as interesting as Lisa's love-life is, poor girl, and I do hope this one deserves her, that isn't the gossip I meant either. Has no one mentioned the Great Bronze Fakes scandal yet?'

'Ooooh no, tell me more. I haven't heard a thing about bronzes. We are talking antiques are we? Not terrible sun tanning disasters.'

'Yes we are talking antiques. Well,' said Nicola, who had finished her lunch and was now walking over to the kitchen serving window so she could share the information quietly, even though there were still no other customers in the tearooms and Caroline hadn't appeared for work yet either. 'It would appear that someone is producing fake bronze statues, and it has sent the whole antiques trade into a right old tizz. It has been the main topic of conversation in the antiques centre for weeks now. But this morning every antiques dealer who has walked through the door of Williamson Antiques has been talking about a discussion on one of the antiques television programmes at the weekend.'

'Really? I don't know much about bronze statues. When I was first married we went to Venice for our honeymoon and saw the horses of St Mark. Oh my goodness they were amazing! Although, thinking about it, I am not sure that the ones we saw outside on the loggia of the basilica were the originals because looking back I think there were another set inside St Mark's, but we didn't go in there. How do you fake bronze?'

'According to the gossip today you cast an item in brass and call it bronze. Or at least in this case you cast the item in brass, paint it, and call it bronze. They are very hard to detect, but the difference in price can vary enormously, for example a sixty pound brass statue could be worth in excess of three hundred and sixty for a bronze version. Remember when the bronze statue by Henry Moore was stolen three years ago from a Scottish country park? That was worth tens of thousands of pounds, but melted down, as probably happened, it was worth about fifteen hundred pounds.'

'Oh yes! Or at least I remember that quite a few bronze statues have been stolen over the past few years. I can't imagine how on earth the thieves organise to steal them; they are huge and very heavy. But then when I was at university a team of workmen arrived in their liveried works' van at about ten o'clock one morning, walked all the way through our four storey building in their overalls, removed every single one of the payphones from the walls and stole them! No one stopped them or questioned them because the men looked as though they were meant to be there.'

'Wow, I know they are criminals but I do feel a little bit of admiration for audacity on that scale. Those old payphones would have held quite a lot of money. Such a waste of beautiful artwork though, going back to the Henry Moore statues, to melt it down like that. But no, the bronzes which are causing such hoo-ha in the world of antiques are tiny in comparison, probably measuring around three to thirty centimetres tall. The craftsmanship that would go into faking large bronzes by famous artists like Barbara Hepworth, or intricately worked Japanese vases for example, negate the financial pay-off if they were cast in brass. However these small statues are based on cold-painted Vienna bronzes or silvered art deco erotica, and are relatively easy for someone with the skill to create in their spare bedroom. They have been around for years, even the original factories used to cast in brass or spelter as well as bronze, but in recent years more and more of them have been turning up which are being sold as genuine bronze, but are in fact modern brass fakes. I am surprised no one has mentioned it in here yet? You

47

usually hear most of the antiques gossip at the same time as me.'

'Someone may have been talking about it, but I probably wouldn't have noticed or realised what they were talking about. Bronze antiques aren't something I have ever paid particular attention too before. But I will now.' They both turned as the bell rang to signal someone else was entering the tearooms and put an end to their conversation.

The newcomer was a man in his fifties or sixties, wearing a patterned flat cap over his greasy dark hair. The cap had the vague appearance of once being brightly coloured but was now darkened with age and grime. He wore thick black rimmed glasses, a cravat, and a three piece suit in similar state and appearance as his cap. After nodding at the two women he weaved between the furniture to a table and chair in the far corner of the room, and studied the menu.

Their opportunity to catch-up on each other's gossip brought to an abrupt halt, Nicola walked over to one of the tables in the window, through which the November sun was surprisingly strong, and sat down as Gemma brought her cappuccino over to her. Gemma then went and took the newcomer's order, and resolved to seat any more customers as far away from him as possible, and to liberally spray the air with a freshener once he had gone.

Chapter 8

Tuesday 24th November, 6.30pm

Lisa Bartlett was in a quandary. She had tried on and rejected several different items of clothing; had re-arranged her hair numerous times alternating between having it long, loose and curly to various styles involving hair clips or bands; and had completely removed her make-up once and re-applied it.

Her date on Saturday night had been fantastic and exceeded all of her, admittedly low, expectations! Robin Morton was everything his online profile and emails had promised. She hadn't counted on him being even more attractive than his photographs on the website suggested, nor had she been expecting such a funny, polite, and intelligent man. Why on earth was he single? They hadn't pried too deeply into each other's past relationship histories; Lisa was reluctant to share because hers had been so disastrous, and Robin didn't think it was relevant to his budding romance with Lisa.

But now they were meeting for a second date in 'real' life, and her expectations for the evening were high. Not so high that she would be inviting him back to her house. She had a no-sex-before-the-third-date rule which she was looking forward to having the opportunity to put into practice, finally. She deliberately left her legs unshaven and had not changed her bed clothes to further support her effort to keep to the rule, just in case there was a chance Robin would be interested. And both of her children were home that evening. A definite incentive to maintain celibacy.

Eventually she chose jeans and a white shirt, with her super warm navy blue wool long coat and high heeled blue suede boots, and left her hair loose. She also opted to drive to the pub, partly because as beautiful as her boots were they were challenging to walk in, and partly so she would stick to non-alcoholic drinks.

Despite her lengthy preparations she was a few minutes early when she arrived at The Ship Inn, but Robin was already there sitting in his car, and walked over as she climbed out of her mini. They kissed each other briefly on the cheek in greeting, and then walked together into the bar.

'Hello Lisa, hello again,' said Mike to Robin. 'What would you like to drink?'

'Hi Mike, this is Robin. I'll have a Virgin Mary please.'

'And a small red wine for me please, Mike. I telephoned yesterday and booked a table in your restaurant, name of Morton,' said Robin.

'Ah, yes, we wondered who that was. Go on through to the dining room, you can sit anywhere you like, and I'll bring your drinks through. Menus are on the table.'

As they made their way through the pub, out of the bar and into the dining room, Lisa was aware of every person staring to see who she was with, and it added to her already high state of nervous tension.

The room was empty, so they chose a table for two tucked away in one of the corners where they could sit without inviting attention. By the time Mike appeared with their drinks they had chosen their meals, and once he had taken their order and left them alone again, Lisa felt much calmer. Robin was so easy to talk to, he didn't seem to be bothered by all of the stares and whispering surrounding their presence, and was only interested in her and how her day had been. Another couple of tables were taken as the evening went on, but Lisa barely noticed the occupants, she was so entranced by Robin and his funny stories and tales of his travels around the country, and beyond.

Robin was some sort of engineer for a company which was a subsidiary of a major German engineering company, and so he spent a lot of time travelling, either driving or taking public transport, and had seemingly endless tales about the people he met as he travelled or while he was staying in various hotels in the United Kingdom and Europe. Sometimes he would also be sent further a field, to Dubai or New York or Australia, but mostly he worked in the south-east of England, where he had a flat. His parents lived in Swanwick, the County town of Brackenshire, and he regularly stayed with them which was why he had added Brackenshire to his geographical dating profile.

The hours slipped away, and the first time Lisa looked at her watch was when they were drinking coffee. She was astonished and disappointed to discover it was ten thirty, and she could see that both Sarah and Mike were going through the motions of closing the pub for the night as the last of the Regulars drained their glasses, so she reluctantly accepted the evening was coming to an end.

'When do you think you will be back to see your parents?' she asked, trying not to allow a pleading tone to enter her question.

'Oh, I checked before I came out this evening,' Robin grinned. 'I would really love to see you again Lisa, I hope you would like to see me again?'

'Oh yes!' ooops, that was a bit too keen, Gemma would tell me off if she was here, thought Lisa.

'Great!' he leaned back in his chair, a huge grin covering his face as he looked into her eyes. 'I have to go up north to Durham tomorrow for a few days, then over to Germany, back to Durham, and will return to Swanwick in three weeks' time, Friday the eighteenth. I could come and pick you up, and take you out to the Italian on the High Street, Amore isn't it?'

'Oh,' Lisa also leaned back in her chair. 'That long?'

'Yes, I am sorry. Now you can see why I am single,' Robin said, a look of concern creeping across his face. 'I will make it up to you, I promise. And we can email, talk on the phone and text until then? Please don't dump me!'

'Oh, I'm not going to dump you, I just don't want to wait that long for our third date!' exclaimed Lisa, before feeling the familiar whoosh of crimson flush her face as she realised what she was saying. 'Er, I mean, um...' come on Lisa, she said to herself, pull yourself together and act like a grown-up. 'Friday the eighteenth of December it is then,' she smiled, before suddenly remembering, 'oh, no, I can't see you then! What about the Saturday?'

'Oh can't you? Yes, Saturday the nineteenth. I'll book a table if they can fit us in amongst all the Christmas parties taking place that evening, and pick you up at about seven o'clock? Let me know your address before then. Oh Lisa, I am so glad you are willing to put up with my erratic and unsociable work schedule. No, no, dinner is on me,' he said as he picked up the bill Mike had placed on their table, and stood up so he could help Lisa on with her coat.

Together they walked out to the car park, and stopped to enjoy a long delicious kiss goodbye, before parting and heading towards their respective cars, both feeling the warm glow of attraction and anticipation protecting them from the chill of the winter's night.

Chapter 9

Sunday 29th November 2015, 6.15am

'Good Morning!' Tony Cookson greeted Cliff with his usual early morning cheeriness. When Paul Black wasn't around, Tony's good humour was evident.

'Morning' muttered Cliff, as he settled himself into the passenger seat of Tony's van. Cliff did not share Tony's enthusiasm for getting up and dressed and on the road for work before the sun rose, although he didn't mind the early start if he was going out running.

'Is it going to be a good day today?' asked Tony as he drove them the familiar route to Drayton Flea Market. 'I think it will be; I have a good feeling about business.' Tony loved these dark early morning buying trips, when no one else was on the road and the day was fully of possibilities.

'Who knows? Weather forecast says it is going to be dry, so that is something good I suppose,' replied Cliff, grumpily.

Once they were at the market they paid their ten pound entrance fee which enabled them to have access to the outdoor stalls for the first hour and a half, before the market was open to the public buyers for free and the doors to the building containing the indoor stalls were finally unlocked. The two men split up as usual to search individually, agreeing to meet a couple of hours later in the cafe.

Tony was primarily a postcard dealer which meant that the majority of his interests were inside, out of the often rainy weather, but he also dealt and collected militaria which tended to be more robust and able to withstand a drop or more of rain, so he headed off through the outdoor stalls to see his favourite dealer in military antiques, Mark Kenyon.

Meanwhile Cliff methodically moved from one stall to another, up and down the rows, ending up back where he started and beginning the process again while the stall holders continued to set up their tables and unpack their boxes. Cliff was the type of dealer who walked carefully, torch in hand, scrutinising each stall, loathe to miss a bargain. Others rushed from one to the next, focused on beating everyone else in the race to win the prize of being the first to find the treasure. Whatever their methods, the dealers were united in their aim to spot a bargain they could sell on for maximum profit. Meanwhile the familiar noises of the market engulfed them as tables were unfolded, their legs clattering and scratching along the tarmac and gravel surfaces, the shouts and calls of the sellers and buyers as they engaged in friendly and sometimes not-so friendly banter. The choking smell of cigarette smoke mixed with welcoming scents of coffee and sizzling bacon from the outdoor toastie van.

By the end of November the antiques trade is usually winding down, particularly the outdoor markets because the freezing temperatures combined with the inevitable

British winter wind and rain makes it too unpleasant to be standing behind your stall for hours at a time, and is particularly challenging when your stock is getting wet or blown off your tables. The sound of smashing glass and cries of defeat are familiar background noise to winter antiques markets (in fact some years spring, summer and autumn fairs suffer too, particularly those on a Bank Holiday), and woe betide anyone who has not securely anchored their gazebo or marquee because their incompetence is likely to not only damage their own stock, but will often take out several of their neighbours' too as the tented structures fly around in the wind.

At the end of the year the 'buzz' that surrounds the fresh-to-the-market stock on which the antiques trade thrives on is missing, not just because of the short daylight hours and grim weather, but also because the overseas buyers are reluctant to travel when the weather is likely to disrupt air, road and rail transport; holiday season accommodation and travel costs are sky high; the housing market and therefore house clearances are drying up; few people are having major building works or renovations, so the number of houses with rooms needing to be cleared out or re-decorated at this time of year are limited; the auctions are also quieter, and the sources of stock are flat-lining.

Antiques dealers try to help each other out, whilst still aiming to successfully run a business to support themselves and their families. There is the old joke about three antiques dealers on an island with only one item of stock between them, a chair, and they all make a profit.

For shop owners like Cliff the antiques markets and fairs are important sources of new stock, as are auctions, house clearances and both trade and private sellers, so it can depend on the time of year which source is the most profitable. Winter antiques markets and fairs in the United Kingdom are only for the hardy and the dedicated, but are essential if you want to survive in business. Williamson Antiques had been home to over thirty other antiques dealers, until earlier in the year someone had broken into the building and destroyed almost all of the stock. As a result the number of dealers who wanted to entrust their stock to Cliff had dropped by more than a half, and he had been struggling to afford to fill the empty spaces with enough of his own stock to make the place appealing for antiques dealers and members of the public with money to spare.

By nine o'clock Cliff's feet and hands were freezing and he was feeling thoroughly miserable. He had not found a single item to buy. Successfully managing the stock in an antiques centre is a catch-22 situation in which the more new stock you have available for buyers to purchase, the more old stock you will sell. Buyers suddenly notice an item which has been gathering dust for over nine months when something fresh is placed next to it, but if all they see are the same objects every time they look then they will stop looking, and reduce the chance of buying to zero. It is important to keep the supply of antiques turning over somehow because unless you sell old stock you won't have the money for new. And yet every year in November and December it is a surprise to the antiques dealers that the trade is quiet, and they all engage in long despairing conversations predicting the End of The Antiques Trade. Cliff was longing for a hot cup of tea to warm him up and decided to head over to the cafe, inside the hangar which housed the indoor stalls.

'Hi Cliff!' he looked over to see Linda Beecham, one of the dealers who currently had a stand in his antiques centre. Linda was bundled up in several layers of clothing, all hidden beneath matching blue waterproof trousers and jacket, with a white woolly hat and scarf. All that Cliff could see of her was her smiling face.

'Hi Linda, how's it going, have you done much business this morning?'

'Not too bad for this time of year, taken about five hundred pounds so far.' Linda was one of those dealers who was always upbeat, she seemed to take all the highs and lows of the antiques trade in her stride, and Cliff was sure that even if she had only taken five pounds that morning she would have found something to smile about. 'Cliff, any chance you could keep an eye on my stall while I pop to the loo please?'

'Yes sure, happy too,' said Cliff in a bright voice, although inwardly he groaned, he wanted to be inside holding a steaming hot mug, not standing out here in this miserable freezing weather. 'You go on. Anything I need to know?'

'No I don't think so. Everything is priced, but I shouldn't be too long so if there is a query they can wait a few minutes for me until I get back. Although it will take me a while to undo and untuck all these layers of clothes I am wearing and then put them all back together again!' she grinned and turned away, walking quickly in the direction of the Ladies toilets.

Cliff stood behind the tables watching the rest of the market going about their own business. It was many years since he had last stalled out at an antiques fair, and had forgotten about the variety of life walking by carrying their latest purchases or pushing laden trolleys: smartly dressed people, at least one of whom he knew was bankrupt; scruffily dressed people, two of whom he knew had fortunes tucked away; a woman who was very warmly dressed, wrapped up in scarf and hat and huge overcoat, but wearing thin socks and open-toed sandals on her feet; another woman who Cliff had seen transition over several years and now looked more masculine in his view than she ever did before the operations; grandfathers with grandchildren, or were they the children's fathers?; husbands and wives; young lads with energy and enthusiasm for the business; old men who remember the Good Old Days; dogs, dogs and more dogs. For a few minutes Cliff forgot how cold he was feeling and enjoyed being a spectator in an environment he was familiar with.

His reverie was interrupted by an abrupt voice enquiring the price of a silver plated candlestick.

'Oh, um, is there a price on it?'

'I'm asking you mate, how much?' The man was in his seventies, an old-timer Cliff remembered from the days when he used to stall out. He didn't have any manners back then either. Remembering this was not his stall, and biting back a rude response, Cliff politely gestured for the man to pass the candlestick to him so he could read the price tag.

'The label says twenty four pounds,' he said politely handing the item back.

'I know what the label says, I want to know how much you are going to sell it to me for.'

'You can have it for twenty.'

'Huh,' said the man and slammed the candlestick down on the table before marching away.

'Charming!' laughed a woman, holding a small silver frame. 'The label says one hundred and sixty pounds, can you do any better please?'

'I should think so, you can have it for one forty,' smiled Cliff.

'Could you do it for one twenty?' she asked.

'Sorry, no, one forty is the best.'

'Thank you, I'll have it for one forty.'

As the woman walked away, happily tucking her purchase into bag, Cliff reflected on how unpleasant some people chose to go through life whilst others were generous with their exchanges.

'Ooooh that's better, thanks Cliff, hope I haven't kept you too long?' Linda was back, smiling as usual.

'No problem Linda, I was enjoying watching everyone go by. Someone just walked past carrying a front door!'

'Sell anything?'

'Yes, a silver frame. I'm afraid someone was trying to buy one of those silver plate candlesticks but I didn't handle him very well. I am out of practise with certain types of customer.'

Linda laughed 'I can imagine the kind you mean. You ban them from the antique centre don't you?'

'Spot on Linda, you know what I am talking about.'

'Not to worry, I start putting the price up when they leave their manners at the gate. Thanks for selling the frame. I can think about packing up soon.'

'Already?'

'Oh yes, the public rarely buy from me, so once the dealers have whizzed round there is little point in staying just to lose the use of my toes!' she laughed.

'Wow, things certainly have changed since I used to stall out. We would still be here at three in the afternoon.'

'Ah, careful, you are starting to look at the antiques trade through rose tinted glasses there Cliff. Think back. How much did you actually sell to people who only came to this fair in those last four hours, and how much did you sell to people you could see anywhere?'

'Well, yes, I suppose you are right, I mostly sold to other dealers, but if I didn't stay they would have bought from someone who did.'

'Times have changed now Cliff,' Linda said sombrely. 'The dealers have usually gone by now, as they have another fair to go to up in Shropshire which opens at two in the afternoon, and then onto Worcester early tomorrow morning. Even the ones who have stalled out, like me, will not be staying much past ten o'clock this morning. Only the indoor sellers and that's because they are not allowed to bring their cars in to pack up before eleven o'clock. When was the last time you were still here buying after half-past nine?'

'True, true, you're right, I'm usually in the cafe by now!' he laughed for the first time that morning. 'Can I get you anything before I go? A cup of tea, or would you prefer a coffee?'

'Ah you are kind, but no thank you, I come prepared with my flask of soup and another of coffee.'

'In my day it was a bottle of wine and another of whisky. Are you coming into the antiques centre later on today?'

'No, I'll pop in tomorrow though. I gave my stand a good clean and re-arrange on Friday so unless you have had a shipper in over the weekend I doubt much will need doing to it. Thanks Cliff, I appreciate your help this morning.'

Cliff walked away from Linda's stall looking at his surroundings with fresh eyes. He had been on such a tight schedule for so many years, rushing here and there, needing to be in certain places at certain times, that he hadn't noticed the world around him, his world, had changed so dramatically. He reached the cafe, ordered himself a cup of tea and a bacon roll, and walked over to the table already occupied by several dealers.

Tony was smiling broadly as he walked into the cafe. He was pleased with the deal he had done with Mark Kenyon, and this had buoyed his confidence and resulted in another very good deal with one of the postcard sellers once the indoor stalls were open for business. He already knew he had an online buyer for the postcards, so had no worries about the lack of available tradable stock or fears about attracting buyers from whom he could make a decent profit. He bought his food and drink and went to join Cliff and the other dealers. Unlike Tony's, their collective mood was glum.

'What's up?'

'Another of those fake bronzes has turned up. Cost John here a grand,' grunted Cliff.

'Oh no, I'm sorry,' exclaimed Tony.

'S'OK, not your fault.' John Robson, an antiques dealer of indeterminate age who had been in the business forever, took another sip of his tea. 'These fakes are turning up everywhere; this is the seventh one I have heard about recently. Just wish I didn't own it.'

'What did it look like?' asked Tony curiously.

John sighed 'She was a beautiful piece of art deco erotica, silvered.' He made a clumsy attempt at imitating the statue's pose, looking anything but erotic. Nobody laughed. The situation was too serious for levity, and John was not playing the clown, he was genuinely trying to describe the item which was responsible for a major dip in his financial stability, and therefore his ability to successfully trade. 'My customer was not happy when it went bouncing back after last week's auction; it will be a while before she will trust me again. This business is hard enough as it is without something like that turning up.'

'How did she find out?'

'Her customer bought it to sell at the Florida Antiques Fair, and weighed it in preparation for shipping.'

'Ah, right. Brass was it then?'

'Yup. Anyway, it's done now. Won't be buying any bronzes for a while, however stunning they appear to be.'

The group sat in grim silence.

John's face suddenly lit up. 'But look at what I have just bought, this beautiful piece of jade.'

The seventeenth century Chinese work of art was passed around the table as the dealers took it in turns to examine it closely, and pass on their congratulations to John on his successful purchase. He was popular if slightly feared by the other dealers, very knowledgeable, highly successful, and in his younger years could out drink and out fight anyone who chose to take him on. The stories of his alcohol intake on the nights they all used to sit in their vans on various runways and private roads waiting for the next antiques fair to open were legendary.

These days he was teetotal, the times of downing a bottle of whisky and sharing a bottle of tequila the night before a long day on an antiques stall long gone. He would look at his grandchildren and wonder at the fact he was still alive to see them.

Despite his apparent willingness to shrug off the one thousand pound loss to his business, and his fears of the inevitable knock to his reputation with one of his most reliable buyers from whom he had earned over three quarters of a million pounds the year before, John was hiding his true feelings very well.

He was seething.

Rumours about these knock-off bronzes had been circulating for years, and every now and then he would suspect an item of his was dodgy, but it usually wasn't a major problem. Bronzes have been faked for hundreds of years, even the nineteenth-century Austrian factories who produced the stunning cold-painted bronzes also legitimately made their own brass or spelter copies. To an antiques dealer like John and his customers these imitation bronze statues were still quality antique craftsmanship, and deserved the hundreds and thousands of pounds that were exchanged for their ownership.

But this item was different. This bronze had been chosen by him and sold to him as a genuine bronze twentieth century piece of erotica. He had loved it, revered it, stroked it, and appreciated it for its beauty and its age.

And he had been wrong.

Once the teas had been drunk, the breakfasts eaten, and the treasures passed around and admired or dismissed, the antiques dealers went their separate ways. Cliff and Tony walked back to Tony's van, each lost in his own thoughts.

Chapter 10

Monday 30th November, 7.00pm

'You three look thick as thieves holed up in the corner here, what are you whispering about?' asked Sarah Handley as she brought over another round of drinks and started to clear away the glasses from the first round.

The three men looked up guiltily.

'Nothing, nothing, just some deal we are trying to put together,' said Paul hurriedly. He and Tony had not resolved their differences, but were carefully skirting around the subject instead.

As Cliff and Tony took their pints from the tray they both took a sip before setting their glasses down carefully, waiting until Sarah was out of earshot again before continuing their conversation.

'We could do without the public getting to hear about this' said Paul nervously. 'Go on Tony, you were saying?'

'It sounds as though it really was a very good fake,' said Tony. 'From John's description I wouldn't have known it was brass, but then bronze figures are not really my field of expertise.'

'Nor mine,' agreed Cliff. 'But I would have thought an experienced dealer like John Robson would have been able to suss it out. He looked like a beaten puppy, I really felt sorry for the man. He has possibly lost a consistently good customer over this, and I know how hard it is to win back customers' confidence,' he tailed off to stare gloomily into his pint glass, as he thought about his own dismal business and personal situation.

'Yeah we know you do mate,' Paul leaned over and gave his friend's shoulder a rub. 'But you are doing really well again now? I thought business in the antiques centre was picking up again. Another two new dealers joined you this month?'

'Yes things are starting to look up again, at last. If you had told me this time last year what was going to happen I would have shut up shop, sold everything, and moved to Turkey like Gary Wadley!'

'Hmmh, and look what is going on in Turkey,' commented Tony.

'Oh, not where Gary is living. Turkey is a huge country and most of the trouble being reported in the news is all going on in the south-east, on the Syrian border. Kalkan and areas further to the west are not affected.'

'Not all of it mate,' chimed in Paul. 'Look at all those suicide bombings in Istanbul and Ankara!'

'Well that is a bit like saying no one should have moved to Northumberland in the eighties because of the troubles in Northern Ireland and bomb attacks in London!' exclaimed Cliff.

'Anyway,' said Paul heavily, 'let's get back to the matter in hand. Where did John buy it originally? And who did he buy it from?'

'Ah well that is the interesting bit. He bought it from a Knocker (*Kathy's note: a Knocker is a cold caller looking to buy antiques, some of whom advertise for specific items in the local paper and refer to the advert as a method of proving their respectability*) who bought it from a lady whose husband had been caught with his pants down - as you have so often mate. She responded to one of the Knocker's adverts for old pens and basically sold him everything in the house which belonged to her husband, including the art deco bronze which now turns out to be brass, and what John thought was a late nineteenth century cold-painted Vienna bronze of a bulldog by Bergmann. He's worried about the authenticity of that, too.'

'Well the Bergmann factory did make spelter imitations of earlier bronzes, so it could have been genuine. Maybe he isn't as far off his game as he thinks he is,' said Tony. 'Did John say what else he bought in that house? Sounds like an interesting haul.'

'Yes, that is where he bought the stonking silver cruet set from the Officer's Mess in Norfolk he sold for seven hundred pounds, and those medals you bought from him back in September. Didn't you know?' asked Cliff curiously. 'I thought you had twigged when he was talking about it all on Sunday?'

'Ah it was that house!' said Tony. 'I still have those medals. They are beautiful examples.'

'Oh what I wouldn't give to see inside your shed,' said Paul longingly. 'I imagine it is a real treasure trove. Have you made a Will? I don't suppose you fancy leaving it all to Black's Auctions to sell for Lesley do you?'

Tony suddenly went very pale 'Don't joke about things like that Paul. It isn't funny.'

'Sorry mate, what's up? You haven't had a dodgy diagnosis from the doctor or anything have you?'

'No! I am perfectly healthy!' Tony seemed to regain some of his former good humour. 'Anyway, I have no intention of leaving anything in that shed after I am dead. That is my pension, and it will all be sold while I am alive so I can enjoy the proceeds of all my hard work. Cheers boys! Another?'

Without waiting for them to reply he got up and went over to the bar.

'I don't want another thanks Tony!' Cliff shouted after him.

'Nor me!' called Paul.

'I'm heading off home for a coffee. Want to come?'

'Um, no thanks, but I'll see you in the morning? Seven o'clock on The Green?' Paul looked hopefully at his friend. They had been running partners for years, but the recent upheaval in Cliff's life meant that he hadn't been putting effort into looking after himself and keeping up his fitness levels, so Paul had been out on his own most mornings. 'There is no ice forecast for tonight so we should be fine. I want to do fifteen miles tomorrow, if you are up for it. Thought I'd try the Trailway and run up and down each set of steps by the bridges five times, rather than do our usual Cosham Hill route. It was really muddy a fortnight ago when I ran it, when you were....er...'

'Stinking in my pit? Engulfed in my own misery? Reaping the rewards of a misspent marriage? It's alright, you can say it.' Cliff grinned, to Paul's relief. It was good to see his friend starting to recover some of his former good humour. 'I'll meet you at seven tomorrow morning on the Green, but I don't think I am back up to running more than eight miles at the moment, sorry. Although if you are going on the Trailway why don't I borrow your bike? Then I can cycle the distance, and get off to run up and down the steps with you?'

'Good idea! I'll bring it with me. See you in the morning.'

Chapter 11

Tuesday 30th November, 9.30am

When Rebecca Williamson arrived for work she was surprised to see that Paul was already in his office. Although he lived next door to the auction house, and was often up early for his exercise routines, he rarely came into work before ten o'clock, so she decided not to disturb him. She had grown to enjoy that first peaceful half an hour alone in the vast Georgian building, relishing the time to switch over from mummy-to-three-teenagers mode into efficient Personal Assistant to the Managing Director of an auction house.

Some days there wasn't much of a dividing line between the two roles, she mused.

Whatever problem Paul had been wrestling with a fortnight ago had not gone away, so she doubted it was anything to do with his love life which usually quickly imploded in messy recriminations from whichever female he had tangled with, or in some cases furious testosterone shouting and threatening the odds if Paul ever came near his wife/ mistress/ girlfriend/ daughter (delete as appropriate) and in one case mother, again.

Sometimes Paul would retreat to his office if there was a dispute with a customer: either a vendor who was dissatisfied with the eventual hammer price of his or her item, or who had not fully understood that the auctioneer's commission of twenty percent plus value added tax on the commission mean the vendor did not receive the price paid by the buyer; or a buyer who also had failed to comprehend that they would have to pay an additional twenty percent plus VAT on top of the amount they bid for an item. But in those cases he would be closeted in with the vendor or buyer, but Rebecca was sure he was alone this time.

The other common problem Paul would need to resolve was that of successful bidders who failed to pay, sometimes leaving it for six weeks before settling their bill, even though the auction house's terms and conditions clearly stated all debts were to be paid on the day of the auction, and meanwhile leaving both the vendor and the auction house out of pocket. Rebecca had read in a trade magazine that it is estimated that fifty five percent of all successful auction hammer prices in China go unpaid. Fortunately that statistic did not apply in Woodford, or anything close to it, but there was still the occasional bidder who failed to pay even after six weeks' grace, in which case the item would either be returned to the owner or put back in for auction a second time.

Rebecca continued with her morning routine of checking the answer phone and writing an abbreviation of the messages in the book they kept specifically for that purpose - one of the changes she had introduced after finding that the previous ad hoc method of listening and then often forgetting or deleting the messages was far more time-consuming than the simple act of taking notes - and sorting the emails which filled the inbox over night into ones she could deal with and ones for Paul to answer. She looked up as a figure appeared at the glass front door, and beckoned for Tony Cookson to come in.

'Hi Rebecca, is he in?' Tony nodded his head towards Paul's office door.

'Morning Tony, yes he is but I am not sure if he is free to talk. Hang on a minute and I'll ask.' She picked up the phone to ring him, but Tony was already heading towards the office door, and had opened it and was through before she could do any more. He was obviously expected because almost immediately Paul had popped his head through the same door to ask Rebecca to make them some coffee, and they spent the next half an hour shut away in the office. When they eventually emerged they were clearly sharing a joke together, and after Tony had left the day continued without any more changes to the normal routine.

Chapter 12

Friday 4th December, 7.00pm

The general sale at Black's Auction had been underway for half an hour, and the Antiques For All contestants had already upset several of the dealers by talking while bidding was taking place. This is an absolute no-no in an auction room, because the auctioneer needs to be able to hear and see bids, and prospective bidders have to be allowed to keep track of where the bidding has reached, so if people are having a chat amongst themselves they are a distraction to the auction process.

The two antiques dealers who were supporting the four male and female wannabe dealers in their competition were looking embarrassed and trying to quieten their contestants without much luck. The director was nowhere to be seen, and the show's host was involved in a bidding war for a mixed lot in which only she and the dealer she was bidding against had spotted a Venetian glass dish worth at least three hundred pounds. The current bid was twenty eight pounds.

Over in one corner a group of regular antiques dealers were making far more noise than the contestants, and Paul had already had to ask them to quieten down, but he wasn't going to be too strict with them because he and the other people in the room were used to hearing their squabbles and giggling, and had developed useful selective deafness against the racket over the years. But the Antiques For All film crew were only present two or three times a year, and their black clothed presence appeared sinister and disrupted the flow of the auction, not to mention forcing regular bidders to sit in different sections of the room to the ones they were used to by taking up space for the film equipment and while they filmed short pieces to camera. Similar to a school staff room where the comfy patterned armchair over by the window is where the Head of Science always sits, and the group of low chairs by the notice board are where the English Department congregate, regular buyers at auction have a spot in which they like to be positioned and woe betide anyone who stands against this patch of wall or sits in one of the Sale Lots of chairs or sofas which are usually positioned in the same place each week.

The soundman and the camera woman were experienced at these events, and had learned to film around the grumpy faces and loud mutterings from disgruntled bidders. They knew they had plenty of footage to make a hilarious video of outtakes, and planned to show it at the Antiques For All Christmas Party, so they were happy for the dealer who kept ringing a school bell every time the host did her piece to camera so she had to start again, or for the person who thought it was funny to stand behind the contestants and make bunny ears, or worse, with their fingers. All the more drinks their fellow staff members would be buying them at the party in a couple of weeks' time.

The show's host was an experienced antiques dealer, who was well-respected in the trade aside from her decision to sell her skills on television. The antiques trade has a love-hate relationship with television: on the one hand there are a minority of dealers who earn a fortune from these shows both in direct fees and from the fresh stock the filming process gives them access to; the rest are left to cope with the 'wannabes' as Mike and Sarah Handley nicknamed them. If you really want to scupper a deal with an antiques dealer at a flea market then pick up a quality, well-priced item from their stand and proceed to rubbish both it and the price. If you would like to see the item smashed on the floor in front of you, or simply withdrawn from sale, offer to buy it for ten percent of the asking price. A few dealers have a sense of humour about this behaviour and start to put the price up during the haggling process, providing their colleagues stalled out around them with a few minutes of entertainment and openly poking fun at the wannabe who has behaved in such an ignorant and insulting manner.

Antiques dealers are respectful towards each other, despite the teasing and micky-taking, and they do not appreciate seeing their profession being reduced to car boot tactics on the nation's television sets, as many of the shows do. But there are one or two which show the real life of an antiques dealer, and when you see a dealer repeatedly haggling an item down to ten percent of the asking price take a good look at what he or she is buying and ask yourself why the vendor is willing to sell something for one hundred and thirty pounds when the ticket price is one thousand three hundred. How long have they owned it? Does the buyer have access to sales outlets the vendor does not? Is the item in need of restoration which will cost several hundreds of pounds, and the vendor is unwilling to pay, or does not have a reliable restorer in his network? What else is the dealer buying from them on which they could be making a decent profit?

The show's host triumphantly won the Lot for forty five pounds, and noticed her assistance was required by the two star dealers. Within seconds she had smoothed the ruffled feathers of the regular dealers, sssshed the contestants and hustled them towards the exit, and reassured her colleagues she would keep them out of the room until they were required for filming purposes. Once she had settled the wannabes in the cafe with a cup of tea and slice of cake each, she went in search of the director, whose job it was to keep order.

She had a pretty good idea where he would be.

She walked out to the car park, found his van, and flung open the back doors. For such a cold night there was an awful lot of flesh on display.

Even though she had been expecting to find him closeted with the female antiques dealer he had been chatting up on their last two visits to Woodford, she was unprepared for the explicit scene which was lit up by the interior light when she opened the doors. There were parts of the director she would rather not have seen, and it would take a while for those graphic images to fade from her memory. It took her a few seconds to find her voice, and when she did she used it to good effect. 'Get

off that woman, put your clothes on, and go inside and do
the job you are being paid to do!'

Chapter 13

Monday 15th December, 7.00am

'Wakey wakey, rise and shine O daughter of mine!'

'Oh dad! You are not going to be like this every morning are you? I'll have to find myself somewhere else to stay,' groaned Jennifer as Peter came into her room. Or rather Gemma's son Daniel's room, but as Daniel, who worked at Black's Auctions, had officially moved out over two years' ago Gemma felt it was time the bedroom's status was changed to 'spare' room and had persuaded Daniel to remove the last of his childhood belongings the week before. No time to decorate before Jennifer moved in, but that was next on Gemma's list. She was planning to put her cottage on the market in the New Year and knew the whole place would need to be re-decorated, so was making lists of what needed to be done and by whom. Painting was something she enjoyed, so the list with her name on it was quite long already.

'Here you are, a cup of tea to get you started,' laughed Peter. 'Would you like a cooked breakfast? I can have it ready in half an hour?'

'Oh no, can't think of anything worse! I'll make myself some porridge when I get up. But thank you for the tea, now that I could get used to,' she smiled, already in a slightly better mood. 'How was Lucy when you went down? I didn't hear anything during the night.'

'Oh she seemed fine, typical greyhound she was hogging the dog bed by the radiator. Suzy was curled up on the floor next to her, so no problems from either of them. I expect they are used to each other by now, they can continue to share the boot room at night while you are here.'

After her father had gone, Jennifer lay back against her pillows and reflected on all that had happened in the last eight days. From the time she received the phone call from Jackie Martin four weeks ago, who was lying in her hospital bed with the pain she was feeling clear in her voice, offering Jennifer a job, until five o'clock last night when she had arrived at Gemma's cottage with a car full of clothes and veterinary equipment, her calm and well-ordered life had been thoroughly turned upside down and shaken about like a snow globe.

Jennifer took after her father in that she liked her life quiet and considered, no sudden changes or impetuous decisions, but neither was she afraid to take on a challenge or a puzzle. This was why she had followed him into the veterinary profession. She loved the factual aspect of science, and she needed to have a purpose to her life, so animal care, and in particular equine veterinary science, suited her personality.

Until last Sunday her career had followed an unerring path, with her decision at the age of seven years old to be a veterinary surgeon sealed when her father saved the life of a cat who had been run over in front of them. From that day on Jennifer had known which subjects she needed to study at school and which grades she needed to achieve in them. She was academically bright, which certainly helped in her desire to train in veterinary science, and, unlike her younger sister Alison, was not particularly keen on partying through her teenage or university years, preferring instead to join various school and college sports teams. Both of her parents supported her ambition, and she spent her spare time after school and at weekends volunteering at the riding stables where her mother worked in or at the veterinary practice in which her father was a partner. While she was away at university she found an animal shelter she could support by cleaning out stalls and runs, and taking the dogs for walks. When she graduated she was offered the first job she applied for, not at her father's practice but at a larger mixed-animal practice nearby, and she had been very happy working there, content there would be opportunities for career progression when the time was right.

But Jackie's offer, out of the blue, had shaken her well-ordered world, and given her the opportunity to assess her life. At the grand old age of twenty six years old that one phone call made Jennifer realise she was now three years behind her own life schedule. She had always known that marriage and children were going to be a part of her life, naturally occurring life events she had assumed would fit in with her chosen timescale. Jennifer thought she would meet the man of her dreams by the time she was twenty two years old, they would marry when she was twenty five, and have their first child by the time she was thirty, before going on to have one or maybe two more, depending on how she was able to cope with motherhood and her career. And yet here she was, with no man, and no prospect of one any time soon.

Her immediate inclination had been to turn down Jackie's offer during that initial phone conversation, as it was far too unexpected and certainly not something that had crossed her mind previously. But something stopped her from a definite 'no', and she asked for a week to think about it.

For Jackie the sheer effort of holding a phone conversation was huge, and she was only too pleased to end the call, even without a firm decision being reached, despite the time-critical nature of her dilemma. She knew that Peter and Alastair were capable of holding the practice together for at least a month, but that it wouldn't be fair to impose on Alastair's good nature for any longer than that, particularly over the Christmas period, and that Peter's wedding preparations and subsequent celebrations would be taking his focus away from the veterinary practice.

The morning after her telephone conversation with Jackie, Jennifer arrived at work and saw the place through new eyes. Was this where she wanted to spend the rest of her life? She tried to book an appointment with her manager with the intention of quizzing him about her future career prospects, but he wasn't able to find time in his schedule to meet that week. She then asked if she could bring forward the week's holiday she had booked in December, but the answer, not surprisingly, was no, and she was concerned to hear that even though her holiday was in the diary, and had been for several months, there was some uncertainty about whether or not she would be able to take it due to a clash of dates with another vet.

That evening Jennifer had sat at her desk in her home office, and made a list. She drew three columns : Reasons to Stay, in which security of job and job satisfaction were obvious contenders; Reasons to Leave, in which she was saddened to write 'employer loyalty' because this was the first time she had asked them for anything, and not only did they not have the time to sit down with her when she requested it, but she realised that all those extra unpaid hours she gave them and the times she had willingly come in at short notice on official days off, were expected rather than appreciated; and Reasons to Move, which was empty for most of the evening.

Later she had prepared her evening meal, eaten it, washed up, phoned her sister for a chat, then phoned her mother, then phoned her father.

And then wrote 'BECAUSE I CAN' in the empty column.

She smiled to herself when the smell of her father's cooking rose through the floorboards and reached her nose. Enthusiastically she jumped out of bed, ready to take on her first day at work as the New Girl again. Maybe she would have a bacon sandwich after all. Come on Life, let's get started!

Chapter 14

Friday 18th December 2015, 4.25pm

'You may kiss your bride.'

The ancient castle room erupted with loud cheers as Peter Isaac theatrically took his new wife Gemma in his arms and swung her around, before they gave each other a hearty snog. Laughing they broke away from each other, only to quickly come back together for a big hug, standing with their arms around each other looking around at their family and friends who had braved the blustery sleeting winter weather to come and help the happy couple celebrate their marriage in Brackendon Castle.

The last five weeks had been a whirlwind of plans, lists, phone calls, shopping trips, emails, and excitement. After Peter proposed to Gemma Bartlett at the top of the hill in Brackendon Woods they had talked non-stop about wedding plans all the way back home. By the time they were having a celebratory meal that evening in The Ship Inn they had already told their children, agreed on the guest list, the venue, and the earliest date possible.

The couple only met for the first time in April earlier that year, both had been married before and had children with their respective partners, but both of those relationships had ended in divorce. Despite their experiences neither Peter nor Gemma had any doubts about marrying again now they had met each other. They were having a real whirlwind romance, and thoroughly enjoying every minute of it.

Gemma's sons Nathan and Daniel, who were both in their early twenties, knew that Peter was going to propose to their mother because he had taken the precaution of checking they approved a few weeks before he asked her to marry him, so when they each received a phone call from the happy couple informing them of their forthcoming nuptials, both boys were genuinely delighted and pleased for their mum and soon-to-be step-father.

Peter usually spoke to his daughters, who were both in their mid-twenties, at least once a fortnight by telephone, relying on texts and emails in the interim to keep in contact. The week before The Proposal he had tentatively raised the subject with them separately on the phone. Both Jennifer and Alison thought it was far too soon after the couple had met to be making such a permanent commitment, but they liked Gemma and were relieved to see their father happy after a very difficult few years, so had jointly given their support, although both expressed their reservations at the speed of the engagement. When their father phoned them individually with his news they both made an effort to sound totally supportive.

In between his veterinary duties the next day Peter had managed to book their one and only choice of wedding venue, the beautiful twelfth century Brackendon Castle, setting the time and date for the wedding at four o'clock in the afternoon on Friday December 18th, and everything else had to fit into place after that. Their guest list was small, and between them they managed to see or telephone everybody by the Friday, and formal postal invitations were received and replied to by the end of the following week.

Gemma asked her sister, Lisa, (who, like Peter's daughters, was a bit concerned about the speed in which her older sister's relationship had progressed, but was also content to go with the fast flow and general excitement) and her niece, Lisa's daughter Caroline, to be her Maid of Honour and bridesmaid respectively, and both eagerly accepted. They gave themselves a fortnight to come up with the wedding theme, and the three girls had a fantastic couple of weeks searching through magazines and online websites for ideas, their sole topic of conversation with everyone around them was Winter Weddings.

Gemma's first wedding was a big traditional Church of England affair, complete with five bridesmaids, two hundred and twenty five guests, and a vintage car for transport, followed by a two week honeymoon in Mauritius, and had taken eighteen months to plan and organise. Lisa had been her bridesmaid then, too, but the sisters decided they weren't going to be superstitious about that. This time she was keen to have the minimum amount of fuss whilst still having a very special day, with only five weeks to organise everything and very little in the way of savings, she knew this wedding day would be different to her previous one.

Gemma, Lisa and Caroline all used the same hairdresser in Woodford, a lovely lady called Paula, so

Gemma paid for an evening with her and with one of the local beauticians, Abigail, so they could brainstorm their Wedding Look.

Gemma and Lisa owned the Woodford Tearooms. The Bartlett sisters had bought the business four years ago and had built a very successful following with the local people, as well as catering for the seasonal holiday-makers, and so for that first fortnight in a very rainy November the main topic of conversation for their tearoom customers had been Winter Wedding ideas. There had been some really lovely suggestions, and some not-in-a-million-years ideas, enabling Gemma to practice her 'Hmmh, something to think about, thank you' response. Once the three women had decided on clothes, hair and make-up they kept their decisions to themselves, simply responding to any enquiries or suggestions for the forthcoming nuptials with knowing smiles and winks.

It was too short notice to have anything made bespoke, or for major alterations, but online they managed to find three long, hooded cloaks in wine with white faux-fur trim, and also found some beautiful hair accessories. Dress shopping was even more straightforward, and having done their homework online the three women spent a wonderful week-day being Ladies Of Leisure by going to one of the big department stores in Swanwick (not somewhere you want to go at a weekend-day in the run-up to Christmas) and after only about half an hour had tried on and bought: one gold with ivory detail long dress for Gemma, and two similar ivory with gold detail cocktail dresses for Lisa and Caroline. They then celebrated their successful and stress free shopping experience by going off to be Ladies Who Lunch and sharing a couple of bottles of Prosecco, having previously booked Gemma's eldest son Daniel to chauffeur them to and fro.

The one area the three couldn't agree on was footwear, so in the end they shopped separately: Caroline invested her own money in a pair of stunning gold sandals with incredibly high heels and straps which went half way up her calves; Lisa chose a pair of ivory Victorian-style heeled ankle boots, and Gemma wore a relatively plain pair of gold court shoes she had owned for years but only worn a couple of times before. As hers was a long dress she argued that no one would really notice her footwear, much to Caroline's disgust who's Very Favourite Thing in the world was to go shoe shopping. Her mother found this hilarious, since her daughter's second favourite activity was running several miles most days, around the lanes and tracks of Woodford and its surrounding villages. Caroline's reasoning was she spent so much time in running shoes or sensible work shoes for her shifts at the tearooms, that splashing out on fancy footwear was a perfectly reasonable balance.

The three women all had similar fair skin tones and blue eyes, so after the evening spent with Abigail updating their beauty skills and collection of cosmetics, they were able to apply their own and each other's Wedding Make-up on the Big Day. Gemma and Lisa both had long curly blonde hair which Paula the hairdresser skilfully arranged a few hours before the marriage ceremony with the gold and ivory decorations they had bought online, Gemma's in a low chignon complete with tiara and Lisa's long and flowing, carefully designed to cope with being covered by the hood of their cloaks if the weather was typical for December. Caroline had straight shoulder-length dark brown hair which she was keen to enjoy loose since she spent almost all day every day with it tied back, so Paula was relieved that after a simple blow-dry into shape with liberal application of product to keep it all there, all she had to do was secure a gold decorated headband to Caroline's head.

The castle setting was stunning, enhanced by the cold and bleak winter weather. As the guests arrived their path was lit by great flaming torches, giving the suggestion of heat even if they were too high to be effective, and the warmly dressed Ushers – a mixture of Brackendon Castle employees and family members – welcomed each guest and directed them to the Banqueting Hall where the wedding ceremony was to take place. Once inside the guests were seated in rows on gold painted chairs with plush maroon cushions, and the simple civil ceremony started promptly at four o'clock in the afternoon, with the only surprise being the inclusion of the tying of an ornately decorated apron's strings in a True Lover's Knot as part of Peter and Gemma's personalised vows. Jennifer had suggested it as a link between Gemma's profession as a caterer and Peter's as a veterinary surgeon.

Gemma and Lisa decided to organise the catering themselves, with the help of Mike and Sarah Handley who they regularly worked alongside at the town's social events. The post-wedding cocktails immediately after the ceremony to accompany the party nibbles at the castle were a choice of body-warming spiced apple cider, mulled wine, or hot chocolate, before everyone piled into a couple of mini-buses to go back to Woodford for the wedding reception in the Garden Room of The Ship Inn, which they had decorated as a Winter Wonderland the day before.

Mike and Sarah were fantastic hosts, as always, but Peter and Gemma also wanted them to be guests and paid for additional staff to be recruited and work alongside the Handley's existing staff, so the pub could be open to customers as usual while the Landlords celebrated with the rest of the wedding guests both at the castle and in their own function room. It was a real treat for Mike and Sarah, who rarely attended social events together, and had never been guests at a party in their own public house before. At the end of the evening, as they waved the happy couple off (they were only walking a few minutes up the road to Gemma's cottage), they both agreed that The Ship Inn was a jolly good place to celebrate a family event.

Chapter 15

Saturday 19th December 2015, 8.00am

'Good morning Mrs Isaac.'

'Good morning Mr Isaac.'

Gemma and Peter grinned at each other as they lay in bed. They decided not to go away for a honeymoon, partly because their wedding had taken place at such short notice so trying to book anything in the weeks leading up to Christmas was going to be difficult, but also because there wasn't anywhere else they wanted to be. This was fortunate because with Jackie now on several months' sick leave, and Peter's daughter only recently installed as the newest member of the Woodford Equine Veterinary Practice team, the timing would have meant that Peter's absence would inevitably have caused an awful lot of stress to several people, including Peter himself. Gemma and her sister Lisa had taken the unprecedented decision to close the Woodford Tearooms for seven days' holiday from the Thursday before the wedding to the following Wednesday. Originally Peter had also been going to have this time as annual leave, but he and Gemma had agreed he would just take the Friday and Saturday off.

They were going to start house-hunting, because although Gemma's cottage was big enough for them both to live in, and was ideally situated on Farnham Road which led from Woodford High Street towards the neighbouring village of Brackendon and faced the large open common land named The Green, it wasn't quite big enough to accommodate both her sons and his daughters for family gatherings. As Peter's daughters lived far enough away to warrant staying over night when they visited, both Gemma and Peter were keen to make their stay as comfortable as possible when they did come. Their children were all old enough to have their own partners, and in a couple of cases dogs and horses too, although Peter wasn't planning to find a house with 'room for a pony'.

'Come on Mrs Isaac, let's get up and open our wedding presents!' said Peter, as he leapt out of bed, patting Gemma's Staffie Suzy, who had crept up the stairs hoping not to be noticed, on the head as he went past. 'I can hear noises downstairs in the kitchen so it sounds as though the rest of the family have turned up ready for breakfast. I'll go and see if there is any coffee and chocolate croissants left and save some for us, while you gather up a pen and paper so we can make sure we send Thank You cards to everyone. Let the wedding present opening begin!'

Despite requesting no personal presents, just the guests' presence at their marriage ceremony, several people had chosen to ignore this and produced deliciously gift-wrapped items in the preceding days and on the wedding day itself. Gemma and Peter had both been married before, they were in their forties and fifties respectively, and had over fifty years of accumulated possessions between them, although Peter's had taken a radical down-sizing in recent years. They had more than enough 'stuff' to fill Gemma's three bedroom cottage.

Peter's mother and his daughters Jennifer and Alison had stayed at Lisa's house, along with Lisa and Caroline, while Nathan who was home for the Christmas holidays had stayed at his brother Daniel's flat, and Lisa's son Robert had stayed at his boyfriend's house. As agreed everybody, minus their girlfriends and boyfriends, were meeting at Gemma's cottage for a morning-after-the-day-before breakfast. Once more of the fresh coffee was brewed and the home-made croissants were hot, crunchy, and the chocolate pieces inside were melted to the optimum tongue-stripping perfection, Mr and Mrs Isaac joined their family, both still in their pyjamas.

'This is better than Christmas Day!' laughed Peter, as he started to untie an elaborate silver bow. 'Oh Gemma, look at this, how beautiful, a framed photograph of our children. When did you all organise to have this taken?'

'Oh!' Gemma's eyes teared up. 'How thoughtful of you all. I bet this was your idea Alison wasn't it? I can't imagine when you all found the time to get together to have it taken.'

Two hours later they had dispensed with the pen and paper, drunk another pot of coffee, and made numerous telephone calls as one after another the celebratory wrappings revealed meaningful personalised gifts, including a perfectly cast beautiful model of a nineteenth century cold-painted Vienna bronze Staffordshire Bull Terrier on a stand with an inscription added to the plate engraved with their wedding date.

'This is far too generous of your workmates,' said Gemma thoughtfully, frowning as she took a sip of coffee. The card said the bronze had been given to them by Peter's senior partners in the Woodford Equine Veterinary Practice, Jackie Martin and Alastair Wilkinson, and the three veterinary nurses and two administration staff. 'But perfect. I love it. I think it should take pride of place here on the mantelpiece, don't you?'

'Yes, it will look great up there. I wonder who found it, and where?'

Neither of them noticed Jennifer and Alison exchanging a conspiratorial smile.

Peter carried on 'These bronzes can be very valuable, we'd probably better check the house insurance covers it. I think a Thank You card would be best, rather than phone everyone individually, and I'll take some cake in when I go back to work tomorrow. One of your fruit cakes, and a chocolate cake maybe, pretty please, oh best sister-in-law in the world?'

Lisa laughed, 'Yes, alright, I think that is an excellent idea.'

Gemma added 'And a card and a cake for everyone at Black's Auctions as well, don't you think? This funny silver framed cartoon of a horse casually drinking a mug of tea while the vet struggles to run around the field is inspired. I'll have a bet with you that Rebecca Williamson found this one. Oh,' she sighed and gave her new husband a hug, 'aren't we lucky to have such wonderful family and friends.' She turned to include everybody in the room. 'We didn't give you much time to help us celebrate our wedding vows, and yet everyone we asked came to the ceremony, and all these people ignoring our request for no presents by coming up with such thoughtful gifts! How wonderful to be starting the day with our close family, drinking coffee and eating chocolate croissants, perfect.'

'Uh oh she's going to get emotional,' complained Nathan. 'Right, enough of this, get dressed you two, let's all take the dogs and go for a walk to burn off some of the booze and cake we have been guzzling for the last twenty four hours.'

'Excellent idea!' said everyone.

Chapter 16

Sunday 20th December 2015, 9.55am

'Good morning Nicola! How are you?' called Cliff from behind the counter of Williamson Antiques, as one of his employees Nicola Stacey walked in through the front door. They were the only two working in the antiques centre, the other two members of staff, Barry and Des, were already on their Christmas holidays.

'Morning Cliff, I am fine thank you. Wasn't it a lovely day on Friday? I am so pleased for Gemma and Peter; they are such a nice couple.'

'Yes it was a good 'Do' wasn't it. Mike and Sarah did them proud as always. How was your head yesterday morning? You were knocking back the fizz a bit weren't you?' he said teasingly.

'Mine was fine,' she retorted sharply. 'I was not 'knocking back the fizz' as you so rudely put it. I only had three glasses all night! It was the sloe gin which did for me,' she admitted, grinning at her boss, as memories of the evening flitted through her brain. 'You on the other hand looked stone cold sober!'

'Oh yes, reformed man, me,' said Cliff proudly. 'Well, after the last few months I thought I owed it to myself and my family not to get into any more embarrassing incidents, and I had to be fit to open this place yesterday,' he said seriously.

'Yes you do owe them that,' said Nicola, a touch more righteously than she intended. Quickly she changed her tone 'Cuppa then Cliff?'

'No thanks, I've already got one, but the kettle only boiled ten minutes ago so go upstairs and make yourself one and I'll see you when you come back down. We have a new stall holder coming in later today so I will need to run through a few things with you after your week off.'

As Nicola ran up the stairs to the antiques centre's small kitchen and made herself a coffee, Cliff sat back in his chair and reflected how things had changed for him over the last few months, and how if Gemma and Peter's wedding had been this time last year he probably would not have even gone. The knowledge that he would have chosen to spend time with his mistress rather than with his beautiful wife Rebecca at a friend's marriage celebrations was painful to him now. He would have done anything to go as Rebecca's Significant Other this year, but she, quite rightly, would not consider his suggestion, and instead had happily gone on her own. Cliff's confidence had taken a battering in recent months, and he had been very reluctant to even go to the wedding at all, but Paul insisted that they close their businesses for the afternoon and go together, as he too was without a date for the event having recently managed to screw up his latest romance. At least Rebecca hadn't found a date to go with; Cliff was grateful for small mercies, and he felt he had behaved appropriately at all times whilst still making sure she knew his feelings for her. Maybe, if he kept up this behaviour, she would eventually give in.

By the time Nicola walked back downstairs a couple of antiques dealers had come in to check their stands and cabinets, and Cliff had pulled himself together and was ready to bring her up-to-date with the previous week's news and the following week's plans. Nicola thought he still looked a bit paler than normal, and wondered if he would ever regain his previous bounce and enthusiasm for life. The events and revelations of the previous few months had been shocking for everybody. He had undoubtedly been responsible for his own behaviour, and as a result of his actions much of the respect she used to have for him for the last nineteen years was irretrievably lost. However she greatly admired the way he had managed to pick himself up, and attempt to re-build his life and the business he so nearly lost. She had always liked him and hoped that things would work out well for him, soon.

Cliff was sitting behind the counter with a list in front of him, and as soon as Nicola was settled in her chair next to him he began. 'I have given permission for one of those television antiques shows to turn up here at any time in the next six weeks. They should ring us a day or so beforehand, but, according to a dealer in Swanwick, when they filmed in his shop the film crew and stars of the show all turned up at his door five minutes before closing time.'

'Oooh is it the one which films at Black's Auctions? What was the name, oh yes, Antiques For All.

Apparently one of the film crew was having sex with an antiques dealer in the car park!'

'Yes I heard,' groaned Cliff. 'We don't want any of that going on here. We have had enough bad publicity.'

Nicola laughed. Poor Cliff, he really had had a tough time of it lately. Sex seemed to follow him everywhere he went, and not in a good way. She steered the subject onto safer ground. 'So if they are not going to give us much notice you need to be ready at any time for cameras to start rolling. Why on earth have you agreed to this? I thought you held the view these shows are ruining the antiques trade?'

'Oh I do, but the business is so poor I decided if you can't beat 'em join 'em!'

'Well don't go giving away stuff for free like they usually do, or every Tom Dick and Harry will think they can do the same,' grumbled Nicola.

'I may not be the one who is here when they come.'

Cliff laughed at the look of horror on Nicola's face.

'You cannot seriously expect me to be on television! No! No way.' Her face brightened as she thought of someone 'If they turn up when you're not here I'll phone Sarah Handley. She would LOVE to be on an antiques show.'

'Right, that's sorted then,' Cliff was still laughing as he looked at his list. 'Next...' but he was interrupted as the door opened.

'Brrrrr, it's cold out there!' said Hazel Wilkinson as she walked into the antiques centre. Hazel was one of those women whose age is difficult to guess. Her hair was all variations of grey from very dark to white, and she wore it scooped up with various pins and combs. Her clothes were usually ankle-length patterned skirts worn with plain coloured fitted tops and jackets, and she had a variety of long earrings and big necklaces, and always wore several rings on her fingers. She could have been anywhere between forty five and sixty five years old, but Nicola guessed she was nearer sixty because she taught Nicola when she was at Woodford Secondary School.

'Ah Hazel, excellent timing Mrs Wilkinson, I was just about to tell Nicola that you would be joining us. Are you parked around the back?'

'Yes I am. Alastair is there too with his estate car which he has had to empty of all his vet stuff, so both of our cars are full to bursting with china. I think today may be the first time since he bought that car twelve years ago he has seen the back seats!'

'Come with me,' Cliff stood up from his chair and beckoned Hazel to walk with him to the back of the huge room, where a set of large double doors opened out to the area at the rear of the antiques centre. Nicola joined them and between the four of them the Wilkinsons' cars were emptied in a quarter of the time it took to pack them.

'That is the last box for today, thank goodness.' Hazel surveyed the pile of boxes and sized up the available shelf space. 'I am so pleased to have all of this out of our spare room, I had forgotten what the carpet looked like! Now all I have to do is unpack it all and display it to its best advantage.'

Nicola laughed, 'I'll go and make you a tea or a coffee now then, if you are going to be staying in one place for a while. What would you like?'

'Oh tea please, lovely, thanks.'

'Milk? Sugar?'

'Just some milk please. Thanks Nicola, that is very welcome.'

Before she retired from teaching Hazel had lived and taught in the Woodford area all of her life. She decided to retire the year before with her husband, Alastair, and the pair of them now spent as much time as possible on their beloved canal boat exploring various waterways, and hiring boats for those unreachable by water in their own boat.

Over the years Hazel had amassed a large collection of china statues, decorative plates, and other ornaments, regularly visiting the monthly local Drayton Flea Market and scouring Black's Auctions catalogues for treasures. But time spent on the canals had given her a new perspective on life, and she no longer felt the need to collect these items but still enjoyed the research and thrill of the purchase, so had decided to be sensible about it and turn her hobby into a little business. She had given herself a year to become established in Williamson Antiques, to see if she could make as well as spend money, and was very excited about the whole enterprise.

While Nicola was upstairs waiting for the kettle to boil, Alastair had returned home with his empty car, Cliff had gone to collect his fourteen year old daughter Charlotte from a friend's house, and Hazel was transferring the contents of several cardboard boxes to the shelves of her new antiques stand, another newcomer to the antiques centre was just starting to bring boxes of stock in from his van parked out in the small car park at the back of the building. When Nicola came back downstairs with two steaming mugs of tea, Hazel whispered 'What's his name?'

'No idea,' whispered back Nicola. 'I saw him in the Woodford Tearooms a few weeks ago, and he seems to know his way around here. Hang on, Cliff wrote a list for me on the counter, here we are, you are number two and under number three he has written Rowland Mitchell. This must be him. I'll go and check.'

Hazel watched as Nicola walked over to introduce herself to the man they guessed was Rowland Mitchell. Their conversation was brief, and he clearly did not want to stop unloading the items from his car in order to be polite, so Nicola gave up and returned to Hazel's stand.

'He is not very friendly is he?' whispered Hazel.

'No, not very. Whiffs a bit too. I have never seen him in here before, have you?'

Hazel shook her head, and they both decided to find something more worthwhile to do.

Chapter 17

Monday 21st December 2015, 10.00am

'Hold on Paul, are you sure? I'm not sure I would be able to tell if they are fake or not. These look and feel like a beautiful pair of bronze greyhounds to me.'

Cliff was having a late breakfast in the next door Woodford Tearooms with Paul Black, and Paul had brought along a couple of items a customer wanted to put into one of his auctions about which he had some concerns. The men had already been out running together that morning, and as the mornings were so dark and they owned their own businesses they were lucky enough to be able to choose their training times. While Cliff kept Williamson Antiques open every day over the Christmas period except Christmas Day, Boxing Day and New Year's Day, Paul closed Black's Auctions for two weeks, and would be re-opening in January. As far as his customers and employees, which included Cliff's estranged wife Rebecca, were concerned the business was shut, it was very much on Paul's mind.

'No, I am not sure, and that is the problem. These bronzes are so hard to authenticate. I do not want Black's Auctions to get a reputation for selling stolen or fake goods, and after having two complaints from customers about suspected fake bronzes already I don't want to risk a third. You know how easily these rumours start.'

'Yes I do,' said Cliff heavily. 'OK, I will have a think about who would be best to ask. I cannot think of anyone off the top of my head. Go on, give me a clue who it is, I don't want to make the mistake of buying off him. Or her?'

'Oh I can't, not yet, sorry mate. But don't worry; it isn't anyone you would be buying bronze statues from.'

'Really? I am intrigued now. And yet he, or she, puts them in your auction for sale? Hmmm.'

Paul ignored his friend who was attempting an impression of Sherlock Holmes on the other side of the table, and carried on with his own train of thought. 'The trouble is they have been put in for the auction on the nineteenth of February, so I really need to know before the tenth of February when the catalogue goes to the printers.'

'Ooooh they are lovely!' exclaimed Lisa, making both men jump. 'Guilty consciences boys?' she teased, and then felt her face and neck flush beetroot red as she looked at Cliff and remembered he had been having a secret affair about which no one in the village knew until a few months ago. Desperately trying to recover her foot from her mouth she tried to focus on the pair of bronze greyhounds Paul was showing Cliff, but they had disappeared. Paul had hurriedly shoved the bronzes back in his bag when Lisa appeared, wishing he had invited Cliff to his house for lunch where they could have talked privately. The less people who knew about this problem the better.

'Bronze aren't they? Someone gave Gemma and Peter a beautiful bronze statue of a dog for a wedding present, although that was a Staffordshire Bull Terrier Has Jennifer seen these? Her Lucy is a greyhound. Are they going in your next sale in January, Paul? No one can walk past without touching and stroking Gemma and Peter's bronze.' She had been looking at Paul in an effort to recover from her embarrassing faux pas with Cliff but too late remembered their brief encounter at this very table a couple of months before, and then again in the pub afterwards. Although she was sure Paul was unaware of the sexual awakening she had experienced as a result of his concerned hugs on two occasions when she had been upset, her body was unkindly reminding her of its response to his touch, and it was beginning to affect her speech. Aware that she was now increasing the size of the large hole she had been digging, and desperately trying to draw together her scattered thoughts so she could STOP talking about touching and stroking, she hurriedly asked 'Would either of you like any more of anything?'

Inwardly she groaned, although it was possible she had done it out loud and now she was so uncomfortable and unsettled that she was afraid she was losing her faculties.

'Yes please Lisa, I'll have another coffee. Cliff?'

'Yes, I'll have another one too; better make it a pot of coffee. Oh, might as well have a couple of mince pies to go with that don't you think Paul? 'Tis the season and all that?'

'Good idea, another pot of coffee and a couple of mince pies please Lisa.' Paul wasn't sure he would be able to swallow anything he felt so ill about the problem he was faced with, and resolved to take any leftover mince pies back home to eat later. He was oblivious to Lisa's discomfort, and had his own problems to concentrate on. The owner of the bronzes was someone he regularly did business with, and he hated to think they may be using his auction house to launder fake items. The penalties for consciously providing false information in an auction catalogue are severe, and Paul was likely to face a prison sentence if found guilty. He was also disturbed by the thought that the person could be deliberately deceiving him. Trust is a vital part of the antiques business. He was finding the whole experience upsetting.

Cliff was unaware of the full extent of his friend's dilemma, but had picked up on Lisa's embarrassment and correctly guessed that at least part of it was to do with him, and also could see that some of it was to do with Paul although he wasn't sure the extent of her interest in Paul. 'Oh well, I have to expect people will stumble over their words for the rest of my life,' he sighed, 'but you were not helping her either. Have you two had a fling?'

'No!' Cliff wondered why Paul was so vehement in his denial. The fact was that Paul's focus was on his business problems, his love life was a mess, and he wasn't in the mood for being teased. 'Anyway I think Lisa's heart is with someone else now. I've seen her with a man, in The Ship Inn.'

'Yes, I have too, a few weeks ago now though, not recently. He looks vaguely familiar but I can't place him. Do you know who he is?'

'No, no idea. Haven't really paid him much attention. Anyway, back to my problem. What am I going to do?'

'Well, it really depends if he is a good customer or not doesn't it? If you don't mind upsetting him by rejecting what he wants to put in your auction then just say no. You must have done that loads of times before? On the other hand, if he is using your auction house as a way to fence fake antiques then there is probably more to this than you know about, and there could even be people watching your auctions to see what happens to these items. If I was in your shoes, I wouldn't risk it.'

'Yes,' Paul sighed. 'I think you may be right. I need to reject his custom, don't I. Trouble is the repercussions could be huge.'

Chapter 18

Thursday 31st December 2015, 11.50pm

Mike Handley had been feeling ill for several days. The Christmas holiday season was always a busy time for The Ship Inn in Woodford, and both he and Sarah had worked as many hours as they could, often not falling into their bed before half-past two in the morning and then up again for seven o'clock deliveries. The pub was host to the Christmas parties for almost all of the local businesses, groups and clubs, as well as being a favourite party venue for families who either didn't have the space to accommodate everybody at home, or who wanted to go where someone else would be slaving in the kitchen both before and after the meal. Even on Christmas Day both Sarah and Mike were up and working by six thirty, despite the fact the Christmas Eve celebrations didn't end until three o'clock that morning, and when they finally locked the pub doors at six o'clock in the evening they chose to cuddle up on the sofa with a cup of tea before both falling asleep where they were.

Every year Sarah vowed it would be the last time they worked such a hectic schedule, and her dream was to either leave the pub in the capable hands of the staff or close it completely for a fortnight. Mike would not even consider closing the pub for one day, let alone a couple of weeks, and it was at his insistence that they worked until they dropped. Many of the town's residents were very grateful for the Handley's continuing hospitality, both as customers and as employees, and so when the subject came up for discussion in public Sarah's was inevitably the lone voice.

New Year's Eve in Woodford was traditionally a Fancy Dress party for anyone who wanted to join in. There were three public houses, and the first revellers would begin as early as five o'clock in the afternoon at The Boot, which was officially in Brackendon but all the locals referred to it as a Woodford pub. After a few drinks the party would make its way along Farnham Road towards Woodford, and after a mile they would reach the next pub, The Royal Oak, where those less energetic would already have gathered. By ten o'clock The Boot and The Royal Oak were empty of customers and so both pubs closed up for the night and the staff joined in with the party half a mile along the road in The Ship Inn.

The theme for 2015 was British Weather, which produced outfits ranging from ponchos over bikinis - a favourite amongst many of the men - to rain drops, bright yellow sun costumes, and one imaginative couple managed to create a windswept look from head to toe. Without fail every member of the party, which by eleven o'clock comprised of over four hundred people, wore wellies.

The Ship Inn was the final destination because it backed onto the village green, where there was plenty of room for overspill from the pub, which legally could not hold that many people, and so every year they prayed for dry weather.

Sarah noticed Mike was looking a bit pale, and left her place behind the bar to go over to him where he was now sitting on the bottom of the stairs between the bar and the kitchen, which led up to their flat.

'Mike, darling, are you alright? You are looking a bit tired.'

'Sarah...'

'Mike. Mike. MIKE.'

Sarah's screams pierced the noise of the party. Starting as a ripple and ending as a wave people began to tell their neighbours to ssssssh, the individual noises silenced all the way through the pub and out to The Green and the High Street. Murmurs and whispers started to build as the message was passed that Mike was ill, an ambulance had been called, and the community collectively broke up their party atmosphere electing instead to stay together in quiet concern.

By the time the rare sound of the ambulance's sirens could be heard the blue lights had been visible for several minutes, flashing their way along the lanes towards Woodford.

At twelve forty two on January 1st 2016 the worst news possible was announced: Mike Handley was dead.

Chapter 19

Wednesday 13ᵗʰ January 2016, 9.30am

The church was booked, the guests had accepted their invitations, the outside caterers were arranged, and she had bought a new outfit suitable for the occasion. As she looked around the Garden Room of The Ship Inn Sarah Handley reflected that of all the events she had expected to be hosting, the first in 2016 would not be her husband's Wake. Mike Handley, landlord of The Ship Inn for nearly eleven years and her husband and the love of her life for almost twenty years had collapsed and died on New Year's Eve at the age of fifty two years old from a heart attack.

The doctors had been warning him for several years that if he didn't change his lifestyle, namely exercise more, eat less, and relax occasionally, that this tragic end would come sooner rather than later. His death had not come as a complete surprise, but that was no comfort to Sarah. The one area of the whole experience she could draw comfort from was that Mike had died very quickly, in a matter of seconds, behind the bar as usual; doing what he loved which was engaging in lively banter with the regulars. But she could find no consolation in that knowledge today when in approximately four hours time this room would be filled with people, and Sarah knew she would never feel lonelier in her life.

She turned as her best friend, Nicola Stacey, walked into the room.

'Come on Sarah, time to get dressed,' Nicola said gently, as she led Sarah out of the Garden Room and steered her in the direction of the stairs which went up to the first floor of the pub, and where Mike and Sarah's living accommodation was situated.

Sarah slowly made her way up the stairs, her legs feeling as leaden as her spirits, with Nicola close behind following at Sarah's chosen pace, careful not to hurry her friend, allowing her to take her own time.

At the top of the stairs Nicola could smell coffee, and knew that Sarah's parents, who were staying at the pub along with Mike's parents, were preparing breakfast for her. When Sarah's mother appeared, Nicola turned and went back down the stairs, leaving the family to share their grief in relative privacy before the rest of the funeral guests started to arrive.

By eleven o'clock The Ship Inn's bar was full of local people who had taken time off work, or former regulars and friends from other public houses the Handleys had run in previous years. All came to celebrate Mike Handley's life, the noise forcing Sarah out of her depression as she heard loud male voices telling 'Mike' stories, and the inevitable laughter which followed. Her husband had been an excellent example of a good village landlord: stalwart of the local community, a typical publican with a warm and friendly personality which encouraged customers to come back time and time again, but tough as old boots with anyone who tried to upset the carefully cultivated ambience of his pub, and with a heart of gold for those in need.

The Ship Inn was their fifth business, the previous four had been run-down inner-city drugs and drinking dens which Mike and Sarah were sent into by the brewery to turn around with a two year deadline and limited budget. They succeeded with the first and third, leaving behind two family-friendly public houses firmly placed in the heart of the communities; but the second and fourth had too much against them, namely that the local communities were so badly fractured with no positive cohesive purpose to see the benefit of a centrally located place in which to socialise without wrecking either the fabric of the building or each other. Working at the fourth pub had been very tough for both Mike and Sarah, and several times they had been in fear of their lives, so when their two year tenure was up and the brewery offered them a fifth pub to turnaround, they declined. By that time they had been searching for a new venture, neither expecting to run another pub, but when Sarah's former local in the town she grew up in became available for sale they were in full agreement that this would be their next adventure.

The Ship Inn had always been a popular meeting place for the locals since the nineteenth century when it was a coaching inn, going through a succession of transformations in the previous two centuries.

The previous landlord had managed to alienate most of the population of Woodford in his short eighteen month tenure by refusing to serve chips (when requests

113

were made the sharp reply of 'You don't ask a Michelin Starred Chef for chips!' was not well received) and by putting the beer prices up by thirty percent. He clearly wanted to encourage London Weekenders into his pub, expecting to live comfortably off the cash-rich bankers and internet entrepreneurs who bought second homes in the area and sent their children to the local boarding schools. What the man stupidly misunderstood was that those people who had bought second homes in Brackenshire and who came to eat and drink in the Woodford public houses did so because they wanted to relax in the County's environment with their children and friends, drinking locally brewed beer and eating home cooked pies and deliciously prepared local meat and vegetables, and yes, often, with chips. He had also miscalculated how much money the second home owners brought into the town, and that they would usually spend the school holidays abroad leaving several weeks of the year when the pub was lucky to have three customers in a day. By dismissing the spending power of the local residents, and by making the walking and cycling holiday-makers in their clothes better suited to tramping through the local woods than teetering across a smart wooden pub floor extremely unwelcome, he managed to run the business into the ground, before doing a moon-light flit one night.

Mike and Sarah bought the Freehouse, their first time working for themselves without the support or restrictions of a brewery, and within the first three days welcomed more customers than the previous landlord managed in his final month in charge. From then on The

Ship Inn was firmly established back in the hearts of the people of Woodford. Customers were welcome to drop in for a pint or come with their families for a three course meal; it was a place a woman would feel comfortable to go on her own; the bar was spacious; there was a beautiful dining room for those who wanted a slightly quieter more intimate atmosphere; there was a lobby area for mucky walking boots and wet coats; the snug which tended to be inhabited by Regulars if they were not propping up the bar; and the garden room and beer garden were ideal for owners to sit with their dogs after a walk in the rain or along muddy tracks. Mike and Sarah were keen to support local events like the Woodford Summer Fête, and were soon providing a venue for birthday, wedding, and Christmas parties, and, as today, a comfortable friendly environment for a Wake.

Although not a trained chef, Mike had worked closely with the ones they employed, overseeing the menus, mucking in when they were short-staffed, and preparing his own meat and vegetarian Monthly Specials which used local meat and seasonal fruit and vegetables bought from suppliers based in the surrounding area.

Sarah knew it had become the norm for people to request funeral guests to come wearing colourful clothing and celebrate, not mourn, the life of the deceased, but on that bleak, cold, miserable, wet winter's day she had no desire to wear anything other than her heavy black wool coat over a matching black dress and cardigan, and didn't want to be jolly and cheerful.

She was furious with Mike.

If he had only done as the doctors advised him to he would be here today, by her side behind the bar as usual, laughing and joking with the customers himself, rather than being the subject of their humorous tales.

The day passed slowly, dragging its heels as she wanted to do on the walk from the pub to the church and back again. She endured the funeral service, not finding peace or solace in the massive turnout or the vicar's words of comfort, or in Mike's brother's light hearted and fond History of Mike.

Once back at The Ship Inn she slipped away as soon as she could. Knowing she would not get any peace upstairs she got in her car and drove away, not caring that she was leaving behind concerned friends and family, hating herself for her selfish behaviour but unable to find the energy to pretend to all these people that Mike had loved her very much, and share stories about how kind and generous he was. If he had really cared about her he would still be here.

It was one of those car journeys where you suddenly realise you have no memory of how you arrived at your destination; did you drive through red traffic lights? Did you stop, look, and wait for other cars at roundabouts? Had the traffic been heavy on the dual carriageway? In Sarah's case she hadn't even known she had a destination, but when she turned into the long driveway of Swanwick Manor she became aware of her actions and of her surroundings.

Sarah first visited the home of the Barker family a few months before. When she wasn't working all hours in the pub she liked to delve deep into family history, and in the last few years had enhanced her research by tracing the families of the subjects of portrait miniatures. One of her discoveries was a portrait miniature of a nineteenth century relative of the Barker family who now live in Swanwick Manor, and the previous September Sarah had contacted them and subsequently been invited to join them for afternoon tea. As a result of this meeting she had been welcomed back several times since then, usually enjoying afternoon tea with Margaret Barker, a lady in her seventies now confined to a wheelchair after a horse riding accident, as the warm Autumn sunshine weakened into the chilly Winter daylight, driving them inside from the sheltered sunny walled garden to the conservatory so they could still enjoy the horticultural view which changed every time Sarah visited. Sometimes Margaret's husband David would also join them, although he could usually be heard mending something deep in his cavernous garage on the other side of the garden's wall, and more frequently Margaret's son, Frederick, a tall handsome man in his early fifties, would sit with them for a while. Sarah wasn't sure what Frederick's job was, but he seemed very knowledgeable about a lot of things, and when pressed would simply murmur that he did 'something boring in the City'.

She pulled up outside the garden gate, suddenly aware that she hadn't telephoned to ask if she could come as she usually did, and unsure what to do next. As she sat and dithered the gate opened and Frederick, or Fred as his parents called him but Sarah felt he looked more like a Frederick, came out, smiling as he recognised their visitor.

'Sarah! What a lovely surprise. Mum didn't say you were coming today, come on inside and I'll put the kettle on.'

Sarah gathered up her bag and heaved herself out of the car before following him back through the familiar gate and into the welcoming atmosphere of the Barker's home.

'Sarah, dear!' exclaimed Margaret. 'How lovely to see you. Come and sit down here while Frederick makes us some tea. Would you like cake too? David brought a fruit cake back from the Farmers Market this morning, just perfect for such a cold winter's day as this. Now, how are you? Pub quiet at this time of year is it?'

Sarah removed her coat and sat down; grateful for the family's hospitality, aware they had no knowledge of the upheaval in her life and finding it a relief not to be greeted with sympathetic looks and pitying comments.

'Yes, January and February are usually quiet, and this year is no exception,' she lied, thinking about the busy pub she had fled, crammed full of mourners all drinking and eating in her husband's memory. 'So, how are you all? Did you have a big family Christmas?'

And so Sarah managed to spend a couple of hours in the company of people who behaved and acted normally around her for the first time in thirteen days, before thanking them for the tea and cake, which was so delicious Sarah ate three slices, suddenly aware she had only eaten half of everything her mother or Nicola had put in front of her for the last fortnight and finding herself ravenous. Frederick accompanied her back out to her car when she was ready to leave, and she could see his tall lean figure in her rear view mirror waving until she was out of sight. At the end of the drive she stopped and checked her phone, and felt a rush of guilt as she saw several missed calls and text messages. She quickly typed one message to Nicola and one to her mother, assuring them both she was fine and would be home in an hour, before putting the car back into gear and driving home.

Home.

As she drove she took care to concentrate on her journey this time, but also pondered the word 'home', and wondered if she would continue to choose The Ship Inn as her home, now that Mike was no longer there to share it with her.

Chapter 20

Thursday 14th January 2016, 11.00am

The next morning Sarah opened the pub as usual, although this was to be her first time behind the bar since Mike's death a fortnight before. By temporarily running away the day before, and having some time out from The Ship Inn, and from Woodford, with people who knew nothing about the tragedy which struck her life at the start of the New Year, Sarah was able to gain some perspective, and to find the strength to make a start and pick up her life again.

Her new life.

Life without Mike.

Both sets of parents were still staying upstairs in the home she and Mike had shared for the last ten years since they bought The Ship Inn, although his parents were due to go home today, and her parents were going home at the weekend. She had found their joint presence invasive, she didn't want their sympathy, or to share their grief, or to comfort them. Sarah knew she was being hard and unreasonable, and resented them even more for putting her in this position. Yesterday she decided that the best thing would be to pretend that everything was business as usual, so they would all go away and leave her in peace to find her own way forward. They were holding her back, and she wanted them gone. Mike had left her on her own, and that was something she was going to have to get used to. The sooner his parents went and stopped forcing her to listen to how wonderful he had been, the better. Sarah was sure she would stop randomly bursting into tears once her own mother and father had gone back to their house and she didn't have to put up with their hushed voices, creeping footfalls, sympathetic looks and enquiries every few minutes.

'Morning Tony, the usual?' she put on her best Welcoming Landlady voice as one of The Ship Inn's Regulars, Tony Cookson, walked in through the door.

'Yes please Sarah. Lovely 'do' yesterday, everyone did Mike proud didn't they? I really should be working today, but imbibed a bit too much of the old whisky with Cliff and Paul last night, so decided to take today off, and start again tomorrow. Although drinking at lunchtime probably isn't going to help me recover any quicker!' He laughed, desperately hoping to get some sort of response from Sarah. She looked terrible, and he didn't think she had heard a word he had said.

'Morning Paul, the usual?' said Sarah, as Paul Black, another Regular, walked up to the bar taking off his coat as he moved.

'Morning Sarah, how are you?' Realising after several seconds of silence he would not be getting a response to his question, Paul continued hurriedly 'Not for me, I'll have a half of orange juice and lemonade please. Have to go back to work this afternoon, but took the morning off as drank too much last night.' He grimaced, looking at Tony. 'You too mate? Although you are obviously feeling better than me, look at you with your pint of bitter!'

'No, I feel terrible, but decided that hair of the dog and a day off work would be my best road to recovery,' laughed Tony, all the time exchanging glances with Paul as they tried to silently and subtly communicate with each other about the awful state of their beloved landlady behind the bar.

At that moment Mike's father appeared from upstairs 'Hello boys, I'm surprised to see you two in here, you were the final ones to leave last night. Did you sleep in the snug?' he joked.

Relieved to find someone else in the pub with whom they could converse, Tony and Paul engaged Sarah's father-in-law in jolly conversation and reminisces of Mike's funeral the day before, soon joined by other locals and Sarah's parents and her mother-in-law. Within half an hour the pub was alive to the sound of story-telling and laughter, and Sarah felt a sudden urge to run away again.

But this time she held her ground.

For one thing she was limited to two other members of staff working that day, as she had only contracted the extra staff until Mike's funeral, and for another she resolved to give herself a month in which to decide if she was going to be able to run the pub on her own, or if she was going to sell up. Everyone had been telling her not to make any rash decisions, that she should leave it at least three months before making any plans, and that it would be better to wait a year as grief takes at least twelve to eighteen months to work its way through your system.

What a load of bollocks, thought Sarah, every time a well-meaning friend or family member handed out their unasked for advice. What do they know about it? None of them have been let down like she had. None of them were in her position. No, she would give it a month and then act on her decision one way or another.

Chapter 21

Saturday 16th January 2016, 7.00pm

'Oh hello, how are you? Are you settled in to your new job now?' Paul Black was back in The Ship Inn, again drinking orange juice. He was entered into a ten mile run in Swanwick the next day and knew that his mid-week alcohol excesses would take their toll on his race time so he didn't want to exacerbate this with any more debilitating libations. On entering the pub his face lit up when he saw Jennifer Isaac walking towards the bar alone. They first met at her father and Gemma's wedding, and Paul had managed to spend quite a lot of time trying to flirt with Jennifer who he thought was extremely attractive. But he hadn't been able to convince her to agree to a date with him since then.

'Oh, hi,' replied Jennifer, her previous good mood evaporating. Here was that annoying man again, all leery and in her face. At twenty-six years old Jennifer was young enough to be this man's daughter, and old enough to recognise a seasoned Lothario when she met one. It was the first time they had met since her father's wedding, although she was now living and working in Woodford she had managed to avoid Paul whose attention had been unwelcome and mildly creepy.

'Yes I have, thank you. Excuse me,' she said firmly, as she continued her journey to the bar to order another round of drinks. Sarah saw what was going on and smiled knowingly as Jennifer reached the bar and pulled a face at her.

'Same again all round Jennifer?' she asked brightly.

'Yes please Sarah' said Jennifer trying to create an aura of intense concentration and focus and touch-me-not prickliness as she felt Paul's presence come into her personal space. Oh hell, now what? These situations are always awkward, the man was clearly interested in her, he appeared to have no idea about body language, seeming to believe he was irresistible to any female he took a fancy too. She had tried to be polite and friendly without encouraging him every time he grabbed the opportunity to monopolise her during the wedding, but she was damned if she was going to allow him to repeat his behaviour every time they bumped into each other.

Sarah saw the look of desperation on Jennifer's face, and could see that Paul was homing in on her for an intense seduction effort which was clearly not welcome, so took pity on both of them and said 'You go back to your family Jennifer and I'll bring the drinks over in a few minutes.'

'Thank you,' smiled Jennifer gratefully, the relief and understanding at what Sarah had done for her positively beaming from her face, and she turned away from Paul and hurried as fast as she could back to relative safety.

Sarah watched Paul as he followed Jennifer's progress through the pub. When he turned back to Sarah she leaned across the bar and said in a conspiratorial whisper

'Take my advice Paul, find someone your own age and settle down. You are not as young as you used to be, you have used and abused all the available and not-so-available women in this town and surrounding area, you are rapidly becoming a laughing stock, and the air of desperation around you is palpable. That young lady is clearly not interested in you, in fact by the look on her face you make her skin crawl.'

Satisfied she had successfully put him in his place she turned away and started to take the drinks order from the person standing next to him, leaving Paul in a mild state of shock with his mouth open. After a few seconds he came too, shut his mouth, and left the pub.

At forty three years old the twice-divorced father of two had been happily living under the illusion that his love 'em and leave 'em approach to life made him the envy of all men and irresistible to all women, and that it was a lifestyle choice he could continue until he decided to stop, which was not going to be any time soon. But Sarah's blunt speech stopped him in his tracks for the first time ever. Despite all the hearts he had broken over the last ten years since his marriage to Christine was destroyed by her discovery of his affair with another woman, the wide wake of misery he trailed behind him and the occasional emotional outburst directed at him by cheated girlfriends and cheated-on boyfriends and husbands, it had never occurred to Paul that his behaviour could be viewed in anything but a positive light. He honestly believed that he was desired by women and the envy of all the men who met him. As he walked the two minutes back to his home, a small cottage he had built alongside his auction house, he started to contemplate the uncomfortable truth that rather than being the object of many people's jealousy and admiration, he was actually turning into a figure of fun.

Meanwhile Sarah was feeling satisfied that she had spread a little of her own bad feeling to someone else, as she continued with her bright landlady façade for the rest of the evening.

'Was that Paul Black you were talking to at the bar?' asked Gemma after Jennifer had returned to the table and they had all been served with their Starters. 'Watch him, he is notorious for seeking out fresh meat and I am very much afraid that a stunning intelligent young woman like you would be right up his street.'

'Hey! Don't describe my daughter as fresh meat!' complained Peter.

Jennifer laughed. 'Don't worry Gem, I have the measure of him. He spent most of your wedding day trying to chat me up. Men like that are just sad, destined to end up bitter and alone. I can't imagine why any woman finds them attractive enough to fall for their transparent attempts to get them into bed!'

'No, neither can I, but believe me we see enough of them sobbing into their teacups in the tearooms to know there is more to Paul Black than his own publicity,' sighed Gemma. 'Anyway, on a much more positive subject, we keep forgetting to ask you where you bought that amazing bronze your dad's work colleagues gave us as a wedding present? When we quizzed her, Jackie Martin said you found it for them.'

'Oh yes! Lovely isn't it. We have an antiques and collectors fair every week in the market square back home, and one of the stalls sells those bronzes. He usually has one or two different ones every time I go there, and when I saw the Staffie I immediately thought of you and bought it to give to you myself. But then I saw that lady who makes those tapestry wedding samplers, and Jackie asked me for wedding present suggestions even though you said you didn't want any, so I gave her the bronze and had a sampler made up to commemorate your wedding day.'

'Really? You bought something as beautiful and well-crafted as that bronze from a market?' queried her dad.

'Yes, they have some really quality antique items there, as well as the typical rubbish you would expect. It all seems to sell,' shrugged Jennifer. 'The sampler lady stalls out at that market too, and that is where I bought your Alpaca wool slipper socks from.'

'Once we buy our new house maybe we should spend some time scouring the antiques markets and car boots Gemma?'

'Mmmmh, maybe,' said Gemma, who thought the idea sounded terrible!

Chapter 22

Monday 18th January 2016, 12.30pm

Rebecca's morning had again been disrupted by arriving for work at half past nine and finding her boss was already closeted in his office. She was still none the wiser about the reason for this change in work routine, and found that it wasn't only his timing which had changed, but also his attitude. For the nineteen years Rebecca had known him Paul had always been a bit of a joker, never taking anything very seriously, and more than likely to take the Mickey out of anyone and everyone he came into contact with. But for the past few weeks his jokes were fewer, his demeanour was more harassed than happy, and his relationship with clients was starting to be affected.

Conflict is inevitable when you manage an auction house, but dealing with it had been one of Paul's strong points up until recently. Because of the variety of auctions they held Paul and his team were usually able to steer items into the most suitable sale, but recently Paul had been turning away potential vendors telling them bluntly their belongings were not of the quality he was looking for. Although this had been the case in one or two situations, Rebecca counted at least five others which she thought Paul would have accepted a few months before, including a couple of items from a dealer who was regularly consigned goods for auction, and was one of Paul's friends.

On the mornings when Paul came into the auction house earlier than usual the workplace took on a slightly disjointed air, as though everybody was waiting for some major explosion to shake everything back into place. So far no explosions had taken place; instead the build-up was continuing to rise.

Daniel Bartlett, Gemma's tall, blonde haired son and another of Paul's employees, usually started work at eight thirty in the morning, when he would either be hard at work preparing items for the online and printed catalogues for the next sale, or he would be out on the road with one or more of the other employees clearing houses or collecting and delivering auction items. That morning he was out first thing, and had just arrived back from delivering some furniture which had been sold in the previous Friday's sale.

'Hi Rebecca, I'm just popping down to mum's, do you want me to get you anything for lunch?'

'Oh yes please Daniel, whatever the soup of the day is and a ham roll would be great. Shall I phone and order it? What are you having?'

'Oh, no thanks. If you don't mind waiting a bit I said I'd help her with one of the lights, the bulb needs changing and she can't reach. I'll be back in about half an hour.'

'OK, thank you!' she called after him, just as he and Cliff did a little dance past each other as one went out and one came in through the door.

'Morning Rebecca, cor it is cold out there. Is Paul in his office?' The initial awkwardness Cliff and Rebecca felt when they were newly separated and she first became an employee of Black's Auctions had long since evaporated. They saw each other most days either here at the auction house, or at the former family home where Rebecca lived with their children, and seemed to have settled into an easy way of coping.

'Hi Cliff, yes he is, and he is on his own. He has been in a troubled mood all morning, so maybe you can jolly him out of it. I am just keeping my head down out here!'

'Ah, another screwed-up romance?' guessed Cliff, and they both laughed. 'How did he get on in the race yesterday? He usually posts on facebook, but I haven't seen anything yet.'

'I don't think he ran yesterday. Daniel mentioned he thought Paul was at home just after lunch when he popped in to return the tables he borrowed for the Swanwick Car Boot.'

Cliff knocked on the closed door of Paul's office, which was not normally shut, and waited a few moments before opening it and walking in, despite not being given the go-head by the man closeted inside.

'Morning Paul, time for a spot of lunch at the tearooms?' Cliff noted that his friend looked drawn and pale. 'Are you alright? Not going down with something are you?'

'No, no I'm fine. Just a bit tired,' sighed Paul. 'Yes, lunch at the tearooms is an excellent idea, thanks. I could do with a bit of fresh air; the walk down there will do me some good.'

'Did you not compete yesterday then?'

'No, no I didn't. I've got some stuff on my mind, mate. Couldn't get in the right headspace for running yesterday.'

'Oh? Sounds more like a pint and plate of chilli at The Ship is in order, than a bowl of soup at the tearooms.'

'No, no way, I don't think I'll be going back in The Ship for a while Cliff. Sarah gave me a right mouthful on Saturday. I know she is grieving for Mike, but she was evil!'

'What on earth did you do to deserve that? What did she say? Please tell me you didn't try to pull her!'

'No I did not! I'm not that bad.'

'You are,' laughed Cliff.

'No, I am not,' said Paul carefully. 'Anyway, I regard Sarah as a friend. Or I did. I am not sure after Saturday.'

'Is that what is up with you then? Something Sarah said to you?' asked Cliff, showing a touch more concern than he had previously.

'Oh, no. Well, yes that as well. But no. I am still struggling to know what to do about these ... items. The vendor is trying to put pressure on me to catalogue them as nineteenth century Vienna cold-painted bronze, but I really want to be sure they are before I do. I can't afford the hassle if I get it wrong. But worse than that, the more I think about it the more I think my client has been deceiving me for years.'

'So you have been brooding about this all weekend instead of getting out there and doing what you love.

Who is it? Do I know them? Are you any closer to finding out the truth?'

'Don't give me a hard time! But no, put like that, no I still don't really have an idea about what is going on, or what to do about it. Come on, let's go and have some lunch.'

The two men walked in silence the five minutes from the auction house at the top of Woodford High Street to the Woodford Tearooms near the bottom of it.

Once inside, they found a table to sit at, ordered drinks and food, and continued to sit in silence for a few more minutes, each lost in their own thoughts.

Eventually Paul roused himself 'Why did you walk up to me if you wanted to come here? You could have phoned me, and then just come next door from your place. You are not still hoping Rebecca will fall into your arms are you?' he said, with a wry smile.

Cliff gave Paul a sideways look. 'No, I have given up all hope that I can win her back. Why would she, or any woman for that matter, want me now after what I have done? I am definitely damaged goods where women are concerned. But any excuse to see her, and if that means walking *all the way* up the High Street and back then she is worth it,' he sighed.

'Oh mate, you really need to move on. Why don't you join an online dating site? Loads of women on those! I can recommend a really good site I am on at the moment.'

'No! Stop! I am not going to start taking relationship or dating advice from you, Paul Black' laughed Cliff.

'Hey, that hurts!' Paul looked genuinely upset.

'No offence Paul, but the seduce 'em, shag 'em, two-time 'em, method isn't a life choice I want to pursue. I loved being married, and that is what I want again.'

'Quite right Cliff, good for you,' the two men looked up as Gemma Isaac appeared with their plates of ham, egg and chips. 'I highly recommend it,' she laughed, before turning to Paul. 'I hear you have been pestering my step-daughter, Jennifer? Lay off Paul, she doesn't need or want your sort of attention.'

'Alright, alright!' Paul looked quite cross as he leaned back in his chair, holding his hands up as though to defend himself from further attack. 'Anyone would think she was some young girl and I was a paedophile the way you lot are behaving. Sarah had a go at me in the pub on Saturday about her too, but all I was doing was making polite conversation.'

'Maybe you should pay attention then, if more than one person has commented on your behaviour,' said Gemma, before walking away.

As she went back to the kitchen she wondered if she had been a little harsh with Paul. His conquests and their inevitable messy endings were the stuff of legend in Woodford, and she and Lisa had previously enjoyed the gossip and latest stories of Paul Black's most recent liaisons being re-told at the tables of their tearooms, but all of a sudden they weren't so entertaining any more. Never having had a daughter of her own she was surprised at how defensive she was about Paul's clearly unwanted attentions towards Jennifer. She had a feeling Jennifer would not be pleased if she knew what had just taken place between them, and resolved to keep quiet in future. She hoped Paul had got the message, but doubted it.

'Alright Boss?' Daniel appeared at Paul and Cliff's table, carrying a large brown paper bag containing his and Rebecca's lunches. 'I thought I would crack on with photographing the Chinese vases this afternoon, is that OK?'

'Yes, that's OK. Everything go alright this morning?'

'Yup, all delivered and installed in the lady's house. What a gorgeous place. She and her husband designed it themselves, and it took five years to finish! She was really pleased with everything, especially the refectory table, the size of it fitted perfectly with their kitchen.'

'So she should have been, that was a real bargain. Once upon a time it would have cost her about eight thousand pounds! Anyway, thanks for that Daniel, hopefully she and her husband will be back for more stuff to fill their new home.'

'Oh I think she will be, plus his grandmother has just died and they want you to go and price up to clear her flat. One of them will give you a ring later today. I'd better go; Rebecca is waiting for her lunch.'

'Nice lad,' commented Cliff after Daniel had left the tearooms and they could see him heading up the High Street. 'Always difficult to find and keep good staff isn't it? If they have anything about them they steal your business, and if they don't they ruin your business. It's a No Win situation!' he laughed. 'Right, back to your problems. Come on, tell me the latest.'

Chapter 23

Monday 18th January 2016, 2.00pm

'Look Dad, I just don't agree with you. There is no chance that a horse with a diagnosis of navicular syndrome can ever be brought back into work without the support of shoes. The damage the navicular bone has caused to the tendons is irreversible.'

'Oh Jennifer, have you not been listening to anything I have been saying? Remember that big dark brown horse belonging to your mother's friend Brenda, who went lame halfway through the Hunting Season about three years ago. Everyone said the same thing about him. Danny, that's his name, but Brenda sent him to a barefoot rehabilitation place in Devon for three months, continued with the equine management advice she was given once he came home, and has been hunting him, without shoes, once a week for the last two seasons with no further signs of lameness.'

'Well that is very fortunate for Danny and Brenda, but you can't convince me based on one horse's lucky result. Not all horses can go barefoot, and once damage like this we can see on these x-rays takes place there is no going back.'

'Danny isn't the only one; there are numerous others I can tell you about. If you remove the causes of poor biomechanics then the horse will do its best to recover. And I disagree with you; all horses can go barefoot, but not all owners can.'

'Ooooh Dad, is this our first professional fight?' laughed Jennifer.

'Yes, I think it is! All I am saying is go and see for yourself next time you go up to Shropshire to see your sister and mother, and talk to Brenda about what changes she needed to make to Danny's management. I am sure she would be happy to share her experiences with you. If Alastair can cover for me I'll come up with you for the day; I haven't seen Alison since the wedding, and it would be good to see for myself how Brenda's horse is doing now. Which day is the market on where you bought our wedding present? Sounds like a fascinating place.'

'It is on every Wednesday. Did you never go when you lived up there Dad?'

'Nope, not something that was of interest to me in those days.'

'In those days!' repeated Jennifer. 'You moved down here less than a year ago!'

'Yes I did,' laughed her father. 'How life has changed since then,' he winked at her and gave her a hug. 'Look, why don't you give the rehab place a call and arrange to go and visit there too? I'll come with you if you like, if Alastair can cover again for a morning or an afternoon. It has been a while since I was over there, and it is such an inspiring and innovative place. I am sure they will have even more experiences to share with me.'

'Oh I don't have time to go on a wild goose chase.'

'It would not be a wild goose chase; it would be an essential and informative part of your continuing professional development, from which your clients could benefit.'

'Alright Dad, I'll have a think about it, I can see how passionate you are about this subject. But if, as you say, not all owners can go barefoot then that causes us a problem because it is the owners who manage the horses.'

'Absolutely right Jennifer, it is the owner's responsibility to manage their horse as best they can, and that is why it would be a good idea for you to go and see Brenda and her horse, Danny, and find out how she manages him. I see it as our responsibility to provide those owners who want to know with the best information and support we can, and that means occasionally following some wild geese! Talking of birds, I'd like to take Gemma to see that gorgeous house over on Swan Hill tomorrow when I am due to be on emergency cover, could you stand in for me please between four and five o'clock?'

'Oh, are you going to look at the one with the fantastic views across to Cosham Hill?'

'Yes, that's the one. If the people who came to view her cottage yesterday make good on their promise of an offer then who knows, we could be all moved in by Easter!'

'No problem, I am booked in to be at the Western riding school tomorrow afternoon for a few tetanus vaccinations, and they are always happy to be flexible if I need to leave. Did I tell you I have booked myself in for six weeks of lessons with them? I quite fancy being a Cowgirl!'

Privately Peter remembered a certain video he had been made to watch a couple of years before and hoped that his daughter wouldn't mention her desire to be a cowgirl to Cliff Williamson.

Chapter 24

Tuesday 19ᵗʰ January 2016, 10.00am

Nicola Stacey and Cliff Williamson were sitting behind the counter, running through the antiques centre's sales figures for the month so far.

'Hazel Wilkinson seems to be doing better than I expected,' commented Cliff. 'I didn't think china and porcelain sold very well any more.'

'I think it helped that she set up her stand in time for all the family Christmas and New Year parties when people suddenly realised they weren't going to have enough teapots or side plates, and they have come back for more in preparation for summer picnics.'

'Summer picnics! That is looking a bit far ahead isn't it? It's pouring down outside,' laughed Cliff.

'Not really. If you think about it what we sell in here is never guaranteed from one week to the next. You are thinking with an antiques dealer's head rather than like a member of the public. The majority of our stock on a daily basis is sold to members of the public who browse when they have a spare half hour, or make a special effort to come in if they are looking for something in particular. Hazel sold about three times as much stock to public buyers in the weeks before Christmas than she has done this month, but the people who have been buying her stock this month nearly all bought from her stand last month.

'The majority of our income, however, comes from the Trade, none of whom are likely to be buying anything from Hazel's stand. Dealers like Hazel appeal to buyers like Hazel. If you think about it some of those antiques dealers who come in like clockwork once or twice a week on the look out for fresh stock may or may not buy something, but they are our bread and butter buyers because when they do put their hands in their pockets it will be for many more pounds than the public buyers, and they usually buy from other antiques dealers' stands.

'The rest of the trade buyers may only come in three times a year, but they sweep the place - regardless of whether it is a public or an antiques dealer's stand because their clients cover both ends of the market - and they spend a fortune, and they are the ones who make it worth our while to stay open.

'Well, your while Cliff.

'Unlike the public buyers, the trade buyers, although they will be looking for a particular type of item, will not usually be looking for a specific colour or pattern of plate or cup, whereas the public buyers know they need to buy it today or it will likely be gone the next time they come in here. That is why Hazel did so well before Christmas, is doing relatively well this month, but will be lucky to sell into double figures next month when her stock's limited appeal will have saturated our local market place. None of her dinosaur antiques, those model cottages, have sold, and they won't unless by some piece of luck a collector who is missing those particular examples stumbles across our antiques centre.'

Cliff sat back and looked at Nicola. He had been running his antiques centre for almost nineteen years and this was probably the longest and most detailed speech he had ever heard her make on the subject of how his business worked. Nicola had been working for him almost since the day he opened Williamson Antiques, and yet he had never appreciated her insight into how the antiques trade worked before. He already knew all that she was telling him, but it gave him a small thrill to realise that here was someone who felt almost as strongly about his antiques centre as he did. Rebecca had always been interested in the day-to-day goings on, but had never shown any interest in how the business worked.

'Sorry Cliff,' she mumbled looking embarrassed because he was looking at her so strangely, she thought she had overstepped her position and upset him. 'I didn't mean to teach you your business.'

'Oh not at all, please don't apologise Nicola! I was just thinking what a smart person you are, and what an idiot I am for not noticing before. You really care about this place don't you?'

'Well of course I do. Why do you think I have stayed here all these years? Particularly after all the awful events last year. It certainly wasn't for the pay. I feel a part of this business, we all do. Does this mean I get a pay rise now you have noticed I can do more than unlock the front door, switch on the lights, and be polite to the customers?' she grinned.

'Steady on,' he laughed. 'You'll be expecting a television appearance fee next!'

'I can't believe that flipping film crew managed to turn up at a time when neither you nor Sarah were within an hour of here, and not a single other antiques dealer came into the antiques centre who I could persuade to replace me! They all stood out of shot drinking tea and sniggering! I think I deserve a huge bonus for that humiliating experience.'

'Ha ha no you don't, but you have earned another cup of tea. Stay there, I'll go and make us one before we move onto the next page when you can tell me why Rowland Mitchell has been selling out every week. His stall must contain the least desirable stock in this antique centre; all those damaged bits of 1950s and 1960s furniture, and mass made china from the 1960s. '

'Now that I don't know,' replied Nicola, thoughtfully.

Chapter 25

Tuesday 19th January 2016, 4.30pm

Gemma and Peter stood together, holding hands, looking out over the breath-taking views of Stormy Vale, which was living up to its name as a dramatic scene of wind and rain supported by clouds of varying shades of grey was moving at speed across the landscape.

'Wow' breathed Gemma. 'I could stand here all day.'

'Stunning isn't it,' smiled Peter. 'I knew you'd like it.'

'Like it? I love it!' exclaimed Gemma. 'Not so keen on the house, though. I think I love my little cottage so much I am struggling to picture myself living anywhere else. The family bathroom is awful and poorly designed; I'm afraid that flowery bathroom suite is hideous and not to my taste at all. The bedrooms are horribly decorated; that one with the primary coloured triangles all over the wall was giving me a headache. The fittings in the two ensuites look as though they were installed by toddlers. And the kitchen! How on earth has a family of six been catering in that? It looks as though whoever designed the layout of the bathroom also planned the kitchen. Everything is in the wrong place; there is no flow between the units.'

'Let's go back in and have a proper look around. Everything you are talking about is cosmetic isn't it? We would expect to replace kitchen and bathroom suites wherever we move into. We did whizz in and out of every room the first time. It has the number of rooms we want, although certainly not in the condition I was expecting from the estate agent's details or photos. Some of those photographs were taken very carefully indeed.'

As they went back inside for a second look, this time with less enthusiasm than the first time, Peter's phone rang.

'Hold on, love, I had better answer this, it is Jackie Martin. Hi Jackie, is everything OK?' he asked anxiously.

'Sorry to disturb you Peter, I was wondering if you are free this evening for a chat?'

'Yes of course, Jackie. Shall I come to Rebecca's house?'

'Ooooh no, any excuse to get out. Rebecca will bring me to The Ship Inn if you can join me there. How about six thirty?'

'Make it nearer six forty five and I'll be there.'

By the time he found Gemma she was standing in the conservatory, lost in thought as she gazed through the windows at the view.

'Jackie wants to meet me for a chat this evening, in the pub. No idea what about or how long for, but shall we eat in there tonight?'

'Good idea,' said Gemma. 'I'll come along with you, and sit by the fireplace with my plans for this place while you two talk.'

'Ah, are you feeling a bit more enthusiastic about it?'

'Yes,' she said slowly. 'I think I may be. How about you; what do you think about it now?'

'Oh I haven't had a chance to look round again, come on, you can't have got far either if you are only in here!'

Chapter 26

Tuesday 19th January 2016, 6.45pm

Jackie and Rebecca were already seated in the snug when Peter and Gemma arrived, so instead of sitting on her own so that Jackie and Peter could have their discussion in private, Gemma joined them too. It was all very mysterious, because Jackie preferred to have her professional meetings in the surgery, and only went to the pub for social evenings with her friends. She had been in almost daily contact with Peter since her accident either by phone, or he had gone to Rebecca's house where she was still convalescing, and he had found her advice and support invaluable. Even though he was a very experienced veterinary surgeon, and had been a senior partner at the previous Practice he worked at, he found Jackie's knowledge of their Brackenshire clients and her willingness to share and discuss different treatment options very important while he continued to become established in the area.

He had no idea why she had called this evening's meeting, and why it appeared to be a social occasion rather than their familiar professional work routine. Peter was a little nervous about what she may want to talk to him about, his mind racing through the various clients he had seen in recent weeks and wondering how many had been dissatisfied with his work. He could think of at least two who had been critical of his recommendations for them to change their horses' diet and exercise instead of reaching for his prescription pad. He was relieved that once everyone was settled with drinks Jackie got straight to the point.

'Peter. I have decided to retire. I do not plan to come back to work, and I would like to give you first refusal for the business.'

Whatever Peter was expecting, it wasn't that. Jackie was one of the most dedicated vets he had ever met; he could never imagine her giving it all up.

'I can see this has come as a bit of a shock to you, Peter!' she laughed. 'The truth is, this accident has given me the time to, no, has *made* me, take stock of my life. As you know being a veterinary surgeon, particularly an equine vet, is all-consuming if you want to be of any use to your patients, and I just don't want to carry on putting the effort in any more. And that is the crux of the matter, it is now an effort, and has been for a couple of years. I tried to go part-time, but realistically that is not working, and I haven't been enjoying it - it really is all or nothing, and I choose nothing. Even though we haven't seen eye-to-eye over a few things, I do respect your professionalism and abilities, and trust that I would be selling the Practice to someone who would take care of it and our clients. I have given this a lot of thought; this is not a spur of the moment decision.' She saw the look of horror on his face, and laughed, 'and yes I do have nightmares of you turning the stable block into an American barn with pea gravel everywhere.'

Peter laughed too, realising he had been holding his breath since Jackie started to talk, and Rebecca and Gemma exchanged glances of relief. Rebecca was privy to her mother's decision prior to the meeting, but had been more cautious about Peter's response than Jackie, who couldn't understand why he wouldn't want to take over her business. Jackie considered it to be a logical progressive step for Peter, but Rebecca could see it would be a massive upheaval to the life he thought was laid out for him when he moved to Woodford less than ten months earlier. Gemma was almost as shocked as Peter, because she had not envisaged Jackie retiring from the profession she loved and was her life's work. Gemma was not sure what Jackie's proposal meant for her new husband and herself, but could see that their quiet plans for a move to Swan Hill were suddenly up for a major re-evaluation.

Jackie, oblivious to the high emotions around her, continued. 'Of course any changes you make will be entirely up to you, it will be your business, so you can do with it as you wish. I have no intention of doing an 'Alastair' and stepping in every five minutes if you need a hand, though. I have plans for what I would like to do with the rest of my life, and they don't allow for maintaining a level of professional veterinary competency. So you needn't worry about me breathing over your shoulder every time you bring in a barefoot hoofcare specialist instead of a farrier,' she winked at Peter, knowing full well this had been one of the few bones of contention between them in the last few months. 'So, what do you think?' She picked up her drink and sat back, watching him as he tried to process her news and her offer.

Peter didn't know what to think. He had only joined Jackie's business in May the previous year, and had been happy to come in as a junior member of the veterinary team which only consisted of himself and Jackie, with retired vet Alastair Wilkinson stepping in whenever they needed an additional body, and the nurses and admin staff who were all extremely proficient in their work. Jackie was such a vibrant and efficient member of the team, always in full control of all of the various aspects of the Practice, it had never occurred to him she was even contemplating retirement, let alone making way for him to step into her shoes. He looked over at Gemma, who appeared to be as stunned as he was.

'Mum, I think you need to allow Peter to have a few days to think about this,' said Rebecca gently, much to Peter's relief. 'Unlike you who has known about your decision since November, the first he heard about it was five minutes ago.'

'November?' queried Gemma.

'Yes,' said Jackie, 'I decided as I was lying on the stable floor after that damned horse had kicked me. That has *never* happened to me before, and I don't intend to allow it to happen again.'

'But you must have been kicked before Jackie?' said Peter.

'Oh yes, more times than I care to remember. But that time I was stupid. I knew the tensions in that stable yard, I knew that bloody woman in charge ruled by terror, and I should have sent her out of the stable to make me a coffee like I usually do, but I got complacent and look what happened. It was entirely my fault, and I could have avoided it. And that is my point; I just don't care enough to make the effort to placate people like that anymore, so it is time to stop before I get even more damaged, or worse cause harm to a horse. Well, you have heard my proposal, and my reasons for presenting it to you. Why don't you have a think about it for a few days, would next Tuesday be too soon to come back with an answer?'

Peter and Gemma exchanged glances before Peter spoke. 'I think a week could be just right Jackie. Same time, same place? You too Rebecca?'

Rebecca nodded in agreement.

'Good, that's settled.' Jackie was satisfied she had said everything she wanted to, and felt sure Peter would come back with a positive answer the following week. She picked up her glass of wine which had been untouched throughout her sales pitch, and continued 'Now, tell me how the whole house-selling house-buying experience is going. Have you heard the Maxwell-Lewis farm is up for sale? Poor Mrs Maxwell-Lewis, she just can't cope without her son Simon propping up the running of that place. Since he was put behind bars last Autumn the place has become even more run-down than it was before. Fortunately they didn't keep horses there so we are safe, but the farm vets over in Swanwick have had great difficulty in being paid for over three years now. Martin Spiers was telling me she owes them well into six figures. He doesn't think they will see much of it, so is pinning all his hopes on getting some of it paid when the farm is sold.'

'Ah is that what is happening to it?' mused Gemma. 'Lisa and I have been noticing more estate and land agents than usual coming into the tearooms, and they all have aerial photographs of the land so we knew something was going on. When does Simon's case go to trial? Do you know Rebecca?'

'No, Cliff hasn't said anything to me about it. I'll ask him if he knows anything next time I see him. It does seem very unfair that Simon is the only one to lose his liberty when he was not the mastermind behind the Country House Thefts, but I suppose he was the only one committing the burglaries. I did wonder if the old lady was going to be able to keep going without Simon.

'The poor woman was deeply shocked by the revelations last year, I don't think she had any idea of what Simon had been upto.' said Jackie.

Everyone sat quietly contemplating the events of the previous year which had caused so much upheaval to the lives of several people in the usually sleepy town of Woodford.

Rebecca's life in particular had been jolted off course, but as she sat in the comfortable surroundings of The Ship Inn with friends and family she reflected that the past few months had been a time of positive transition, and she was excited about her future. Her mind turned to practical matters. As Woodford Summer Fête Coordinator the logistics of organising the event were always on her mind.

'I wonder if the Maxwell-Lewis farm will be sold before the fête in May? Mrs Maxwell-Lewis generously allowed us to use the drive and one of the paddocks for the horses for the last two years. I think we would struggle if we didn't have access this year Mum.'

'That reminds me Rebecca, I had better organise to meet up with the others and put our programme together for this year's Horse Show. I'll go and see Mrs Maxwell-Lewis for you and ask what her plans are, if she knows them,' said Jackie, making a note in her diary. 'I think the whole place is being sold as three lots. The reason I mention it, Peter, is because the lease on the surgery is due for renewal in the next eighteen months, so if you are thinking about altering the emphasis of the Practice in any way, you know, to something which may require more of a rehabilitation emphasis for example' she winked 'then some of that farmland may be ideal.'

Chapter 27

Wednesday 20th January 2016, 12.35pm

Rebecca and Christine Black, Paul Black's first ex-wife and Rebecca's best friend, were sitting in the Woodford Tearooms. They were the only customers, and Lisa Bartlett was enjoying the relative peace and quiet after a very busy few days. She was developing a recipe for a pheasant curry; their freezers were full of pheasants from the local shoots so she had plenty of ingredients with which to test a variety of flavours. Lisa and Gemma tried to keep their menu seasonal, using local suppliers where possible; although now the shooting season was almost over they were not sure if pheasant would still be popular.

'Morning ladies, do you know what you would like to order? In case you haven't decided there is a free dish on the menu today, pheasant curry. I'd like some guinea-pigs to tell me if the flavour is chilli enough or too much.'

'Ooooh yes please, I'll be a guinea-pig for you!' Lisa smiled; Christine Black was always so enthusiastic about being a Taster for the dishes Lisa and Gemma wanted to try out on their customers.

'Not for me thanks,' said Rebecca. 'I don't want to smell of curry all afternoon; I don't think the clients of

Black's Auctions would appreciate it. Parsnip soup and a wholemeal roll for me please Lisa.' She turned back to Christine once Lisa had left them. 'So come on then, what was so important we had to meet for lunch at short notice then Christine? Please don't tell me you are pregnant!'

'Good grief no,' Christine shuddered and smoothed down her already perfectly straight blond hair with one carefully manicured hand. 'Two are plenty for me, thank you very much. No, this is about you,' she gave Rebecca a sly look. 'Remember Benjamin Francis from school? You and he had a 'thing' for a while in Year Eleven didn't you?'

'Oh yes Benjamin! Oh he was so cute; he used to have a gorgeous denim jacket he would let me wear sometimes. You were already dating Paul by then weren't you?'

Christine groaned, 'Yes I was, and he couldn't keep it in his pants even then! I forgave him everything, I was totally in love with the idea of going out with a much older man, rather than any of the teenage boys at our school. But enough about my Ex, come on, back to Benjamin.'

'Fine by me. What made you think of him?'

'Well,' said Christine, leaning closer towards Rebecca as though imparting a state secret, 'Benjamin contacted me through Facebook last week and we have been chatting through the private messaging service, and your name came up.'

'Uh oh,' groaned Rebecca.

'Wait wait, don't jump to conclusions, I didn't tell him anything about You Know Who and You Know What, all I said was that your marriage broke down last summer and you were currently single, he is too, and he wants to meet you! Isn't that exciting?'

'No.'

'Yes it is, let me tell you about him. Do you remember he was always into music, and he and a couple of the other boys formed a band - I forget what it was called' Rebecca shook her head, she couldn't remember either 'well, he now works in the music industry, has homes in New York, Majorca and London. I told him about your son Michael and his band, and he said maybe he could do something to help him in his career. He was impressed that a sixteen year old had been playing with his own band for three years.'

'You two seem to have been having quite a conversation. You are still with Dave aren't you?' said Rebecca sullenly.

Christine Black was dating one of Woodford Secondary School's mathematics teachers, Dave Truckell. They had been seeing each other for a few months, and from what Rebecca had seen of them they seemed to be a lovely couple.

'Hey don't be like that! I am only thinking of you. Look, he is coming back to Woodford this weekend to see his parents, they still live here, and he would like to meet you for a drink in The Ship Inn on Friday night. Me and Dave can come too so it isn't too awkward...'

'No, not much' muttered Rebecca

'...and it is only a drink' Christine carried on excitedly, pointedly ignoring her friend's unenthusiastic comments. 'Come on, it will be good for you.'

'How do you work that out!' exclaimed Rebecca. 'I am perfectly happy with my life thank you very much. I do not need or want a man in it. I am still getting over the last one.'

Lisa appeared with their food, so Christine grasped the opportunity for reinforcements.

'Oh tell her she has to come, Lisa. Don't you think it would be good for Rebecca to have a nice male friend?'

'Oh no,' laughed Lisa backing away with the empty tray, 'don't you drag me into this. I am the *last* person to be handing out relationship advice.'

'But you are all loved up these days aren't you?' teased Christine. 'I have seen you in the Ship Inn several times with a mystery man. Who is he, by the way?'

'His name is Robin Morton, he works for an engineering company, divorced, no children, and his shoe size is eleven. Enough information?' she asked, with a light edge to her voice.

'How did you meet him Lisa? Was he a customer?' asked Rebecca, who although wasn't interested in having another man in her life had been wondering how people meet new partners.

Lisa recognised Rebecca's question as one of genuine curiosity rather than probing for gossip. 'Oh, I met him online, through a dating site. Are you interested then Rebecca? I can help you get started.'

'No, no, no,' said Rebecca, raising her hands up in horror and laughing. 'I haven't entirely got rid of the last one yet!' she grinned. 'But IF' she glared at Christine, her eyes appearing to be more black than their usual soft brown, 'I do decide I am ready for some romance in my life, then you, Lisa, will be the first person I shall come to.'

'Good grief don't do that!' laughed Lisa. 'This is very early days for me. Look what happened to my last attempt, and the one before that,' she chuckled happily as she hurried back to the safety of her kitchen, secure in the knowledge she was at last having fun in her love life.

'You don't need to start scouring the internet for a date,' said Christine grumpily. 'I have found you a real life man, whom you know. Or at least knew, once upon a time. Look, you don't have to sleep with him or anything, or even be on your own. I told you, Dave and I will be there too.'

'Oh, yes, you think it would be better for me to date this man who found you on the internet? Oh, and you have asked Dave if he is OK with this then?'

'Oh yes!' said Christine, totally missing the warning icy tone in Rebecca's voice. 'He is all for it, he thinks it is an excellent idea.' She sat back, and started to tuck in to her lunch. 'Mmmh Lisa this is wonderful!' she called through to the kitchen. 'You should try some,' she said offering Rebecca a forkful of rice and curry.

'Should I Christine? Should I? I have already said No Thank you to the curry, and explained my reasons even though I don't see why I should have to explain my food choices to anyone, least of all you. And no, I won't be meeting Benjamin Francis, or any other man, on Friday night because I have a Fête Committee meeting and I would rather be there with my friends than sitting in a pub making small talk with a man I haven't seen for over twenty years.' She took a breath and started again, more calmly. 'Thank you for thinking of me, and thank you for your concern about the state of my love life, but I am perfectly happy as I am at the moment, and the last thing I need is a man!'

Chapter 28

Wednesday 20th January 2016, 6.30pm

Sarah Handley whispered to her newly appointed barman, Tom Higston, whose family ran an organic farm in nearby Brackendon. 'Watch those two. Something has been brewing there for a while now, and I don't like the look of either them this evening. Any trouble call me, DON'T get involved, you are not ready.'

Tom nodded in agreement, but resolved to ignore his new employer's advice if things kicked off as she seemed to expect. He had grown up on a farm and was well-versed in handling dangerous situations, and certainly wasn't going to leave it to a middle-aged woman to handle on her own.

Sarah's warning came just in time.

'What are you trying to do, get me sent to prison? I told you I wouldn't do it, but you won't leave it alone. Don't bother putting anything into Black's Auctions in future; I am not interested in working with you any more!' Paul Black furiously slammed his partially beer-filled glass down on the table, shoved his chair backwards so he could stand up, and roughly grabbing his coat from the back of the chair he stormed out of the door leaving Tony Cookson sitting slightly opened mouthed on his own.

'Well! What was that all about?' asked Sarah, as she went over to the table with a cloth to clean up the spilt beer Paul had left there.

'Oh, er, nothing much.'

'Nothing much! Well of course it is about something, you two are good friends. I have never seen Paul behave like that with anyone before. And what was all that about not putting anything in his auction? You are always putting stuff through his auction.'

'Oh, honestly it is nothing. It will blow over.' Sarah didn't look as though she was going anywhere, so Tony lowered his voice causing her to lean down to hear what he was saying. 'Look, I didn't want to say anything, but you know what Paul is like. He had a go at trying to seduce my daughter, Lizzi, and I told him where to go, so he's got the right hump about it. She split up with her husband a couple of months ago. They were only married four years. None of us know what it is all about and we are hoping it is something of nothing, so I really don't want Paul "Shag 'Em" Black getting in the way. He didn't mean what he said, his pride has been injured that's all. It will blow over. I'll have another pint please, Sarah, and one for yourself, and whatever young Tom is drinking, thanks. Lesley will be in later, we're eating in here tonight, so please *please* don't say anything, she doesn't know anything about this business with Lizzi. Lesley has a low-enough opinion of Paul as it is!'

'No, of course I won't. But Paul really needs to stop behaving like a randy teenager and start living like the middle-aged father of two that he is. His behaviour is beginning to verge on anti-social, and he is going for younger and younger women. I had to warn him off pestering Jennifer Isaac in here the other day.'

'Probably because he has exhausted the supply of women of his own age in the area.' Tony laughed, desperately but unsuccessfully trying to ease the tension in the bar. 'Jennifer is a sensible girl, more interested in horses than men from what I have seen of her. I hear Jackie Martin is retiring, is that true?'

His attempt to change the subject was lost on Sarah, who continued with her train of thought as she walked back to the bar, with Tony following her. 'Or the women of his age have more sense than to get entangled with a man like that. If I didn't find his behaviour so distasteful I would feel sorry for him. He is a nice man underneath all that ridiculous way he behaves towards women.'

'Ooooh who are we talking about?' Nicola Stacey joined them at the bar, empty glass in hand and nodded in agreement at Sarah's sign language question for Same Again.

'Paul Black,' said Sarah, shortly. 'Here's your pint Tony,' she nodded to him to go back to his table. 'I'll come over with a couple of menus when Lesley appears shall I?'

'Yes please, thanks Sarah,' and he hurried away before Nicola could start to question him.

'What's Paul been up to now? Or should I ask who?'

'Oh just the usual, chasing skirt too young for him. How is Cliff these days? He seems to be looking a lot happier.'

'Yes, I think he is on the road to recovery. Such a contrast to Paul, and yet of the two of them none of us would have been shocked if the revelations about Cliff last year had been about Paul instead, would we?'

'No, you're right,' laughed Sarah. 'Of the two of them Cliff would have not even been on my list of suspects! So business in the antiques centre is picking up again?'

'Hard to tell at this time of year, but at least the number of stall holders is starting to build up again. Not sure how long one of the new ones will last. Does he come in here, Rowland Mitchell?'

'Name doesn't ring a bell. What does he look like?'

'Um, he is tallish, probably just under six foot, dark hair and moustache, late fifties or early sixties - hard to tell - and wears a filthy three piece tweed suit with matching cap. I am sure you would know him if he came in here Sarah, he is quite distinctive.'

'No, no, can't say I recognise your description. Why don't you think he is going to last?'

'Well, he rarely comes in to clean and tidy his stand. He has been in the antiques centre for about two months and has only come in three times! And his stock is real dinosaur antiques stuff, you know like bureaus and tall boys with the odd Staffordshire figurine thrown in for good measure, or cheap mass produced dinner plates and bowls. When he does bother to come in and re-stock it all seems to sell though. Very curious. Mind you, we don't mind him not coming to see us very often; he absolutely reeks of stale cigarette smoke and alcohol. Cliff makes a point of walking round with the air freshener when Rowland is in the room.'

Sarah laughed 'Oh yes, Mike does the same....' She stopped. 'Mike did the same when we had a less-than-fragrant customer. Here is his can of air freshener,' she said as she picked up the can from under the bar. 'Yes, what can I get for you,' Sarah turned on her best Pub Landlady charm to serve the couple who were now stood at the bar next to Nicola.

While she was busy with her customers, Nicola sat quietly waiting for her to finish.

'Have you thought anymore about going to Zumba? There is a class on a Tuesday night in the village hall. I thought I might give it a go next week,' said Sarah once the couple had left the bar with their drinks and menus. 'I need to start getting in shape for horse riding this year. Mrs Barker suggested a yard up near them in Swanwick as a good place to start with our riding lessons. Tom is settling in well and Tuesdays are normally quiet in here, so it could give him a fair opportunity to start taking responsibility for the place on his own without me breathing down his neck.'

Nicola noted her friend's decision to carry on as though nothing traumatic had recently happened in her life, and sighed to herself. Ever since Mike's death Sarah had refused to talk about him and her little slip a few minutes earlier had been the first time she had used his name in Nicola's presence since his funeral.

'Zumba? Oh I'm not sure Sarah. It all looks a bit complicated to me.'

'No, it'll be fine. Jackie Martin was in here yesterday, poor lady. Her bones are healing but she is still struggling to move around normally. Anyway, she said that everyone gets it wrong, but it's not called that, it's called Freestyle!'

'Oh I like that! Well, I'll give it a go if you do,' laughed Nicola, 'but I'm not sure it will be for me.'

'OK, why don't we plan to go for four weeks in a row, and then if we don't like it we can say we have tried? I'll organise Tom to work here for the next four Tuesdays, and you and I can go to the Indian afterwards to recover. How does that sound?'

Nicola thought is sounded excellent that her friend was planning to take one evening away from the pub every week for four weeks; to her knowledge since Sarah and Mike had taken over the running of The Ship Inn eleven years previously they had rarely spent any evenings elsewhere, even on their days off. Nicola wasn't quite so keen on the idea of spending the next four Tuesday evenings at Zumba though, but she was willing to try for her friend's sake.

'That sounds perfect, Sarah. Let's do it.'

Chapter 29

Thursday 21st January 2016, 3.00pm

'Penny for them Rebecca?'

'Mmmh? What? Oh, sorry Paul, I was miles away!'

'Yes, and you have been for the past half an hour,' he said, kindly. 'You were going to proof read the auction catalogue, but I can see you haven't got past the second page yet. Is everything alright?'

'Oh yes, everything's fine thank you Paul. Sorry, I'll crack on with this now.'

Rebecca frowned in concentration as she checked and double-checked that the descriptions of the paintings for the following Friday's Art Auction matched the photographs, and that the reserves listed were the ones agreed with the vendors. She was interrupted twice, once by the ringing tone of the telephone which Paul answered in his office before she could reach for her handset, and once by Daniel coming through from the auction warehouse to make himself a cup of tea.

'Cuppa Rebecca?'

'Oh yes thanks, green tea please.'

'Rebecca, can I ask you something please?'

'Yes, OK,' said Rebecca slowly. She had had enough of people telling her what to do, and questioning her choices, and really wasn't in the mood for a young lad like Daniel to start on her too.

'Well, is everything alright with my work do you know? Paul has been in a funny mood with me for weeks now, wanting to check every single thing which comes in for the auctions before I start processing them, rather than his usual manner of coming in and out while I am working and discussing individual items as they are laid out, or being happy to only come out when I ask for his expertise. Do you know what it is I have done wrong? I have been going over it and can't think of anything.'

'Oh Daniel, yes as far as I know your work is excellent! If you have made any terrible mistakes then I am not aware of them. But you are right, Paul has been in a funny mood for a while now, but it is with all of us, not just you. Ever since those stolen medals turned up in the auction last October he has been more concerned than ever about the provenance of all of the items for sale. I wouldn't worry about anything, but may be worth having a word with him about it? He won't bite your head off, if you were consistently doing something wrong he would have told you by now, I am sure of it.'

'Oh that is such a relief! I have been really worried, and it has started to affect my sleep which is very unusual. My girlfriend says I can sleep through an earthquake, and she has been threatening to come in and speak to Paul, which I really don't want her to do. Can you imagine how embarrassing that would be?'

'Ha ha yes, that would be excruciating,' laughed Rebecca.

'What are you two laughing about?' asked Paul as he emerged from his office. 'Oh has the kettle boiled? Make me one will you Daniel? How is the catalogue?' he asked, turning his attention to Rebecca.

'So good so far,' she smiled up at him. 'Another half an hour and I'll be finished. Do you want to check it or shall I email it to the printers?'

'Oh no, if you are happy with it I will be, thanks Rebecca. Anything new come in today Daniel?'

'Yes, another seven Lots for the antiques sale in February.'

'Right, I'll come back with you and have a look. Is that my mug? Come on then.'

As Rebecca watched them go she thought about what Daniel had been saying, and wondered if it would be appropriate to question Paul about his change in management style, or if that would be a step too far out of her role as administrative assistant. She had been truthful with Daniel; she really didn't know of anything he was doing wrong to cause Paul's new-found cautious approach to the items which sellers were bringing in for the various auctions. No wonder he was coming in earlier than normal, he was trying to do three people's jobs! In the end she decided to say nothing. She didn't want to invite Paul to start confiding in her about anything personal or professional; that would bring a new level of intimacy to their relationship, and she was very happy with the way they treated each other now that a few ground rules had been established. But her natural caring nature meant that she would be a little more alert to reasons which may be behind this change in behaviour.

Once she had completed proof-reading the auction catalogue and emailed it to the printers as usual, her mind returned to her friend's attempt at match-making. She was furious with Christine for assuming she would be willing to meet her old boyfriend, or any man, so soon after her own marriage break-up and she was particularly upset that Christine had seen fit to involve other people, namely her own boyfriend Dave Truckell who was her children's mathematics teacher! How embarrassing to think they would have been talking about her, discussing 'poor Rebecca' or worse 'poor man-less Rebecca'. The urge to walk round to the estate agency on the High Street where Christine worked and tell her exactly how betrayed she felt was strong. How DARE she talk about her, let alone set-up a date for her? Just at that moment the front door open, and Cliff walked in.

'Oh what do you want now?'

Cliff was rather taken aback by her venomous tone. She had not raised her voice to him since that awful day last July when she discovered he was having an affair. What now? Surely there were no more secrets, please let there be no more revelations, he really didn't think he could cope with anything else.

'Sorry to disturb you Rebecca, is Paul free?'

Instantly Rebecca felt the heat of anger dissipate at the sight of Cliff's frightened-looking face. It wasn't his fault Christine was interfering in her life. Or was it? He was certainly responsible for most of what had gone on over the previous few months.

'Sorry Cliff,' she said wearily. 'I am having a bit of a bad time today. Paul is in the warehouse with Daniel Bartlett. Go on through, I'm sure he won't mind.'

'Is everything OK? Anything I can do? Just tell me Rebecca, you know I will help if I can.'

'Nothing you can help with Cliff, not now. Go on, go and find Paul and leave me to... oh my goodness I am late; I should have been out of here ten minutes ago! I said I would collect Mum from her hospital appointment!'

'Can I help? I could pop round later with a takeaway. Would you like Pizza or Indian? It would be nice to see Jackie, and the kids, and would save you cooking for everybody.'

'Now that is a good idea, thank you. Give the kids a ring and let them choose, I think it is Nick's choice tonight. Won't be long before he has gone to University, will it, we should make the most of it while we have all three of them at home.' She smiled sadly at Cliff, before pulling herself together and dashing out of the door to her car, desperately hoping the traffic lights out of Woodford would be in her favour and not make her any later to pick up her mother than she already was.

Cliff watched her go, his face a picture of misery. He no longer had three children at home, because he had moved out to live above the antiques centre last summer. He pulled himself together and went to find Paul, who was exactly where Rebecca had told him he would be, in the warehouse with Daniel. Daniel's face was a picture of frustration.

'Is this a good time?' asked Cliff, tentatively.

'Yes, yes,' said Paul. 'Come on in. We are just finishing here. Thanks Daniel, good job. Finish up and then you can go home, and I'll see you in the morning.'

Once Daniel was out of earshot Cliff commented 'Well he didn't look very happy.'

'Didn't he?' asked Paul, surprised. 'I didn't notice anything. He's a good worker, is Daniel, I just hope he stays here.' He gestured to Cliff to follow him out of the warehouse to his office. Once they were settled inside, and had finished making small talk about the general problems of managing staff and dishonesty and lack of loyalty in the antiques trade, which took them a good ten minutes, Cliff took a deep breath and launched into the conversation he had been trying to pluck up the courage to start for several weeks. The news of the events in The Ship Inn the previous evening had given Cliff a tangible reason to tackle his friend about the awkward subject, and he felt the time was right to talk to him about it.

'Paul, mate, we've been friends for a long time.'

'Yes, we have. So?' Paul was already on the defensive. Damn, thought Cliff, this wasn't going as planned. Oh well, might as well continue.

'I know why you and Tony have fallen out.'

Paul's face was a picture. His jaw dropped, his eyes were wide, and the look of astonishment lasted for approximately three seconds before he snapped his mouth shut and looked away from Cliff.

'How?' he asked in a careful tone which matched his expression.

'He told Sarah Handley, who told Nicola, who told me.'

171

Paul's face took on a slightly sneaky look. 'Tony told Sarah what. Exactly.'

'Oh come on mate,' said Cliff, suddenly realising he had been hunched forward clasping his hands together as if in prayer, and made an effort to relax his shoulders and lean back in his chair. 'Don't make me say it. You know what you did, why don't you just apologise and move on with your life. It isn't as bad as anything I have done, after all. And Tony has every right to be angry with you, don't you think? You were out of order. OK, it's nothing you haven't tried to do before, I mean even you would have to agree that Jennifer Isaac is too young for you. And as for this business with Tony's daughter, well, that's a bit close to home isn't it, even for you? Just apologise to Tony and Lesley, and then we can all get back to normal. This tension between the two of you is horrible; I need my friends around me not fighting with each other. I can understand Tony being upset with you, but why are you behaving in such a childish way with Tony? Admit you were wrong, and get it over with.'

Paul sat very still and stared at his friend of almost nineteen years.

'So you have all made up your minds have you? Even you. You, who I have stood by, with no judgement, through everything you went through last year. I have been tried and found guilty with no opportunity for defence.'

Cliff shivered, his friend's voice was so cold, his expression steely. But, as the father of a daughter, albeit a good few years younger than Tony's daughter and definitely too young even for Paul Black, he could understand Tony's need to defend his daughter against a known serial womaniser like Paul. Cliff was also wary of Paul's intentions towards Rebecca, and had seriously considered the possibility of killing him if he ever treated her in the way he treated all of the other women in his life.

'What defence could you possibly have Paul?' asked Cliff. 'We all know what you are like. The girl was vulnerable, her marriage had recently broken up, and you pounced. As you always do.'

'STOP! How dare you. Get out.'

Cliff stayed where he was, looking in amazement at his friend. Paul had clearly lost all sense of reality if he thought his behaviour towards Tony's daughter was acceptable. Cliff and Paul had always been able to tackle each other about any issues, however personal or in the wrong they were, but for some reason Paul was behaving differently about this subject. Could it be that he really cared for Tony's daughter? Or was it the old chestnut of wanting something he couldn't have?

'Paul, don't be like that. Come on, someone had to say something to you...' Paul cut him off before he could finish.

'I said get out and I meant it.' As he spoke in a low angry voice Paul stood up and walked purposefully around his desk towards the door. As he opened it he looked at Cliff, who was staring, not moving. 'What part of "Get Out" do you not understand? Move before I do something I regret!' Paul's voice was getting louder and his furious presence was filling the room. Cliff left.

Chapter 30

Saturday 23rd January 2016, 3.00pm

Peter, Jennifer and Gemma were sitting around the kitchen table in Gemma's cottage. It was five days since Jackie Martin had dropped her bombshell, and Peter was still no clearer about how he felt about it. He was made senior partner at his previous Practice before his thirtieth birthday, and for over twenty years had found the responsibility fairly onerous. The relative freedom of being a junior partner at the age of fifty two years old had been liberating, and he really enjoyed being able to concentrate on his own job without having his time taken up with budget sheets and staffing problems.

However, the opportunity to walk into a ready-made small equine practice, one which he already knew and enjoyed working in, and bring in his own approach across the board was extremely tempting. Jackie's nudges and hints about upgrading the facilities to incorporate his desire to be able to rehabilitate horses on site was keeping him awake at night with excitement and anticipation as he ran through all the possibilities.

Jennifer, meanwhile, was not at all enthusiastic about any of it. She was so tired. Almost every horse owner she saw either in the equine hospital or out on her calls viewed her with suspicion, such was their loyalty and respect for Jackie and Alastair, and she was fed-up of treading on eggshells in the way she spoke to them.

Here in Brackenshire she was expected to work independently of her father, although he, Alastair and Jackie were always willing to listen to her fears and questions. They would discuss her treatment options rather than point her to this tried-and-tested plan or that we-have-always-done-it-this-way method. It had reached the point the week before when she caught herself looking back favourably on the days when she had to work within clear boundaries and guide-lines, when only a few months ago she had found them restricting, and at times stifling.

Alastair's wife Hazel was making noises about the amount of time her 'retired' husband was spending on veterinary duties, and Jackie was making it clear she would not be emulating his approach to retirement and would probably be living abroad for at least part of the year. The thought of being without these two people with their wealth of experiences to support her was terrifying. She felt she was out of her depth as things were now; if the Practice was reduced to only herself and her father she would sink.

Gemma couldn't see what the problem was. She and her ex-husband had established their own business when they were in their early twenties, and then when Lisa asked her five years ago to go into business with her, which resulted in them buying and re-vamping the Woodford Tearooms, she had jumped at the chance and loved every minute. There were even a few months when she ran both businesses until she and her husband agreed to separate both their personal and professional lives. Gemma thrived on the kind of stress created with a healthy dose of adrenalin, and she loved challenges and puzzles such as the one Peter was currently faced with. But she had no interest in horses, or veterinary work, so appreciated that there were issues to be faced of which she had very little idea.

'So what do you think about exploring the possibility of buying part of the Maxwell-Lewis farm and establishing it both as our home and my veterinary surgery?' Peter asked Gemma.

'I am quite happy to live above the shop, so-to-speak. I did it for all of the years my first husband and I ran our catering business.'

'But didn't you fall in love with that house on Swan Hill? The views were fantastic.'

'Yes they were, and I did like that house, but I didn't love it. I do think we could turn it into a house that I loved though. But realistically, as beautiful as those views were, how much time would we actually have to enjoy them while we were at home? I see them regularly when I am out with Suzy.'

'Well yes, there is that. Neither of us have much time for sitting around when we are at home. I suppose I am very lucky in that I see those views while I am out and about on calls. I do love stopping the car and standing by the side of the road breathing the country air and enjoying the stunning vista of Stormy Vale.'

Jennifer looked up in amazement. Over the last few weeks she had been so busy trying to find the various yards and fields where her patients lived that she had not been paying any attention to the scenery, and she certainly didn't have time to stop and get out of her car in order to gaze at it for a few minutes. With vague addresses and a sat nav which regularly sent her to the wrong side of the property for access, or on one memorable occasion to the wrong yard completely where she sat for over ten minutes before having to phone the Woodford Equine Veterinary office for help, Jennifer was beginning to think she had made a big mistake giving up her dependable job up in Shropshire. She grew up in the County and was familiar with the lanes and tracks up there, but down here she felt like a fish out of water.

'What do you think Jennifer? Jackie has given you a permanent part-time contract for when she returned to work, but if she isn't coming back then obviously you would have a full-time one. And I would love you to be a junior partner in my practice, if you would like to join me.'

'Oooh yes, that would be wonderful!' said Gemma, sitting up in her chair as the possibilities began to flood her brain. 'Between the three of us, assuming I can sell this cottage fairly quickly, we could buy at least one of those parcels of land. Do you have any savings you could put in Jennifer?'

Jennifer looked at her step-mother in horror. 'Savings? I haven't even paid off the last of my debts from vet school Gemma.'

'Oh, of course, I was forgetting how young you are. You are so professional and competent I keep thinking you have been in the workplace for a lot longer. Sorry.'

'Well I do have the money from when they bought my share of the practice in Shropshire stashed away still, combined with your money from the sale of this cottage we would easily be able to afford the dairy part of the farm. I had a look online on Tuesday night after Jackie talked to us. We would have to work out some figures for renovation, and Jackie wants to sell the practice to me for about three hundred thousand pounds. I think we could probably do with a third full-time vet, don't you Jennifer? So there may be a bit more flexibility with the money if we opt for a senior partner to join us.' Peter and Gemma were feeding off each other's enthusiasm, their plans becoming more extravagant as the afternoon passed by.

Meanwhile Jennifer was still trying to take in the words Gemma had said to her. When Jackie Martin phoned her back in November Jennifer was feeling dissatisfied and unappreciated. Now she was feeling exhausted and unconfident. But Gemma clearly didn't see her like that. And neither could her father or he wouldn't be including her in his plans for the business, and talking about making her a junior partner. She couldn't think straight while the pair of them were chattering on about converting this building and knocking down that shed. At this rate they would have bought the entire Maxwell-Lewis Farm and opened a veterinary theme park with cafe and restaurant on site!

'Sorry Gem, Dad, I have to go. I'll take the dogs out. I'll sort myself out for supper tonight. Thanks.' She wasn't sure they even noticed she had left, such was their excitement at the possibilities their imaginations were exploring.

Chapter 31

Saturday 23rd January 2016, 5.45pm

'Sorry girls, it still gets dark earlier than I think it will.' Jennifer, Lucy the greyhound and Suzy the Staffie were still ten minutes away from the car, the only ones on the Trailway, and without a torch. It was a beautifully still evening, and the owls were noisily hooting to each other up in the trees.

A different sound caught her attention, and Jennifer stopped to listen. She could hear regular rhythmic noises coming towards them. She turned and recognised the sight of a head torch bobbing up and down as the wearer ran along the track. Oh Lord, she thought as she moved herself and the dogs over to one side, is this friend or foe? At least I have the dogs with me. She looked down at Lucy and Suzy who had both obediently sat down when they realised she was waiting for the runner to pass them.

'Well you two wouldn't be much use as alert dogs would you, or protection,' she whispered to them.

'Hello Jennifer. Is everything OK?' The runner stopped alongside them, but Jennifer couldn't make out who it was other than a male with strong calves because the head torch was shining in her eyes. 'You're out a bit late aren't you? Are you on your own?'

Ah, now she recognised that voice. It was Paul Black. Oh brilliant, what good timing, she thought sourly. Of all the people to meet at this time of night on the deserted Trailway, her walk has to coincide with her least favourite Woodford resident's run.

'Oh yes, we're fine thanks Paul. I just got caught out thinking the evenings were getting lighter than they actually are,' she laughed in an effort to hide the bad temper she was in.

'Here,' he was fishing around for something and then unclipped it from his belt and handed her a small torch. 'Have this. Or I can walk back with you if you prefer?'

'Oh thank you! No, no, you carry on. I don't want to interrupt your run. We'll be fine. You are very kind, thanks Paul. I'll bring it back later.' All her ill-feelings towards him dissipated, and were replaced with a lighter one of feeling grateful for his kindness and consideration. This was short-lived.

'It's a date,' he grinned and ran off.

'Oh flipping marvellous, I walked into that one didn't I girls.'

Chapter 32

Sunday 24th January 2016, 7.30am

Cliff sighed; another Sunday morning spent wandering aimlessly round the stalls at Drayton Flea Market. This time last year he had been tucked up in bed, his own bed, content in the knowledge that his business was working well for him. This year he was freezing, miserable, and broke, struggling to keep his head above water in an ever-dwindling marketplace. What an idiot to let things get to this stage. Perhaps he should find himself a proper job, a nine-to-five job with a guaranteed steady income, and weekends off, and six weeks' paid holiday a year.

'Alright Cliff, how are you?' the man whose stall he had just walked past called him back. 'I thought this might be up your street, you buy things like this don't you?' He held out a small heavy object wrapped incongruously in bright blue tissue paper. As Cliff started to peel back the layers of paper his heart began to sing as the small jade bowl appeared. *This* is what dealing in antiques was all about, he thought to himself. Finds like these, falling into your lap. He had never worked out the statistics, but he knew the odds of having something beautiful and perfect and valuable just handed to him were way below those for chipped, cracked and broken cheap goods. Cliff was one of those antiques dealers who got a thrill from seeing and handling quality antiques; he always felt a slight tightening in his chest and a tingle up his spine when in the presence of items like this one.

'You know about that sort of thing don't you?' the man asked.

'Yeah, yeah, well I think I do. This is lovely. How much do you want for it?'

'We cleared a house yesterday, brought most of the furniture up here today and only found it just now in the drawer of that cabinet up there.' The man pointed to the far depth of his van where a large solid wood cabinet was lurking. 'Don't know much about that sort of thing myself, I showed it to Andrew Dover and he reckoned it four hundred. Everyone knows he's a mean bastard, so if he is offering me that it must be worth more.'

'Do you want me to bid for it?' asked Cliff.

'Yeah, if you like. What would you pay me for it?'

'Double Andrew's offer,' said Cliff confidently, and putting the bowl and its wrappings down on the table reached into his trouser pocket for the roll of notes he kept there. 'Will you take eight hundred now?'

'Sounds fair,' said the man, happy to have made a sale, his first of the morning. It was always hard to stall out when the weather was rainy and cold, the buyers didn't want to hang around and had often left before the fair officially opened, leaving the label turners who then came in to kill an hour or so while they waited for an appointment in town, or for their train.

'You have checked the other drawers are empty haven't you?' Cliff asked.

The man laughed. 'Yes! No more treasures to be found.'

Cliff walked away much happier, buoyed up by his purchase. He decided to skip the rest of the stalls and head straight for the cafe. As soon as he walked into the building he could see something was wrong. The little group sat around the table had an uneasy air about them, the tension was palpable. Cliff bought himself a cup of coffee and a sausage roll, and went to join them, deciding not to mention his find until he knew what was upsetting the group.

'Hello lads, have you all decided to stay out of the rain too?' he asked, trying to lighten the mood without risking turning their collective bad temper towards himself.

'Alright Cliff, still pissing down is it?' grunted John Robson, barely looking up from his tea, clearly not expecting an answer.

No one else acknowledged his presence, so Cliff got the silent message loud and clear and settled down to drink his coffee and eat his breakfast without making any more attempts at conversation. After a few minutes Rowland Mitchell also joined them, bringing with him his usual stench of ingrained cigarette smoke and exuding alcohol fumes.

'What's this I hear that you know who robbed you, John?' he asked with his customary bluntness.

'You've been robbed?' asked Cliff incredulously. John Robson was well-known as a hard man in the Trade, not someone you would want to upset, and certainly not someone you would steal from. 'What, someone stole from your shop in Portobello?'

'Behave,' John glanced at Cliff. 'He means the bronze that came bouncing back end of last year.' Turning to Rowland he said 'I do have an idea about who is behind it all, yes. I think you do too.'

'Right, I see,' nodded Rowland.

Cliff became aware he was sitting slightly open-mouthed as this exchange took place, the air of menace around the table was stifling, and he suddenly shivered. Rowland Mitchell had been a stallholder in his antiques centre for several weeks, and this was possibly the first time Cliff had even been aware he was an accepted member of the clique which surrounded John Robson. Cliff was sure he had never seen Rowland talking, or even sitting down, with any of the other antiques dealers. He looked at his customer with fresh eyes, and wondered if maybe he had underestimated the man.

Rowland Mitchell seemed to have heard all he wanted to hear, and abruptly left the table, leaving behind his own unpleasant fragrance. No one commented on the exchange, or showed any curiosity about John Robson's assertions. Cliff was dying to ask who John thought was responsible for the fake bronze figure which had caused him so much financial pain, but didn't dare.

The group's focus changed to a Chinese vase which one of them had sold on eBay for forty thousand pounds, and then on to Cliff's newly purchased jade bowl which one of the other dealers bought from him for nine hundred pounds.

After that the group broke up, the dealers either going back out for another tour of the flea market, or heading out to a different fair, or off for Sunday lunch with their families. Cliff stayed where he was, waiting for Tony to come and find him. He didn't have to wait long before Tony appeared, shaking the rain off his hat.

'Would you like another drink, Cliff?'

'I'll have another coffee, thanks Tony.'

When Tony came back with the tray of food and drink, Cliff said 'You know that chap who took a stall in my antiques centre last month, Rowland Mitchell. Do you know anything about him?'

'Other than he stinks? No, why do you ask?'

'Well, just before you got here John Robson and his gang were sitting at this table, and Rowland Mitchell came over and joined us as though it was the most natural thing in the world! John and Rowland clearly know each other very well, I couldn't believe my eyes. I had no idea he knew that lot, but no one else batted an eyelid when he joined us.'

'I wouldn't have thought Rowland dealt in the sort of things John does; he's mainly a bit of this 'n that type of dealer isn't he? I'd have thought John was way out of his league. Still, you live and learn. What were they talking about?'

'Ah, well that was the interesting thing. Apparently John knows who is behind the fake bronze he bought last year. From the way they were talking Rowland does too.'

'Oh? Who is it?'

'Now that they didn't say. I was a bit surprised to find Rowland Mitchell was more in the know about these things than me, and that he was clearly included in the secret while I wasn't. I suppose in their eyes I am little more than a shop owner. My dealer credentials have been tarnished.'

Tony chose to ignore Cliff's moment of self-pity and focus on the interesting part of his information. 'Really, he was welcomed into the conversation? So what did they say then? Does everybody else know? Who is it?'

'No idea, no one was saying anything much. Just that John knew who was behind it, and Rowland did too. Whoever it is I wouldn't like to be in their shoes. John Robson has a hard nut reputation; I wouldn't cross him.'

'No, me neither.' Tony shivered. 'Didn't he put someone in a wheel chair permanently once? Years ago.'

'Oh yes, that's right. A dealer in Bermondsey Market who cheated him on some scrap silver wasn't it? I'd hate to think what he would do to someone who deliberately sold him a fake.'

They both sat silently for a minute or two, until Cliff roused himself. 'Right, are you finished here?' he said as he collected all the empty debris from various drinks and breakfasts which had been left scattered all over the table.

'Yup, you?'

'Certainly am, let's head home.'

Chapter 33

Monday 25th January, 9.30am

Paul's change in routine of coming to work earlier than Rebecca continued, as did the requests for no disturbances while he was in his office. For a man who was usually so interactive with his staff, always out and about in the warehouse or the main office, chatting with customers and getting involved in queries and problems with his staff, and whose office door was rarely closed, he was transformed into a quiet introverted character who rarely left his desk. He still hadn't confided to Rebecca what the problems were, and her curiosity was beginning to get the better of her. The atmosphere at work had become permanently unsettled; everyone was on edge waiting for the next slight on their work from Paul.

Rebecca decided that today was the day to ask him what was going on. As far as she could see there was nothing wrong with the business, and yet whatever the problem was it clearly had something to do with the auctions because Paul was still being unusually picky about the goods they were accepting for sale. Daniel commented more than once to Rebecca that Paul had changed the goal posts and he no longer knew whether or not to say yes to items he would previously receive for auctions with no hesitation. Rebecca could see it was starting to undermine Daniel's confidence, and thought that if Paul didn't change his management style soon then Daniel would be off to another auction house. Similarly Paul's recent behaviour had changed their office dynamics, and while she welcomed the more business-like relationship between her and Paul, she missed the banter and laughter. If things didn't improve soon then she also may start scanning the vacancies pages of the Brackenshire Post.

The rift between Paul and Tony had widened to the extent that Tony was now banned from the Black's Auctions premises, and after last week's fallout it appeared Cliff's name was also added to the list of people who were persona non grata. Cliff told Rebecca and Jackie all about Paul's treatment of Tony's daughter when he joined them for a family Sunday lunch cooked by Rebecca and their musician son Michael, and about Paul's failed attempts to hook up with Jennifer Isaac. They were all in agreement that Paul was rapidly heading in the wrong direction and had taken on the mantle of desperation, and it wouldn't be long if he carried on in this way he would be labelled a sex-pest. Michael and Charlotte, Cliff and Rebecca's daughter, were friends with Christine and Paul's children who were in the same school years, so the adults tried to keep the conversation from them, unsuccessfully.

Despite the general consensus that Paul was travelling down a slippery slope with his treatment of the women he came into contact with, Rebecca could not see how Paul's failed attempts at romances could be resulting in his change of business practice. He had always behaved in this way towards women, although recent events suggested his modus operandi was changing from casting his hook and enticing the unfortunate women to follow it willingly back to heartbreak, to actually catching them and dragging them into his net before discarding them. Rebecca knew of several women through her Parent Teacher Association and Fête commitments who deliberately entered into relationships with Paul believing that *they* would be the one to make him change his ways. His reputation was so well known that no one in Woodford could possibly be unaware of it. That couldn't be said for the unfortunate women he met online, and by hers and Christine's calculations he had been online dating for at least twelve years, even before he and Christine had split up.

The front door opened and Peter Isaac walked in. Rebecca's heart sank. Was this is it? Another disgruntled father coming to have it out with Paul about his treatment of his daughter?'

'Hi Rebecca, are you well?' asked Peter.

'Yes, fine thank you!' replied Rebecca as brightly as possible. 'We don't usually see you in here Peter, how can I help you today?'

'Oh thank you, but I think I need to see Paul about this little matter,' responded Peter gravely.

Here we go, thought Rebecca. 'OK, I think he is in the middle of something at the moment.'

'Oh don't worry, he is expecting me,' and Peter walked over to Paul's door, knocked, and then opened it and went into his office.

Fifteen minutes later the door re-opened and Peter came out. Rebecca studied his face but could see no clues as to what had been going on. At least there had been no shouting that she could hear, and Peter's face and hands appeared to be unmarked.

'Bye Rebecca,' he said as he walked on out of the front door without pausing.

Minutes later Paul came out of his office and walked over to the kettle. 'Tea, Rebecca?'

'That would be lovely, thank you Paul.'

'Anything I need to know?' he asked, quietly. Now she thought about it, Paul had been unusually quiet and unobtrusive since Cliff's visit the previous Thursday. Paul was normally a live wire, similar to Cliff in that you could sense his presence even if he was concentrating on reading something or examining an item for the auction. But for the last few days his demeanour was a strange mix of simmering anger and defeat.

'Nope, nothing I can think of Paul,' replied Rebecca in as bright a tone as she could manage.

Paul looked at her intently. She looked away.

'You too?' he murmured, and returned to his office without completing his tea-making task.

Well that was uncomfortable, thought Rebecca, and tried to concentrate on the list of answer phone messages and emails which usually filled the first hour of her Monday mornings. Suddenly Paul's door opened.

'I'm just going out. Don't know when I'll be back,' he said over his shoulder as he exited through the front door.

Rebecca sighed. Whatever was going on was interfering with their work now. Paul always let her know where he was, and he was always courteous when he spoke to her. For the last few days he had been abrupt and secretive about his movements. What to do? Presumably Paul's pride had taken a battering, and he was feeling embarrassed and defensive if he thought everyone knew. But all he had been doing was behaving in typical Paul Black-fashion, so what was so different about this one? Maybe he actually cared about Lizzi? Or Jennifer? Or was there someone else?

Daniel walked into the room. 'Hi Rebecca, is Paul in his office?' he asked, peering through the open doorway as he asked the question.

'No, he has just gone out. Is it urgent?'

'Oh, no, nothing much, it is not really important. Where's he gone? I thought he was going to help me work out the logistics for Wednesday. We have two house clearances to do: one in Swanwick and one here in Woodford. I need to know which we are doing first so I can book the guys who are helping with the one here in Woodford. It is Mrs Maxwell-Lewis' old farmhouse so will be a massive job. Have you ever been in there?'

'Ah, yes, a couple of times she invited me into the kitchen for a drink while we discussed Summer Fête affairs. One of those lovely old houses, crammed with knick-knacks and family history. You'll never clear that in a day! Particularly not if you are clearing another house in different part of the county.'

'No, that's why we're using the Higston lads and one of their vans. Mrs Maxwell-Lewis has already moved out, and taken everything she wants. She has also taken Simon's belongings too. Cliff is meant to be going in tomorrow to sort through most of the saleable stuff, but when I saw him in the tearooms on Friday he seemed to think he wouldn't be needed after all. I haven't managed to speak to Paul since then, but I will need to take a van tomorrow and help Cliff if he is doing it, and I need to let the Higstons know what time we need them.'

'OK, hang on a minute, I'll try his mobile.'

Seconds later they both turned towards the sound of Paul's mobile phone as the familiar ring tone of the theme tune to the Antiques Roadshow played in his office.

'Ah, right,' said Daniel. 'Has he not told you where he is going? He can't be far if he hasn't taken his phone with him.'

'No, no, he didn't say.' Secretly she wondered if he had gone down the road to Williamson Antiques and was healing the rift between himself and Cliff. Aloud she said 'Are you clearing the house in Swanwick first?'

'Yes, we're picking the keys up from the estate agents at nine in the morning.'

'And you are taking both Black's vans up there?'

'Yes.'

'So do you think you will be finished by twelve noon?'

'I should think so, yes, it's a straightforward job. The house was a mid-terrace two bedroom holiday let so no personal belongings and only the bare minimum of furniture. One and a half vans for the dump and less than half a van back here with saleable goods.'

'Right, I will speak to Cliff and find out what is going on. In the meantime why don't you assume Cliff will be at the Maxwell-Lewis Farm with you tomorrow, and you can sort out the first dump load and the first auction van load from there between you, plus leave enough directions for what is rubbish and what are auction goods to keep the Higston boys busy the following morning until you get there, say, about one thirty in the afternoon?'

'Yes, I think that will work,' said Daniel, rubbing his chin as he tried to calculate how long it would take to ferry the rubbish to the dump, bring the items for auction back to Black's and unload them, and then drive back down the road to the Maxwell-Lewis Farm which was less than two minutes away.

'Hard day tomorrow with no time for a lunch break, and I reckon we will be working late into the afternoon. But the electricity hasn't been switched off as far as I know, so at least we will be able to see what we are doing. I remember last year we were trying to clear a big old former rectory at the other end of Woodford where the electricity had been turned off so that by half past three in the afternoon we couldn't see a thing! But the farm is still up and running, so they need the power. The cows are due to be auctioned off next month, but they still have to be fed and milked until then.'

'Poor Mrs Maxwell-Lewis. She was absolutely heart-broken by Simon's behaviour. And now she has to move so she can be nearer the prison just so she can see him. He is bound to be given a custodial sentence when his case comes to Court in April. They wouldn't have kept him behind bars for this long if there was a chance he would be given a suspended sentence.' The previous year the residents of the town of Woodford had been rocked by the revelations that a local couple, the Wildes, had masterminded a series of burglaries which became known as The Country House Thefts, and had used a local antiques dealer, Simon Maxwell-Lewis, to acquire the goods. Rebecca felt that of all the people who had been victims of the Wilde's criminal businesses, Mrs Maxwell-Lewis was the least well-known but most affected.

'Not just that, it was his ill-gotten gains which had been keeping that farm running for years. She couldn't have afforded to keep it going without his financial input. She is lucky not to have been charged as an accessory.' Daniel did not feel the same sympathy towards Mrs Maxwell-Lewis as Rebecca. He did not believe she was the innocent party Rebecca believed her to be, and in his view turning a blind eye to robbery and living off the proceeds was as bad as committing the original crimes. Rebecca thought it was an admirable point of view for a young man who dealt with valuable goods belonging to other people, and decided not to challenge him on his fixed black-and-white opinions.

'True. I wonder who will buy the land? I don't imagine anyone will want to keep it as a dairy farm.'

'Not unless they need their heads examined!' laughed Daniel. 'No money and unsociable hard-working hours. My brother had designs on working there when he left college, so he is gutted it is being broken up. I expect he will end up at the Higston's farm over in Brackendon, that's where he has done most of his work experience and now that Tom is making his living from pulling pints they could do with someone like Nathan. I expect the Maxwell-Lewis land will go for development won't it?'

'I don't think it can. Woodford has some sort of ring-fencing whereby only the land to the east, where I live, can be built on for domestic housing. I think the Maxwell-Lewis land has a covenant on it which means it has to stay as agricultural land.'

'I think if you have enough money you can do whatever you want in this country,' said Daniel.

'Sometimes it does seem that way,' agreed Rebecca.

Chapter 34

Monday 25th January, 12 noon

'Hello darling, how lovely to see you. Are you having an early lunch?' Gemma greeted her eldest son with a hug and a kiss, which a few years ago he would have squirmed and complained about, but now he reciprocated with affection.

'Yes, Paul has gone AWOL so I have come down here to fetch some lunch for me and Rebecca,' said Daniel. 'The warehouse is spotless, and I have left the others washing the vans.'

'Paul? He walked past here about two hours ago. Hazel Wilkinson came in for a coffee and a hot cross bun earlier and said she saw him going into the police station. We wondered if it had anything to do with Simon Maxwell-Lewis and those stolen medals?'

'Did he? It would be news to me if it is. I don't think Rebecca knows either, I asked her earlier where he was and she said she didn't know. How weird. Mind you, he has been behaving out of character for the last few weeks; keeps coming into work earlier than me!'

'Can I settle up please Gemma?' Tony Cookson interrupted the Mother-Son conversation by waving a ten pound note between them.

'Yes, of course Tony. Five pounds exactly, thank you. Bye! So, my baby boy,' she said, turning back to Daniel. 'What would you like for your lunch? Do you know what Rebecca wants or do you need to phone her once you've seen the menu?'

'She already knows what she wants, parsnip soup and an egg and cress roll please. She sent me down with this flask for the soup, so I'll take it back up to her once I've finished my lunch. I'm going to take a lunch break here and have something hot, it's freezing outside!'

Daniel went and stood over by the wood burning stove which was kept permanently lit at this time of year. He checked the stack of logs next to it was sufficient for the next twenty four hours, and then stood with his back to the stove, warming the backs of his legs.

While Gemma was busy in the kitchen she heard the bell ring to signal the arrival of more customers, and heard her son welcoming and settling them at one of the tables. When she came back out she was unpleasantly surprised to see one of the dealers from next door, Rowland Mitchell, sitting at the table, while her son pulled faces behind him. When you run a business with open access to the public you quickly learn to cope with those who are less-than-desirable, but having someone as pungent as Rowland Mitchell in an eating establishment is particularly challenging. Gemma was pleased that her son had the common sense to place Rowland in the far corner of the room, away from both the wood burner and the kitchen. All the same, she hoped he wouldn't be staying long, and only wanted a quick drink or bite to eat.

She plastered on her welcoming smile 'Hello Rowland. What I can get for you today?'

Chapter 35

The morning was crisp and cold and had the hallmarks of a beautiful bright sunny day to come. Cliff and Paul were the only human beings on the multi-user Trailway, running in time with each other, their strides perfectly matched, the noise of their running shoes crunching on the surface and their breath pumping out of their bodies and clouding before them the only sounds. Their outward appearance of unity belied the major fracture which had taken place in their friendship a few days before. They had met as usual for a run the following morning, but barely spoke more than two words to each other.

Cliff had finally managed to recover his previous fitness, although was disappointed to discover he could no longer drink as many pints of ale or glasses of whisky as he had previously been able AND run the distances he wanted to. All part of getting older, he thought to himself.

When the two men completed their eight mile circuit and reached Woodford Green they slowed down, swinging their arms and shaking their legs as they walked, before stopping at the benches positioned next to the pond. The water had a thin layer of ice covering most of the surface, but it still looked very inviting to Paul who, like Cliff, was sweating despite the low temperature of the winter's morning. They started their stretching exercises in silence, each concentrating on those muscles which had felt a bit tight at the start of their session and revelling in those which stretched easily.

'So what's all this about you spending Monday morning in the police station?' Cliff asked.

'Oh, for goodness' sake,' muttered Paul. 'Is nothing private in this town? How did you know?'

'Why what's happened now? You were spotted by a member of the Woodford Grapevine,' Cliff laughed in a vain attempt to warm up the atmosphere between them. 'Come on, what's going on?'

'Oh well, I might as tell you. But please don't breathe a word to anyone else; this is all getting out of hand.' Paul stood up and looked around, checking nobody was within earshot. 'Tony wants me to put a brass figure in my auction and catalogue it as bronze.'

'What? Oh come on Paul, you've made that up! And even if it were true, surely that isn't something you would go to the police about. This isn't anything to do with his daughter, Lizzi, is it?' Paul moved towards his friend so that he and Cliff were standing almost toe to toe as the temperature of the argument started to rise, even if the morning air was still below freezing. Paul looked as though he was going to thump Cliff, who shivered and took a slow but big step away from his friend.

'Lizzi? Yeah right, like I would involve the police in my auction business because of something which isn't even happening in my personal life. Don't you know me at all Cliff? Let me spell this out to you, even though you do not deserve any explanation since you didn't even bother to ask my side of the story before jumping to the same conclusion as everybody else in this town.' Paul carefully enunciated every word. 'I did not and have not and will not try to get into the knickers of Lizzi Cookson, or whatever her married name is.'

'Oh.' Cliff stood still, trying to understand what was going on. 'So this has nothing to do with Tony's daughter?' He paused, and then spoke as the thought entered his brain, regretting the words almost before they left his mouth. 'Or is it about Lesley, his wife?'

Paul very slowly shook his head whilst maintaining a furious and dangerous look on his face, his dark eyebrows drawn together, and his brown eyes sending a piercing stare into Cliff's.

'Well then I don't understand. Why have you and Tony fallen out? I can't believe you would be so petty as to report him to the police for an honest mistake such as thinking brass was bronze. It is an easy mistake to make.'

'Don't you understand Cliff? I could lose my business over this. I could go to prison! Knowingly describing brass as bronze is a serious offence in my line of work, not a silly mistake anyone could make. That man knows what he is doing; believe me, and looking back over the years I can see he has been doing it two to three times a year for at least twelve years. He has been pretending to be my friend whilst using my business and the good trustworthy reputation my father built up, to sell his dodgy goods. I can't bear that a so-called friend of mine would cold-heartedly and deliberately use me in this way, piggy-backing on all the hard work that me and my family have put into building and maintaining a successful auction business with a solid reputation, when all the time all he wanted to do was flog his dodgy brass figurines.'

Paul slumped down on the nearest bench and put his head in his hands. Cliff didn't know what to do, so he stood awkwardly nearby. He could see that Paul was close to tears as he continued speaking. 'And then when I challenged him about it, and tried to get him to stop, he started to spread all these vile rumours about me to anyone who would listen. Sadly there were enough people who wanted to hear something bad about me and then pass it on to others, for it to stick. I thought bullying stopped when we grew up and left the playground. It has been a hell of a shock to discover it carries on into adulthood. Trying to prove you are innocent of something is terribly difficult.'

Now that he had started talking Cliff could see Paul wasn't going to stop, so he sat down on the bench next to him, wincing at the freezing touch of the cold slats of the bench beneath his thighs.

'I talked to Christine about it at the weekend. The rumours had reached her ears and she came to give me a piece of her mind. She said my love life was upsetting the children because Lizzi is a teacher at their school. I haven't even spoken to the woman other than a passing "Hello" in the street or in the pub! As far as I know nobody has even asked her if it is true, they are all walking on eggshells around her, as she and her husband try to resolve their differences, which, by the way, have

NOTHING to do with me! It is so unfair that someone can start a rumour like that and everyone believes it.'

Cliff started to say something about Rebecca and Christine's tiff, then switched to a comment about Paul's track record with women, but then thought that kicking someone when they are down was an awful thing to do, so kept his views on their ex-wives' disagreement and of Paul's treatment of women to himself.

'Luckily Christine believed me. Christine said that I couldn't allow him to ruin my business, or my reputation, and that if I had proof that he knows what he is doing then I should go to the police, and if I didn't then I should keep quiet and continue going about my daily life as normal, but cut him off from having access to my business. I tried to do that, Cliff, I really did, but these rumours have been getting out of hand. I can't even go into the Woodford Tearooms or The Ship Inn without somebody giving me a piece of their mind. And then yesterday morning Ian, or PC McClure as he was contacting me in an official capacity, phoned me at the auction house and asked me to meet him and that DS you know down at Woodford police station.'

'DS Patty Coxon? So what did PC McClure and DS Coxon want to see you about?' asked Cliff, as memories of his own relatively recent encounter with the police officers tried to push itself to the forefront of his mind.

'They had another man there, I didn't catch his name, something like Ribena or something, I am sure I have seen him somewhere before though, can't place him just at the moment. Anyway, they said they had evidence that I had been cataloguing brass items as bronze, and selling them at prices reflecting the buyer's understanding that they were genuine bronze figures.'

'Oh, phew, I thought you were going to say Lizzi or Jennifer had put in a complaint!'

Paul glared at his friend, but was finding the need to share with somebody overwhelming and carried on regardless of Cliff's obvious lack of understanding of the seriousness of the situation. 'Ian did most of the talking. It was like being in a room with Good Cop Ian, Bad Cop DS Coxon, and Not-Sure-Who-He-Is-But-He-Doesn't-Talk Much other bloke. Ian was telling me that they have intelligence on a criminal gang who have been producing these bronzes for a few years now, based in the UK somewhere. They have been casting and painting them, which as we know isn't illegal, and then selling them through legitimate channels like my auction house as bronze, which is illegal. Every now and then your DS would chip in with a comment inferring I was part of the gang. When I asked what was in it for me, she laughed and pointed out the fact I get twenty percent commission from both the vendor and the buyer adding up to forty percent. I pointed out to *her* that if I was part of it then I wouldn't be charging anyone the vendor's fee so would only be getting twenty percent from the buyer.'

Cliff grimaced. 'That wasn't too bright, Paul.'

'No, it wasn't. That just set her off on a whole string of questions about who were the vendors and where were they making the brass figures. How many different ways can you ask someone the same two questions? Mind you, Peter Isaac came in yesterday with a brass figure which was sold to his daughter Jennifer, who I have not been pestering either by the way, as a cold painted Vienna bronze at a flea market up in Shropshire. The police didn't seem surprised when I told them about it, and Ribena, or whatever his name was, just nodded, so they must have more information on that. It was actually very good, the paintwork was very skilled, and the only way I could work it out was by weighing it. Fortunately Jennifer didn't pay the full bronze price for it, but she paid a higher price than a brass one would be worth.'

'Who do we know up there we could ask about it?'

'Oh I don't want to be any more involved than I have to be Cliff, this whole thing has caused me enough grief over the last few weeks. I am dreading going into work every day in case another piece of shit turns up in the warehouse for auction, I am fed up of the whole bloody thing affecting my business like this. I am obsessed with checking and re-checking the provenance and authenticity of everything, and I know it is driving my employees mad. Your wife has the patience of a saint, and if this keeps up I am worried that young Daniel will be moving to work for someone less erratic than I have been.'

'But surely you always check the provenance and authenticity of everything which comes into your saleroom?' Cliff didn't mean to provoke his friend, but he couldn't understand why Paul was getting so worked up about the situation.

'Within reason, mate. But there are certain people who put stuff in and you know it will be quality. I look forward to seeing their names on the list; to recognising their van pulling up in the car park. At the moment I can't feel that excitement because I don't trust anyone. And I really don't like being under suspicion by everybody in the town for something I haven't done. It's the repeated deliberate acts of destruction towards my reputation and that of my family business which makes this whole situation a personal betrayal by someone I was proud to count on as a friend of many years. The tittle-tattling and character assassinations are like a physical pain. I appreciate that saying about being stabbed in the back, although I am feeling it in my guts.'

Cliff could see his friend was getting even more worked up as he spoke, rather than finding any sort of relief from sharing his burden with his friend. In an attempt to try to diffuse the situation a little he said 'But surely now you have been to the police you can rest easy? From what you have just been telling me they know who is behind it all.'

'Yes but I don't know who is behind it all, I am suspicious of everyone. I only know the person who is putting them in to my auction, and that is Tony Bloody Cookson!'

Chapter 36

Tuesday 26th January, 6.30pm

Rebecca and Christine had not spoken since their lunchtime get-together the week before. This was not unusual, with their individual families and other commitments to concentrate on the two friends could easily go for several weeks without communicating with each other, and they had different likes and interests to occupy their leisure time, and even went to Zumba sessions on different days of the week.

But this time the circumstances for the silence were different. Rebecca was unsettled by her friend's behaviour towards her, and it had caused her to question her own certainties about herself. Was Christine right to start thinking about Rebecca's future love-life? Although she wasn't just thinking about it, Christine had acted on it. That was the part which upset Rebecca the most; someone else as close as she thought Christine was to her putting into motion something which directly affected Rebecca's life whilst having nothing to do with Christine's.

Christine was someone Rebecca admired. Paul's treatment of her during their marriage knocked her almost as low as a person could get, and yet she had turned her whole outlook on life around and was one of the most positive and balanced people Rebecca knew. Rebecca was one of only a handful of friends who were willing to stand by her during the worst of years; when Christine hated herself so much that she would lash out cruelly at anyone who threatened her own fragile equilibrium.

It hadn't been easy. There was one occasion when Christine had been ranting in her kitchen about how awful her life was, how terrible her future was, and complaining about Paul and Monica (the woman Paul left Christine for, and later married, before repeating his pattern of cheating so they too are now divorced) and their happiness, when Rebecca ventured a suggestion about how she coped with her own challenges and Christine had slapped her down. Not literally, but viciously spelling out to Rebecca that she, Christine, did not view Rebecca as a person who should be dishing out advice on how to be content and happy. It had been a harsh thing to hear from someone as desperately unhappy as Christine was, and Rebecca had taken a little step away from her friend at the time, understanding the reasons for her behaviour but vowing not to attempt to help her again by offering advice. Neither would she ever confide in her in ways she had previously, or share her inner most fears and insecurities. The trust which had developed between them over their years of friendship was irretrievably damaged that day.

The two women continued to socialise occasionally together, sometimes meeting in the Woodford Tearooms for a coffee or lunch, at other times easily pairing up for various school events where they had children in the same classes. But Christine's easy dismissal of Rebecca's belief in herself had permanently scarred their friendship. Rebecca wasn't sure that Christine even realised the damage she had done to the bond between them, and despite plucking up the courage on numerous occasions to talk to Christine about it, her friend's attitude towards her that day had put up a barrier which prevented Rebecca from having the confidence that her distress would be fairly heard. There was also the question of what such a discussion would achieve were it to be addressed. Would Christine understand Rebecca's upset and as a consequence feel even worse about herself? Rebecca's own self-belief was unaffected by Christine's judgement of her, but her respect for Christine was severely dented.

Years later Christine confided in Rebecca that she had contemplated suicide on a particularly bad night around that time, when the children were staying with their father and his new bride. An empty house at night is possibly the worst place to be alone with your own thoughts when you are as miserable as Christine was, and used to having young children around you to care for and be responsible for. The whole vision of her future had been shattered, and she didn't know who she was any more, or what her role in life should be. Even the thought of her children wasn't enough to keep her from killing herself because she honestly thought they would be better off without her; she didn't think she had anything useful to offer them. It was only because she became bogged down in the practicalities of which method, where, and how awful it would be for the poor person or people who found her body that she didn't go through with it. Rebecca understood the causes of her friend's hurtful comments towards her at the time, and forgave her friend almost immediately.

But she never forgot them.

It was a strong lesson about trust for Rebecca to learn, and more recently she wondered if it was why she had been able to take the news of Cliff's incredible deceit relatively well. Certainly her father's desertion of the family when she was a teenager contributed to Rebecca's strength of character. He announced he was leaving, and walked down the garden path, out of the gate at the end, and that was it. Rebecca, her sister Annette, and their mother Jackie watched him go. Neither Rebecca nor Annette knew why he left, and if Jackie understood she chose not to explain. For the next few months and years Rebecca witnessed her mother turning a devastating incident in her life to her advantage. Her mother was both her inspiration and source of support when times were hard. There were days, however, that Rebecca wished life didn't have to be filled with these stabs to the heart in order for peace to be achieved.

Now as she sat at a table in the bar of The Ship Inn waiting for Christine to come and join her for a rare evening together, she wondered if finally the time had come to bring up the subject of the hurt from all those years ago, or whether to leave well alone. If it was still on her mind then maybe it was meant to be brought back out into the open?

'Hi Rebecca!' Christine appeared by her chair and leaned in for a welcoming hug. 'You look gorgeous, I couldn't believe it when you said you were going to have all your lovely long hair cut, but this style really suits you, and looks fabulous.'

Christine was right. Rebecca had always worn her black curly hair long, almost down to her waist, and it had suited her. But her recent decision to have it shortened by a few centimetres so it now hung to just below her shoulder blades gave her a younger, more carefree appearance than before.

'Oh, thank you Christine! I decided it was time to have my hair a bit shorter and Paula promised me she would cut it in a style which was flattering. I am really pleased with it, I keep swishing my hair and checking out my reflection in windows as I walk by.'

'Well I think you look really good. And before we go any further I want to apologise for my behaviour last week. I was totally out of order discussing you with Benjamin. And with Dave. I am so sorry, I really didn't mean to go behind your back or make any assumptions about how you choose to live your life. You do know I am the last person to think we need a man to make our lives complete don't you Rebecca? I wasn't thinking, and I am sorry. I know you are perfectly capable of finding your own friends. Your life is none of my business, and I should never have presumed to create a situation on your behalf.'

As Rebecca looked at her friend's apologetic expression she knew she had been right to refuse to go along with Christine's plans last week, and that there was no need to bring up the words said in another time, but to enjoy the hand of friendship being offered this evening, and relax in the company of someone who loved her. After all, with hindsight Christine had been right all those years ago, although neither of them knew it at the time.

Chapter 37

Tuesday 26th January, 8.00pm

Gemma and Peter walked in to the pub at the same time as Jackie Martin. Rebecca waved them over to the table where she and Christine were just finishing their after-dinner coffees.

'Come on over and join us. Are you all eating in here tonight?'

'No, not tonight, although the cheese board looks good, what do you think darling?' Peter turned to Gemma, who nodded her agreement.

'Ooooh and a nice dessert wine to wash it down with,' she grinned. 'I love your new hair-do Rebecca, very glamorous.'

'Doesn't she look gorgeous?' agreed Jackie. 'I'm eating, but no alcohol tonight. I am celebrating finally being allowed behind the wheel of my car! Oh I have missed the independence of being able to drive myself around the place.'

'Oh my goodness, are you driving already?' exclaimed Gemma.

'Yes! I have bought myself a car with an automatic gearbox, because a manual one with the clutch and gear stick is too difficult in my weakened state. So, before we get down to the business of eating and drinking, have you made a decision Peter? Would you like to buy my practice?'

Peter laughed at Jackie's directness. 'The short answer is 'Yes'. The long answer is 'It depends'. Sorry Jackie, we need more time and information to work out the finances and project plans.'

'Good, I thought you would. I have brought the proposal with me. Have a look at it now, take it away with you, but most of all I am really pleased you are seriously considering it. I know that Martin Spiers from Swanwick vets will make me an offer once it reaches the Brackenshire grapevine that I am retiring, so I am not worried about my future, but I would like to be sure you have had the opportunity to choose yours. Take another week to think about it a bit more. My deadline is March 31st for setting things in motion, but obviously selling the veterinary practice is going to take a lot longer than that.'

'What will you do Jackie?'

'Oh, I have plans to buy a small apartment in Portugal. A friend of mine has one and she goes out three times a year, the rest of the time it is rented to holiday-makers. I have booked to travel out with her at the beginning of April with the intention of finding somewhere similar of my own.'

'That sounds exciting Jackie,' said Christine. 'But won't you miss your children and your grandchildren?'

'Oh no! I'm not going to be living out there permanently. Just spending a few weeks here and there, enjoying the weather, the food, the wine, the pace of life. There are so many beautiful places to visit I won't have time to miss anybody. And of course I hope they will come out with me sometimes too,' she smiled fondly at her daughter.

'Oh I love Portugal!' Christine smiled hopefully at Jackie. 'Is there any chance the invitation is open to friends of your children too, nudge nudge wink wink.'

Jackie laughed. She had always liked Christine, and thought she was good for Rebecca who could sometimes take her responsibilities in life too seriously. 'I take it you would like to come and stay now and then?'

'Oooh yes please!'

'Christine, you are always welcome. With or without Rebecca, although if you could drag her with you at least once a year that would be wonderful.'

Rebecca had never been on holiday without her children, and Jackie thought it was high time she started to find out what adulthood was really all about.

Chapter 38

Tuesday 26th January, 9.30pm

Lisa leaned back in her chair and smiled as she watched Robin making their post dinner cup of tea in her kitchen. After all the stress and effort of her previous two relationships, this one was easy, exciting and uplifting. If it wasn't for the long gaps between their dates it would be perfect. Robin's work schedule was erratic, and he was often abroad for several days at a time or working on projects elsewhere in the United Kingdom, and would then need to spend a few days in the London office to write reports or make presentations. Lisa worked out they had only met six times since that first date in November, but it felt as though they had been together far more because they were usually able to email or text each other several times a day except when Robin was on a plane or in an area where internet and phone signals were poor.

Both of her children had now met him, albeit briefly in passing when he arrived at their house as they were leaving: Caroline already formed the opinion that he was a bit boring; and Robert said he was going to reserve judgement until he had seen more of him than their fleeting meetings and greetings. Both children were out tonight so Lisa had taken the opportunity for the third time to invite Robin into her home for dinner. She was enjoying having his company all to herself, and wasn't ready to share him yet, which seemed to suit him too. Unlike her last dating experience Robin seemed only too happy to stay in with her.

Since Gemma had met and now married Peter the closeness the sisters had become used to was altered, and Lisa had been feeling distinctly left out of cosy family get-togethers for several months. Even the family Saturday night fish 'n chips evenings had stuttered to an end; partly because of the development of Gemma and Peter's relationship and partly because all four children were often out with their own friends or away from home. Caroline had been seeing her boyfriend for over a year now, and had practically moved in with him, and Robert was spending more and more time at his boyfriend's house too. Lisa had always known her son was gay, but it had taken him a long time to accept, and even to publicly acknowledge to himself and his family. When he finally plucked up the courage to 'out' himself a few months before, at one of the family fish 'n chip suppers, he was faintly disappointed to realise that it was no surprise to anyone there, and his big news was received with a similar degree of fuss as his cousin Nathan's announcement that he was buying yet another car because his last one - his fourth in two years - had broken down permanently.

Lisa had stuck to her 'no sex before the third date' rule, and they spent those first three dates in The Ship Inn (the Italian restaurant Robin wanted to take her too for their third date was fully booked, so they ended up back on familiar territory), but as soon as she was comfortable to invite Robin into her home she knew they would end up in her bed together.

And they did.

And it was fantastic.

Finally Lisa, at the grand old age of forty two years old, experienced those wonderful exhilarating full-body sensations with a man who wanted to please her and whom she wanted to please. Her only previous experiences had been with her ex-husband, who had been under the strong impression that sex was a competition, and one in which he would set the rules and he would always win. In contrast Robin was skilled and gentle with her, taking his time to discover what she liked, allowing her to learn what he liked, and the entire time making Lisa feel as though she was the most important person in the world to him.

Tonight was going to be particularly special because it would be the first time Robin was able to stay the whole night, before flying out to Dubai the following day for three weeks.

'What are you smiling about?' asked Robin, as he brought the mugs over to the table. 'You look very happy.'

'Oh, I was just thinking about how wonderful my life is, you know, the usual,' laughed Lisa.

Chapter 39

Thursday 28th January, 6.50am

'Morning Cliff, I wasn't sure if you were going to make it this morning!'

'Why wouldn't I Paul?'

'Wasn't it Rebecca's birthday party last night? She took the afternoon off so she could go off and do something or other with her mother before they went home for some big family party. I assumed you were invited? Have I put my foot in it?'

'Oh yes, I was there, it was great. The kids all pulled together and cooked a fantastic meal for us all, Jackie and Rebecca's sister Annette and her husband and children were there too, so there were ten of us sitting around the table. Jackie commissioned Lisa Bartlett to make a cake, which was stunning to look at and delicious to eat. But it was all over by ten o'clock because Annette and her family had to get back to Swanwick, and Charlotte has swimming practice this morning.'

'I thought you would be well stuck into the champagne and the whisky, and maybe even manage to persuade Rebecca to let you stay the night!' Paul winked at Cliff in a highly suggestive fashion, clearly feeling better about their friendship after the disclosures he had made a couple of days earlier.

'Give it a rest Paul,' grunted Cliff. 'Come on, less chatter more action,' and he set off along the Trailway at a slightly faster pace than usual.

Cliff was cross because Paul's suggestive teasing was entirely on the mark of what he had hoped and planned for the night before. He was very surprised when Rebecca invited him to her birthday dinner, and took it as a step in the right direction for a reconciliation. He missed the purpose of the invitation from her point of view that he was her children's father and this was a family celebration at which they would like him to be a part of.

His breath was literally taken away by the sight of her with her new hairstyle, complimenting stronger make-up than was usual, and a figure-hugging black jersey dress with sparkly detail around the neckline and cuffs. For almost the entire evening he sat between their son Nick and daughter Charlotte, watching Rebecca who sat at the top of table to his left as she laughed and joked with her family, looking relaxed and happy in a way he didn't think he had ever seen her look before.

As the evening drew to a close and Annette and her family prepared to leave, Cliff began to make preparations to stay, but his mother-in-law could see what was on his mind and pulled him up short.

'Here's your coat Cliff, there's room in Annette's Galaxy for you too. Don't worry about your car; you have clearly had too much to drink to even think about getting behind the wheel. Nick can drive it over tomorrow evening. You won't need it before then will you?' said Jackie, propelling him through the front door as well as she could with her healing injuries, and not giving him a chance to make any meaningful protest.

'Oh, er, right, yes, I mean no, thanks. Bye everyone, good bye Rebecca. Thank you for inviting me tonight; I have had a lovely evening.'

As he got into the Parker family's people carrier he saw the look which passed between Jackie and Annette, and knew they had been in it together. He loved both of them, particularly Jackie who he also respected as a hard-working business woman, but just at that moment he didn't like either of them very much.

Later, when he was sitting in his old leather chair in the flat above Williamson Antiques, he brooded on how he had been thwarted in his attempt to spend the night with Rebecca. He accepted that things couldn't get back to the way they were, and after realising how terribly he had behaved throughout their marriage he didn't want them to fall back into those old habits. But he had changed, and he wanted the opportunity to show Rebecca that he was different now, and he could be the husband she deserved.

The last few months had also shown him what a useless father he had been to his children, and he was humbled and grateful that all three of them forgave him and allowed him to become a more integral part of their lives. All he wanted now was for Rebecca to do the same. If only she would give him a chance he would prove to her that she needed him back in her life. And in her bed.

Chapter 40

Sunday 21st February, 3.30am

The antiques dealer was going through his usual early morning routine on a market day. He regularly stalled out at markets, and had boxes of stock pre-prepared for the different customers who attended the various venues, so the evening before it had taken him less than ten minutes to pack his van. A light evening meal, bath, and he laid his clothes out on a chair in his bedroom before he went to bed. When the alarm on his phone woke him at ten past three in the morning he rolled out of bed, dressed, and headed for the bathroom. Once finished he walked into the kitchen to fill the kettle. Because the morning was frosty, while the kettle was boiling he went out to his van to start the engine and turn on the windscreen heaters, leaving them to defrost the windows for him. Back indoors, he made himself a travel mug of coffee, and carrying it in one hand he checked he had his hat, scarf, coat, gloves, phone and wallet in the other.

By half past three he was ready to leave so he opened his front door, and bang. He dropped everything he was holding and managed to hold his arms up to try to prevent the baseball bat from hitting his head a second time. The shock of the attack and the pain was making it difficult for him to think. All he could concentrate on was curling into a ball on the floor in his doorway and waiting for the onslaught to end.

Chapter 41

Sunday 21st February, 7.30am

'Sorry I'm a bit late, I overslept. Cliff was quite cross with....Bloody Hell Mark, what's happened to you?' Tony Cookson stopped dead in his tracks at the sight of the antiques dealer he had come specifically to Drayton Flea Market to see.

'Someone knows,' muttered Mark Kenyon through his swollen and split lips.

'Not here,' hissed Tony, as he went to grab Mark's arm and manoeuvre him away from prying ears, but Mark yelped and broke free.

'Don't touch me,' he whimpered, 'I think my arm is broken.'

'Christ, you need to see a doctor. Come on Mark, get back in your van. Did you see who did this?'

'No I didn't see his face; he jumped me when I opened my front door this morning. It was dark, I couldn't see a thing. I think he must have used a baseball bat though, you know, like that attack on the art dealer a couple of years ago. I opened the door and whack, whack, whack. He got me in the face, and then twice on my arm when I put it up to protect my face. I fell down and by the time I could sit up he was gone. No sign of him.'

'Hey Mark!' the knock on the side of the van and then a face appearing at the window made them both jump. 'Are you not stalling out today? I've got another box of clocks for you here. Why aren't you...bloody hell what's happened to you?'

'Oh nothing, nothing, thanks, just leave the box out there, thanks. I'll settle up with you later this week.' As he spoke Mark was trying unsuccessfully to shield the sight of his bruised and damaged face from the antiques dealer. The man left, quickly.

Once they were alone again Tony continued 'You are sure it was a man?'

'No woman would do this would they? I think I'm going to be sick.'

'You alright there?' another antiques dealer appeared at Mark's window, impatiently waiting for him to open the back doors of his van and unpack the boxes of stock onto the empty tables. 'Oh my god, what happened? Have you called an ambulance?' The man looked horrified, and then when he noticed Tony sitting in the cab next to the injured man started to back away.

'Hey it wasn't me!' yelled Tony after him. 'But he's right, you need to see someone, you shouldn't be here. I can't believe you drove all the way here from Shropshire. I would have thought a beating like that would have you locking your doors and windows and staying inside for a few months.'

'I had to come and see you, to tell you. Someone knows.'

'How can they? What did the man say? Why do you think he beat you up?' asked Tony quietly.

'Nothing, he didn't say anything, he just hit me. I couldn't defend myself, I couldn't do anything,' Mark started to cry, his face a blackening mess as the bruising, the blood and the tears began to form irregular patchwork on his skin.

'Oh for goodness sake, come on, I'll drive your van to the hospital and get Cliff to come and pick me up in mine. Get in the passenger side before anyone else sees you.' Tony was shaking, the horror of Mark Kenyon's injuries was hard to witness, and the usually quietly self-contained man Tony was used to dealing with had been replaced by a terrified broken helpless individual.

'Thank you Tony, thank you,' Mark sobbed, the shock of the morning's events rendering him incapable of finding the courage and strength to take care of himself, he was glad to hand the responsibility over to someone else.

Once the attacker had run away, Mark manoeuvred himself off the floor, picking up his scattered belongings except for the travel mug which he left where it had landed, and continued with his routine. The pain was intense in his head and arms, and he was having trouble seeing through the blood and tears. Nevertheless he turned off the hall lights and locked the front door, before slowly making his way over to his van. He had instinctively held up his right arm first to protect his face, and then his left. Although he was right-handed he was capable of managing light switches and doors and locks with his left which wasn't so badly damaged, but climbing into his van had proved to be the first time he had started to comprehend how damaged his arms were.

Fortunately the indicator stick was on the left. His van had manual gears, so he tucked his right arm inside his jacket, and let go of the steering wheel with his left hand every time he needed to change gear in an incredibly dangerous move, but it meant that he successfully drove from his home in Shropshire to the antiques fair in Brackenshire, wincing and whimpering the whole way down.

Chapter 42

Tuesday 23rd February, 6.50pm

Nicola walked into the village hall with a feeling of dread. Oh God what was she doing here? She was thirty seven years old, never did any exercise, and had to raid the bottom drawer in her wardrobe just so she had something to wear this evening. Everyone else would probably be in slim line lycra while she was in baggy t-shirt and shorts. She had never been any good at dancing in the days when she and Sarah had frequented the nightclubs in Swanwick, and hated showing herself up in public.

Nicola meekly followed Sarah as she walked confidently past all the brightly dressed fitness fanatics lining the walls on either side of the room, drinking from a variety of water bottles and laughing excitedly. Nicola could feel her limbs become heavier, her face reddening, and her heart racing as they approached a woman with ZUMBA INSTRUCTOR printed across her top.

'Hello, my name is Zoë.' Yes it would be, thought Nicola, Zoë Zumba, typical, probably made up. Nicola tried to force her face into a smile but suspected it was more of a grimace. Could everyone else in the room see she was sweating before they had even started? Oh this was hell. At least Sarah was genuinely smiling for the first time in weeks. Come on Nicola keep it together, you are doing this for Sarah. Nicola guessed Zoë was in her thirties, dressed in a fluorescent pink top with black cargo pants and silver high tops. She was quietly spoken and looked like many of the other women in the room, rather than an obviously fit athlete running on adrenalin which had been Nicola's pre-conceived idea of what a Zumba Instructor would look like. Nicola began to relax, thinking that maybe this wouldn't be too strenuous after all.

'Hello,' grinned Sarah. 'I'm Sarah and this is my friend Nicola.'

'Have either of you tried Zumba before?' asked Zoë.

'Nope, we are Zumba Virgins!' Sarah's enthusiasm was making Nicola anxiety rise again, she just wanted to shrink into the ground, or better yet leave.

'Ah great, you'll love it,' smiled Zoë. 'Now, any injuries I need to know about?'

'Not yet,' muttered Nicola.

'Good, well take it easy as this is your first time. Stay near the front so you can see me. (Oh Hell! thought Nicola. I don't want to be at the front! A nice discreet spot at the back, or better yet in the car park, would be preferable) and probably best to just concentrate on where your feet are to start with, your arms will catch up later. Take a break whenever you need to, don't worry about getting it wrong, we all do, even me. You know your own bodies better than anybody else so please keep within your limitations, and step the moves if you can't jump or twist. You both have water bottles? Good, make sure you drink plenty, the water in the kitchen is drinkable so feel free to go and re-fill your bottles if you need to. The toilets are at the back of the hall. Do you have any questions about anything else?' They both shook their heads. 'Great! Enjoy yourselves' she said looking directly Nicola.

Nicola felt herself go even redder, if that was at all possible.

'This is brilliant, thank you so much for coming with me,' Sarah was buzzing, she had wanted to come along to a Zumba class for years but didn't feel she could justify the time away from the pub or from Mike. Now she could do whatever she wanted when she wanted, so long as she could pay the staff wages. Are you watching Mike? Maybe if you had done something like this you'd still be alive today.

Since his death Sarah had got into the habit of chatting to him, sometimes about events during the day, but more often she was chastising him for leaving her on her own. They had always known that with the fourteen year age gap between them Mike would probably be the first to die, but they had believed it would be when he was in his eighties or nineties. Neither had considered he would die in his early fifties. Sarah was cross with him, believing he could have prevented his early death if he had tried harder to change to a healthier lifestyle. So she told him so. Frequently.

Nicola was still struggling with her nerves, as more and more people were arriving who clearly knew what they were doing. She was quite pleased to see there were several people much older than she was, and also quite a few larger-than-she-was-expecting bodies clad in

231

exercise gear emblazoned with various logos. There were also a lot of very athletic looking women. In fact looking around the room she could see that the class consisted of a whole range of sizes and shapes and ages. Maybe she wouldn't stand out too much after all.

Zoë turned the music up and launched into the first dance. Nicola had thought the music was playing loudly when they arrived, but now the noise was at nightclub levels. She also realised she had underestimated Zoë's athletic abilities. Did the woman have springs in her high tops? And look at her arms! They never stopped moving! The previously softly spoken voice was now whooping and yelling words of encouragement and instruction, to which the rest of the class were responding with enthusiasm.

Nicola and Sarah had settled in the third row, far enough forward to be able to see Zoë's feet, far enough back to feel surrounded by other people and not prominently positioned. Just as Nicola worked out which movements they were doing Zoë made a hand signal and changed to something else. Now it was alternate knees up, now it was side to side, now it was stepping forward and back. Good grief how did anyone ever remember all of this? What time was it? How much longer? She glanced at Sarah whose face was a study of concentration, as she moved to the left while everyone else was moving to the right.

'Sorry, sorry' Sarah called out, the woman next to her laughing as they collided.

'Don't worry; you'll get the hang of it.'

'I'm not so sure!' called back Sarah with a grin on her face.

Finally the music faded, and the floor emptied as everyone moved to the side to suck water out of their bottles. In no time at all the next song started, just as Zoë called out 'Now you are all warmed-up let's get moving!'

WARMED-UP thought Nicola. I'm exhausted already! What on earth are the rest of the dances going to be like?

She carried on struggling for the next forty minutes. She knew it had been forty minutes because she kept checking her watch to see how much longer she had to endure this ghastly noisy sweaty experience.

All of a sudden the tempo changed and Zoë called out 'Make sure you are drinking lots of water. Time to stretch and cool down now. You have all worked really hard, well done.'

What? How did that happen? Nicola checked her watch; she couldn't believe that the last fifteen minutes had flown by!

After they had all stretched every muscle, even ones Nicola didn't know she had, the music finally stopped and everyone stood around clapping and cheering, thanking Zoë, and agreeing to the same again the following week.

'Phew that was brilliant!' said Sarah.

'Yes it was,' said a surprised Nicola. She couldn't remember the last time she had felt so free, an almost permanent smile on her face once she had let go of her inhibitions. She was dancing with abandon, enjoying the rhythm of the music, stepping in time with the beats, whooping along with everybody else, and her whole body felt alive. It was exhilarating, and she wanted more. 'We will be coming back same time next week?'

'I'm up for it!'

'Me too. I think I would rather go home and have a shower and change before we go out to eat though Sarah. I wasn't expecting to get that hot and sweaty, and there is no way I want to sit down for an hour or so in this state.'

'Oh I agree,' Sarah was nodding vigorously. 'I know, why don't we split up and go home to shower and change, and then I can pick up a takeaway on my way to your house and we could eat it there?'

'I like the sound of that! I'll order it on my way past. What do you want?'

'The usual: chicken biryani and a peshwari naan. Shall I bring some cold bottles of lager or would you prefer red wine tonight?'

'At this precise moment I could bathe in the lager,' laughed Nicola. 'But I think by the time we have cleaned up then red wine would be perfect, please. We can swap information about this poor chap who was beaten up at the weekend. I have heard at least three versions of the attack, so I am sure you must have heard a few too.'

Chapter 43

Wednesday 24th February, 2.30pm

'Oh no! You didn't tell me your mother was going to be here,' groaned Peter as his daughter drove them into the yard. Peter and his now ex-wife, Diana, separated after several years of misery for both of them, finally divorcing the previous year. They were now in happy new relationships, but they hadn't settled their differences and rarely spoke to each other. Peter couldn't remember the last time he had seen his ex-wife.

Peter and Jennifer travelled up from Brackenshire together that morning to visit Brenda, the owner of the horse Danny, who had been successfully rehabilitated barefoot from his injuries, but first they visited the market where Jennifer originally bought what she believed was a cold painted Vienna bronze of a Staffordshire Bull Terrier for Peter and Gemma's wedding present. After all the talk of bronze versus brass in the tearooms over the last few weeks, Gemma and Peter had discussed it, and in the end Peter took the figure to Paul Black for verification that it was bronze. But Paul had broken the bad news that the figure was actually made from brass. Peter and Gemma decided they didn't care; they still loved it, and appreciated the thought behind the gift. Jennifer wasn't so pleased, after all she had paid for a bronze figure, not a brass one, and she wanted some money back. She intended to find the stall holder and demand compensation.

The market was full of vendors, and Peter couldn't believe the array of goods for sale: clothes, ornaments, china, glass, furniture, food, vinyl records, jewellery, silver, paintings, and statues. They searched the market but Jennifer couldn't locate the stall where she bought the brass figure three months earlier.

By the time they arrived at the yard they had eaten paella and venison burgers, two hours apart, and had a bag containing several pots of olives in an assortment of oils and herbs and spices to take home to Gemma.

'I didn't know she was going to be here. Brenda must have told her we were coming up. I wonder what she wants?' Jennifer got out of the car and walked over to where her mother was standing. Diana Isaac was a small petite woman, always smartly dressed even at the stable yard, and wore her dark hair in short soft waves.

'Hi Mum,' Jennifer said as they hugged and kissed. 'This is a nice surprise! I don't think Dad is so pleased to see you though.'

'Hi darling, lovely to see you too. No, I don't suppose he is, but I'd like his advice. I have brought Monty over with me for him to have a look at. For all our differences I am sure he won't refuse.'

'Oh no what's happened to Monty?' Monty was Diana Isaac's nineteen year old dressage horse, a Belgian Warmblood who had been in the family since Peter bought him for his then-wife eighteen years before.

Jennifer couldn't remember family life without him, although she was eight years old when he arrived.

'Oh I don't know. The farrier has been excellent and kept him going for years with different type of pads and shoes, but even he has now run out of ideas on how to keep him sound. I thought maybe your father could wave his magic barefoot wand over him and fix him,' explained Diana, in a mildly derogatory tone.

'Now now mother, don't start a fight. We're here to see Brenda and Danny, Dad wants me to be as enthusiastic about barefoot as he is but he's got a job on his hands convincing me. The poor man doesn't need you on his case as well!'

'No, you are right darling, I don't want to interfere. I know Brenda is terribly keen for him to see Danny again. She has been trying to explain this whole barefoot rehabilitation process for hoof and leg injuries to me, but I just can't get my head around it. Surely these damaged hooves need shoes for support? It doesn't make sense. Maybe your father will allow me to listen in to their conversation?'

Jennifer looked over to where Peter and Brenda were leaning over the stable door. 'Well I'll ask him if you like, but you must promise not to say a word. No bitchy comments or put-downs. Please Mum.'

Diana gave a big sigh. 'Yes, OK, Brenda said more or less the same to me when she confessed yesterday that he was coming up here. I'll be good, look, zip!' and she mimed zipping her lips together.

Brenda Davies had been around horses all of her life. Her parents owned a specialist yard where they would take in horses belonging to other people and train them to win competitions. Brenda's mother had been a keen horsewoman and regularly competed in dressage, show jumping and cross country events throughout Brenda's childhood, and so Brenda followed her mother's example and continued the family business after her parents retired. She still lived in the same house she grew up in, and she was still married to the local farmer's son who had moved in with Brenda and her parents after their wedding, and he managed their land and farm animals. Brenda and her husband had three children, none of whom showed any inclination to make farming or horses their careers. Diana and Brenda became friends at school, and had always stayed in touch, sometimes competing against each other at equine events.

'Diana.' Peter and Brenda had walked over to join them. 'Brenda says you would like to join us for our discussion about managing a horse barefoot?'

'Hello Peter. Yes I would. Please. If that's alright with you?'

'Yes, OK.' Peter turned to Brenda, 'come on then, let's go and see Danny, and you can tell me all about how you have been getting on for the last year. When did I last see you both? At that One Day Event last March?'

Off they went, chattering away, with Jennifer and Diana trying to keep up behind them. For the next hour and a half Diana had no problem keeping her promise to Jennifer as Brenda and Peter talked non-stop while looking at the contents of the feed room, walking around the fields where Danny spent most of his time when he wasn't being worked, before Brenda rode Danny up and down the concrete yard in walk, trot and canter while Peter videoed them, before she took him into the outdoor school and they jumped a small course of show jumps.

'Thank you for letting me come up and see Danny, and for sharing all your experiences Brenda. It really is great to see him looking so well three years on. Jennifer,' Peter said, turning to his daughter as though suddenly remembering the point of the visit was to educate her. 'What do you think? Do you have any questions for Brenda?'

Jennifer had been watching the whole thing with increasing interest, having come along with the attitude of if she showed willing her dad would leave her alone, because she really didn't believe in all this barefoot nonsense. But Brenda had shown them Danny's final Magnetic Resonance Imaging report which detailed the extensive damage to soft tissue within in his leg. The vets and farriers were united in their view that there was nothing more they could do to help him back to work, and it was against their advice that Brenda had sent him to the barefoot rehabilitation centre in Devon. Jennifer was amazed at how sound and comfortable and athletic he was three years later.

'Yes I do. You have spent all this time talking about what he eats and where he lives and the work you do with him, but you haven't mentioned anything about who trims his hooves, and which barefoot trimming school they trained with?'

'He trims himself Jennifer!' Brenda laughed.

'Does he? But who makes sure his hooves are balanced properly?'

239

'We both do. It is up to me to feed him correctly so he isn't footsore, to work him over enough abrasive ground so his hoof walls can wear away as much as they need to and not to overwork him beyond our preparation. It is also up to me to make sure I don't let him slob along on his forehand or, just as bad, all tense with his head and neck up and a hollow back.'

'Right, I see,' said Jennifer, who clearly didn't really understand.

'May I ask a question?' Diana tentatively stepped forward, all her earlier antagonism and cynicism having evaporated within minutes of watching her friend having so much fun with her horse. Diana remembered the two years of dark days before Brenda had discovered the rehab yard; the seemingly endless heartbreaking tears and despair into which her friend had fallen into as her beloved horse's health deteriorated before their eyes. But she hadn't really paid all that much attention to Danny's recovery, and it was only now that her own horse had been diagnosed with a similar injury that she was starting to question whether her previous understanding of hoofcare was as comprehensive as it could be.

'Go on,' said her ex-husband, cautiously.

'Brenda, I can remember Danny was crippled. Every time the farrier took his shoes off to re-shoe him you had to have a folded towel on the floor for his unshod hoof to stand on or he couldn't even put it on the ground, and yet here you are cantering him up and down this yard before going into the school and jumping seven jumps. What do you put on his soles and frogs to make him comfortable enough to do all that?'

Brenda laughed, kindly. 'Nothing! I changed what I was putting into him, Diana. Once he was eating food which was supporting and not detrimental to his whole body then his hooves stopped being so unbearably, literally, sensitive.'

Peter smiled as he looked at his ex-wife and his daughter, both of whom had identical puzzled expressions on their faces. After a lifetime of believing that horses needed shoes, they were so far out of their comfort zones at seeing a horse they knew had been incapable of even standing with one unshod hoof on the ground, now comfortably showing off his paces with four unshod hooves, their brains couldn't comprehend what their eyes were seeing.

'Come on you, two,' he said. 'Let's go and see old Monty and you can tell me what's been going on with him, Diana.'

While Brenda untacked Danny and turned him back out to join the rest of the herd in the fields, the Isaacs went over to one of the stables where Diana's horse was looking very sorry for himself; a contrast to Danny who was now checking that everyone else in the herd remembered that *he* was boss, even if he had been missing for an hour or so, and was taking them all for a gallop and a rearing and bucking contest to counteract the bitter winter wind which had blown in.

By the time Brenda called them into the kitchen they were all ready for the tea and cake she prepared for them, and Diana had some homework Peter had given her so she could start to do some research into how to rehabilitate Monty herself.

'So, Jennifer, how is your love life? Found anyone gorgeous down there in Brackenshire yet?' asked Brenda, cheekily.

'Oh don't ask!' groaned Jennifer. 'There's this one chap, an antiques auctioneer, who is a right pain in the butt. He is old enough to be my father but thinks he is in with a chance. He has a string of ex-girlfriends, a really poor track record with two divorces behind him, and yet still thinks I will give him the time of day!'

'An antiques auctioneer? You know the elderly couple I clean for,' Brenda directed her question to Diana, who nodded. 'Their son is an antiques dealer. When I went over there yesterday he was there. He was attacked as he opened his front door on Sunday; I think they said someone hit him in the face with a baseball bat. Oh, his poor face! He also has a broken arm; it was a really vicious attack. He is going to be staying with them for a few days while he recovers, but I don't know that he is going to want to go back to his own house again after that.'

'That's awful!' exclaimed Jennifer. 'Who did it? Did they steal anything from him?'

'No one knows who his attackers are. He didn't get a chance to see their faces although he thinks there were at least two of them. He thinks they were going to break in to his house, not realising he was up and about. In the end he doesn't think they did steal anything. He was had already started his van engine to defrost the windscreen before leaving for some antiques market, and his van was loaded ready for the fair, but they left all of that behind. His parents are very worried for him. I think they do some work for him, restoring various items in their workshop in the back garden, but neither of them would be capable of stalling out at the antiques fairs for him so they are all concerned about how he is going to be able to earn any money for the next few weeks. Poor chap; I do hope he recovers soon, for all of their sakes!'

'That's awful. What's his name, maybe Paul knows him?'

'Mark Kenyon. Apparently this sort of thing happens in the antiques world. Probably best you stay away Jennifer!'

'Don't worry, I intend to.'

Chapter 44

Wednesday 24th February, 6.30pm

'Good evening Gemma, we don't often see you in here on your own.' Sarah Handley was writing up the evening's Specials on the menu board as Gemma Isaac walked in through the front door of The Ship Inn.

'Hi Sarah, no I am home alone this evening. Peter and Jennifer will be back later, they have popped up to Shropshire for the day to see a horse, as you do!' she laughed. 'So, Lisa and I decided to treat ourselves to a Works' Night Out, and here we are. Well, here I am. Lisa won't be far behind. Are you OK? You seem to be moving a little oddly?'

'Oh I'm fine. Nicola and I went to our first Zumba class last night, and I can feel it.'

'Oooh you be careful, you'll feel worse tomorrow. Was it good? I hear people talking about it in the tearooms but can't say it is something I have ever felt the urge to do.'

'Oh it was brilliant!' enthused Sarah. 'Couldn't get a step right all evening but it didn't matter. You should come with us next week.'

'Oh, er, I'll have a think about that Sarah,' said Gemma, clearly not jumping at the invitation. 'Can we have a bottle of Cabernet Sauvignon please? I can make a start on that while I am waiting for my little sister.'

The door opened again, and both women turned to see who was coming in.

'Hello ladies, oooh I'm a bit stiff today Sarah, how are you feeling?' Nicola walked carefully doing a good but involuntary impression of a duck, towards them.

'I think I am feeling a bit better than you from the look of you! G&T?'

'Yes please, although it is a school night, but I think after today I have earned it. There has been one topic of conversation this week in the antiques centre, has it been the same in the tearooms Gemma?'

'Do you mean the one about that antiques dealer up in Gloucestershire or wherever who was beaten up?'

'Yes, that's the one. I think he lives in Shropshire though, unless this is another one? I first heard about it on Sunday when they said he had been surprised as he opened his front door and bashed with a bat, and by this afternoon he had been beaten up at a petrol station so badly all the fingers on one hand had been broken and all his teeth had been knocked out, and all his stock had been stolen. Honestly, antiques dealers do love a good gossip, even if one of their own has had a horrific experience!'

'Oh yes, we've been hearing about him all week in the tearooms too. It does sound very frightening, whatever happened to him. No one down here fortunately, but they are all taking extra precautions.'

'It is quite hard to know what more they can do though isn't it?' queried Nicola. 'I mean, I do know of one of the silver dealers who has a number of stop-off places around the country where he can swap vans so it will make it harder to follow him home, and he varies the times and even the days he leaves for fairs, but if someone wants to find you they will.'

'Is that what he dealt in, silver?' asked Sarah.

'I don't know, do you?' Gemma shook her head. Nicola carried on 'I'm not sure anyone has said what he deals in. How curious. Cliff and Tony helped him on Sunday, but Cliff hasn't been saying much. Ah thanks, cheers!' she raised her glass to the other two, just as Lisa walked in through the door.

'Hi Lisa, just in time, pull up a chair and have a glass of wine. Would you like to join us Nicola?'

'Are you eating here tonight? Thank you, yes I will, that is very kind of you both. Have you ordered? I won't take long to choose.'

Once Sarah had taken everyone's food orders to the kitchen and returned the front door opened, and all four women turned to see who else had come in.

'Evening ladies,' said Paul Black cautiously. 'Can I come in, or are you all going to bite my head off and give me a piece of your minds about my chatting-up technique?'

'Oh Paul, have people been giving you a hard time,' laughed Sarah. 'If you can desist from hitting on any of us then I am sure we can resist criticising your ... technique. You're a big boy, you can handle it. What would you like to drink; the usual?'

'Yes please. And OK, it's a deal,' Paul grinned, relieved to be back on speaking terms with his fellow locals. He was having a hard time in his working life; he didn't want to feel alienated during his leisure time too.

'We were talking about the antiques dealer who was beaten up at the weekend, Paul. Do you know anything about him?'

'Oh do you mean Mark Kenyon? Poor man. It sounds as though he went through a terrible ordeal. But no, I don't know any more than you three probably. Doesn't Cliff know him Nicola?'

'Only to speak too, I think Tony Cookson dealt with him more than Cliff did when they go to the Drayton Flea Market.'

'Ah,' said Paul thoughtfully. 'That's interesting. Anyway, I'll take my pint, thank you Sarah, and leave you to carry on without me. Excuse me.'

They watched Paul as he walked away from them and into the snug.

'He is very subdued isn't he?' commented Lisa. 'Not like the usual Paul Black we are used to.'

'That may be my fault,' admitted Sarah. 'I had a go at him about his behaviour towards women a few weeks ago.'

'Oh, and there was me feeling guilty because I did too!' laughed Gemma.

'Did you? Well then maybe he is finally taking some notice. I don't know how Rebecca puts up with him. I'm not sure I could work for a man like that.'

'Oh isn't she amazing?' said Lisa. 'I really admire her, after all she has been through she just picked herself up and got on with her life. But she has known Paul a long time, and since she has been working at Black's Auctions I think she has been very happy there, don't you?'

'Oh yes,' said Gemma. 'Daniel thinks a lot of her, he says the place has been transformed since she joined them last August. Didn't she work there before she married Cliff?'

'Yes she did,' said Nicola. 'It was Paul's dad who ran the place in those days.'

'Oh of course, you have known them since before they were married.'

'I did too,' said Sarah. 'I grew up here, Nicola and I were best friends at school, the same school year as Rebecca and Christine, and I think we were five years below Paul? Cliff moved into the area about twenty odd years ago.'

'Mind you, Daniel hasn't been enjoying working at Black's for a few weeks now,' Gemma lowered her voice, even though there was no way Paul could hear what she was saying from where he now sat in the snug. 'He says that Paul has been quite difficult to work for, and has even upset a few long-term customers. You know that Tony Cookson won't put anything into Black's now?'

'I understood that was because Paul thought that Tony's daughter was fair game, and Tony got the hump about it?' Sarah had left her place behind the bar to join them and was whispering too.

'Not according to Cliff,' contributed Nicola. 'He was quite upset because he and Paul fell out a few weeks ago over it, and it turns out Tony made it all up. Paul and Lizzi Cookson haven't even spoken to each other. Why would you do that to a friend? What a horrible way to treat someone.'

While the rest of the group digested this news the kitchen bell rang to signify their meals were ready, and Sarah disappeared to fetch them. Gemma in particular was feeling a little awkward.

'Tony made it up that Paul had tried to move in on Lizzi?'

'Yes, according to Cliff. Paul was upset that Cliff had believed it even after he denied it.'

'Well yes, I should think he would be upset about that, after he stood by Cliff all through his troubles last year. And we all saw what Cliff had been up to!'

'Oh yes,' laughed Lisa. 'I for one could do with having those images erased from my mind.'

'What's the joke?' asked Paul. 'Another pint, and can I order a lasagne please?' he said to Sarah as she walked in with the starters.

'Yes of course Paul. Do you want to eat in the snug or out here?'

'Oh sit with us Paul,' invited Gemma. 'So long as you don't mind watching us eat our starters.'

'Well thank you, I will join you,' Paul said as he settled in next to Lisa.

By the time Jennifer and Peter arrived back from Shropshire, Sarah had left Tom in charge of the bar and was sitting with Gemma, Nicola, Lisa and Paul where they were sharing a plate of cheese and biscuits and sampling the dessert wines.

'Hello darling,' said Gemma enthusiastically as she jumped up from her chair and weaved unsteadily towards her husband.

'Hello darling,' he laughed as he caught her before she fell past him. 'Have you had a good evening? You look as though you have.'

'Marvellous evening, thank you. Are you hungry? There is plenty left,' she waved in the general direction of the table.

'No thanks Gemma,' replied Jennifer. 'Brenda fed us plenty of cake and biscuits before we left, and we ate loads of food at the market before that. I wouldn't mind a coffee though, if that's OK?' she looked at Sarah.

'Yes of course, no hot food now, but hot drinks we can do. Just ask Tom, he'll sort something out for you.'

'Would anyone else like tea or coffee?'

There was a general murmur of agreement that coffee all round would be a good idea.

'I'll come and give you a hand,' offered Paul, who had drunk two pints all evening and was the only sober one of the party.

Once they were at the bar, waiting for Tom to finish serving another customer, Paul took his opportunity. 'Jennifer, I just wanted to say I am sorry if I have been making you uncomfortable for the last few weeks. I know what people say about me, and some of it is true. I don't have a great track record where relationships are concerned, and I am guilty of only looking for the next conquest rather than anything more meaningful. So, I apologise, and promise I won't make any attempt to ask you out in the future.'

Jennifer looked at him as he stood slightly away from her with his hands up as though surrendering, and thought that if this was another of his moves it was truly pathetic.

'Thanks Paul,' she said, shortly, and turned back to the bar where Tom was now waiting for her order.

They waited in awkward silence while Tom worked the coffee machine and produced six cups of coffee, a couple of jugs of milk, and a bowl of sugar, divided between two trays which Jennifer and Paul carried back to the snug, maintaining their uncomfortable silence until they rejoined the others.

Chapter 45

Thursday 25th February, 6.30am

Jennifer was having a pig of a day, and it wasn't even daylight yet! She had been called out to an emergency at eleven o'clock the night before, when she was still up and dressed having only just arrived back at Gemma's house from The Ship Inn. By the time she arrived at the stable yard an hour later there was no one about to let her in through the electronic gates, and she did not have a phone number she could ring because the person who telephoned from yard where the colicking horse was kept had withheld the number when they telephoned the surgery for her help. The call was automatically forwarded to her phone, and she forgot to ask the caller for their number.

After twenty minutes trying to find a way in she accidentally woke up the occupants of the neighbouring house with all the noise she was making and by constantly setting off the security lights. They did have the yard owner's telephone number, much to Jennifer's relief, but when she finally made contact with them they said the horse had relieved itself ten minutes after they called her and seemed much more comfortable so they had gone home to bed.

Resolving to put them on the practice's blocked list Jennifer collapsed on her bed at half past one in the morning, fully clothed except for her boots which she had removed at the back door on her way in. At quarter to six her phone rang again, and this time it was a very panicky lady who arrived at a livery yard to find her horse trapped upside down on his back against the wall in his stable. Horses will often lay down in their stables, and sometimes they roll over and hit a wall, find they don't have enough space to get back up, and are cast. The horse had clearly been stuck in this position for some time because he was dripping with sweat under his rugs and his metal shoes had made deep grooves on the wooden wall against which he had been thrashing around trying to find some purchase from which he could push himself over and upright. Jennifer was able to give the woman some calming advice over the phone while she made her way downstairs to the kitchen, where she made herself a quick cup of coffee to drink in her car on the way to the yard.

Fortunately this yard was only twenty minutes from Gemma's cottage, but a few minutes after leaving home the car slowed and died to a halt. No fuel. In her fury during the early morning drive back to Woodford Jennifer had failed to notice the warning light.

She jumped out of her car and phoned her father while she started to walk quickly back to the house, so that by the time she was half way there he and Gemma had driven in convoy so Jennifer could swap to his car and Gemma could drive Peter back home.

With many thanks and apologies she re-started her journey, arriving at the yard to be greeted by an extremely grateful owner of an upright horse, who hugged her and insisted she make her another coffee while Jennifer checked the big grey gelding for injuries. Other than being very sweaty and having a slightly higher heart beat than his normal resting thirty five beats a minute, he seemed happy and was tucking into his hay as though he hadn't eaten for hours. Which he probably hadn't. They discussed adding extra table salt to his feed to help him replenish the electrolytes lost during his ordeal, and changes the owner could make to his rugging and his bedding and his turnout so he would be less likely to want to roll in his stable and become cast again.

While she was still there her phone rang again and her next emergency was in a field fifteen minutes away where a horse had stuck his front leg through some sheep fencing and was now attached to it with the wire firmly fixed between the shoe and his hoof.

Fortunately her father's car carried an almost identical veterinary surgeon's kit to hers, and she was able to quickly and efficiently remove his shoe and treat the minor cuts to the fetlock. By the time she left that field, it was daylight and eight o'clock, and she was no longer on emergency call out duty, but she was still a good half an hour away from home, and needed to drive there, wash, dress, breakfast, and be at the surgery ready for a packed morning of routine appointments by nine thirty.

She arrived back at Gemma's house to find it empty; Gemma had obviously already left for the tearooms although Lisa would have opened them by seven thirty that morning, and judging by the absence of her own car, either where she left it by the side of the road or here on the driveway, her father and Gemma must have resolved the lack of diesel problem and he had taken it to work with him.

Jennifer moved about the house on automatic mode. She showered, re-dressed in clean clothes, made herself yet another cup of coffee and a couple of slices of toast which she ate sitting down at the kitchen table with her greyhound Lucy and Gemma's Staffie Suzy paying close attention to any spare crusts which may be left over.

Jennifer was absolutely exhausted. It had been a long day yesterday. She had chosen to drive all the way there and back, and had found the time they spent with Brenda mentally challenging.

As she mulled over all she had seen and heard the day before she felt as though everything she thought she knew had been turned upside down, and it wasn't a nice feeling. Jennifer wondered, not for the first time, if she had made the right decision three months ago when she resigned from her safe job in which, although the hours were similar to the ones she was working here, there had been no requirements for extra-curricular activities like driving an eight hour round trip, unpaid, just to look at a horse which defied everything she was taught at veterinary school.

Seeing that horse yesterday, and listening to Brenda and her father chattering away about roadwork and minerals had been a strange experience, and Jennifer had not found it a pleasant one. She felt much more comfortable dealing with horses who were cast in their stables or had minor wounds. Even major wounds she found fascinating and enjoyed assessing, cleaning and stitching, and then keeping a close eye on the wound over the next few weeks with regular dressing changes and working out which drugs to prescribe to treat any new symptoms which appeared.

But if she had understood correctly, Brenda's horse Danny had rehabilitated without veterinary intervention. Bar shoes, pads, pain relief and box rest were the treatments Jennifer was familiar with for treating navicular syndrome and tendon injuries. If Brenda was to be believed Danny's 'treatment' had been the removal of his supportive shoes, turned away for three months on a pea gravel track with other horses, a complete change of diet to something designed by someone with no qualifications which Jennifer recognised using a whole combination of ingredients she was unfamiliar with and which were not available in any of the local animal feed shops she frequented.

And now her own mother was thinking about going down that route too! Her mother who, for as long as Jennifer could remember, had been the complete opposite of fluffy bunny and tree hugging horse owner. Next she would be clothing her horses in rope halters and waving orange sticks at them, or even worse riding them without bits in their mouths. Although, she thought, Brenda didn't do any of those things, so maybe it didn't follow that taking the shoes off meant an end to everything that was familiar and logical to her.

Jennifer suddenly realised she had been sitting at the kitchen table for far longer than she should have done, and quickly gathered up her bag, coat, and her father's car keys, called the dogs to come with her, and dashed out of the door.

Marvellous. Now she was going to be at least ten minutes late for the first appointment, a lameness examination. Great. After yesterday's insights what on earth was she going to prescribe as the treatment?

Chapter 46

Thursday 25th February, 6.30pm

Jennifer sat in her car, on the driveway at Gemma's cottage on Farnham Road. She was so tired she seriously considered going sleep where she was, in the driver's seat. She summoned up the dregs of her energy to undo her seatbelt, pick up her bag from the passenger seat, open the car door and heave herself out. Peter had brought the dogs home with him a couple of hours earlier so at least she didn't have to take them for a walk as well; she could just walk into the house, climb the stairs, strip, pull back the covers, and fall into bed.

A tremendous crash startled her into being on full alert. The sound appeared to have come from the auction house a few doors down. After a few seconds dithering she tentatively ventured along the pavement towards the origins of the noise. Although the sun had disappeared a while ago there was a full moon, for which Jennifer was grateful as she did not want to draw attention to herself by turning on her head torch if Black's Auctions was being burgled. As she walked she could hear other sounds coming from the direction of the crash, but she wasn't sure what was making them, and no one else seemed to be around.

She fished her mobile phone out of her bag ready to dial 999 if she saw anything suspicious, and continued to walk carefully and quietly. She still could not make out either what the noises were, or where they were coming from. By now she had reached the main entrance to the auction house and all seemed quiet and intact, the noise filling her ears was the sound of the blood pumping around her body. She remembered to breathe.

Jennifer turned and crept back past the auction house, and heard noises again. This time she could make out they were coming from behind the building, so she walked down the alley towards them, by now having pressed the first two nines, with her thumb poised over the third.

She reached the door to Paul's house, or at least where the door should have been, and the source of the crashing sounds a few minutes earlier were clear to see. His front door had been smashed in with a post banger which was now lying on the oak floorboards of Paul's hallway. Jennifer took a few steps back and pressed the third nine. She took even more steps away when the call handler answered the phone because the woman's voice seemed to be shockingly loud in the relative silence of the evening.

'Police,' whispered Jennifer. 'Police, quickly please, to Black's Auctions at the top of Woodford High Street, on the Farnham Road. No I don't know the postcode, sorry, but someone has broken into the home behind the auction house and I think the homeowner is in there too. No, I don't know anything else. Yes I will. It may be a good idea to have an ambulance too, the door was smashed down so whoever has broken in is violent. No I don't know if there are any guns.'

'Hi Jennifer! What are you doing skulking around out here?'

'Sssssh!!!' Jennifer almost leapt out of her skin, before she quickly walked out of the alley as Cliff Williamson was starting to walk in, pushing him before her so he had to walk backwards, until they were both standing out on the pavement.

'Move, Cliff, move. Come on, we need to get out of here. Yes, yes, someone else is here,' she said to the call handler who was squawking out of her phone wanting to know what was happening. 'Cliff, come on, I have called the police, they are on their way. Someone has smashed down Paul's door and I think they are still in there with him.'

'What? I'm going in,' and Cliff dashed down the alley and through the splintered wood that had once been a barrier to unwanted visitors.

'Oh god,' muttered Jennifer, 'sorry' she whispered into her phone and pressed the off button to silence the squawking, and followed him.

She carefully stepped through the damaged door and tiptoed towards the sound of men's voices. On the way she admired Paul's taste in home decoration, realising what a peculiar thing to be thinking whilst her heart was in her mouth. She arrived at the doorway to a living room, but stayed out of sight, straining to hear the low tones inside. There appeared to only be one other person beside Cliff and Paul, and from the sound of it that person was threatening to kill Paul.

Jennifer had heard enough, this was more than a break-in. She needed to let the police know how urgent the situation was, so she backed away quickly, dialling 999 as she went.

'Police please,' she whispered urgently, before screaming 'AAARRRGGGGHHHHHHH!' as she tripped over the post banger and crashed to the floor, dropping her phone and bag as she went. She heard an oath and someone ran past her and out of the doorway.

'Jennifer, Jennifer, are you OK?' Cliff was there, gathering up her phone and bag and putting his hand out to help her up.

'Yes, yes, I'm fine, just banged my elbow when I went down. Oh god I am so sorry, I was trying to creep back out and phone the police.'

'Well I am sorry you got hurt but thank goodness you did make a noise. Because of you, Tony ran away before he could finish the job he came here to do.'

The welcome sound of sirens filled the air, and Cliff checked she could stand before going back out to the road to guide the emergency services in. Now back on her feet and holding her injured arm against her body, Jennifer walked into the living room, where she stopped dead in her tracks. Paul Black was lying on the floor, covered head to toe in blood. His face was unrecognisable, and one of his legs was clearly broken with the shards of bone visible through the torn trouser leg.

'Oh Paul, are you alright?' What a stupid thing to say Jennifer, she thought to herself. Out loud she asked 'Can you speak to me?'

Paul grunted through what must have been his mouth but it was so swollen and discoloured she couldn't be sure where his lips were. He looked at her through one tear-filled eye, the other was a closed puffy mess which appeared to be swelling even more as she watched.

'Oh Paul!' Jennifer felt useless, she wanted to touch him, to reassure him, but his whole body looked as though it had been battered and she couldn't be sure where was safe to put her hand without causing even more damage.

At that moment a couple of paramedics came into the room and all decisions were taken out of her hands. They were accompanied by several policemen, including the local PC Ian McClure and PCSO Sophie Boston, both of whom left as soon as they had seen that Paul was not going to be able to speak to them. Jennifer sat down on the sofa, recognising it as a Chesterfield and thinking again how inconsequential her priorities seemed to be. As she watched the paramedics calmly and quickly gain Paul's trust and completing their assessments of his traumatic condition, she marvelled at their skills and confidence in this environment where horrific violence had been taking place only a few minutes previously.

Cliff came back into the room with PC Ian McClure, and they walked around the medical action to join her at the sofa.

Cliff sat next to her and put his arm around her. 'Jennifer, are you OK? You are shaking. Shall I make you a hot drink? Ian needs to ask you some questions. Is that alright?'

Jennifer suddenly became aware of her own situation; of her throbbing elbow and her shaking body. She had a second's notice enabling her to turn and lean over the arm of the sofa before throwing up.

'Ian, there is a roll of paper towels on the window sill in the kitchen behind the sink, and the glasses are in the cupboard on the wall up on the left,' Cliff said quietly, all the time with his hand gently stroking her back.

'Oh I am so sorry,' gasped Jennifer. 'I had no idea I was going to do that.'

'It's OK, it's the shock. You'll be alright now. Thanks Ian,' as the PC reappeared with the emergency tissues and reviving water.

'I didn't know I had eaten enough today to throw anything up,' Jennifer tried a weak smile, before looking at Cliff. 'Are you alright Cliff? You were in here with them. Did you say it was Tony Cookson who did all this?' she exclaimed with disbelief.

'Can we start at the beginning?' asked Ian as he took the opportunity to take some control of the situation now that the two eyewitnesses were both in the same place and capable of speech. His questioning was delayed for a minute or so as Paul was carried out of the room on a stretcher, the paramedics assuring Cliff he was going to be alright, and that the air ambulance had landed on The Green and would be taking him to Swanwick Hospital.

Jennifer and Cliff related their experiences to Ian a couple of times while other police popped in and out with various questions for Ian to answer, disappearing again once they were satisfied. Cliff was getting more and more agitated that they were wasting time sitting on

Paul's sofa instead of going out and hunting down Tony Cookson, but Ian was firm that he and Jennifer had done as much as they could for Paul that evening, and they were to leave Tony Cookson to the police.

Eventually Ian was satisfied that Jennifer and Cliff had told him everything they could, which really wasn't very much other than Jennifer had heard a noise at approximately half past six which could have been the start of the attack on Paul, and Cliff had found Tony with a baseball bat beating Paul as he lay on the floor of his own living room two minutes later. From the time Jennifer first dialled 999 to the time the police and paramedics arrived together was seven minutes. The whole incident had taken less than ten minutes, but the build-up and repercussions could be counted in years.

PCSO Sophie Boston came into the room to tell Jennifer that Peter and Gemma were outside waiting for her. The dogs had alerted them that she was home, and yet when she didn't walk through the door after a few minutes Gemma had gone out to look for her in the immediate area, thinking she might have tripped over something on the way from the drive to the back door. When she heard the sirens and saw the blue flashing lights - not a weekly, monthly, or even yearly occurrence in Woodford - she worried that something had happened to Jennifer and had rushed inside to fetch Peter. They were very relieved when Sophie reassured them that Jennifer was not the one needing emergency treatment, although one of the paramedics suggested she go to the Accident & Emergency Department to have her arm x-rayed as it was swelling at an alarming rate. Gemma drove all four of them, including Cliff, to Swanwick Hospital and left Peter and Jennifer in the radiography department while she and Cliff went to find out what Paul's condition was.

Fortunately there were no equine emergencies that night requiring Peter's attention, nor were there any other human ones requiring the radiographer's attention, so Jennifer was seen straight away. Nothing was broken, just bruising, an ice-pack and instructions to take ibuprofen. Jennifer always carried arnica with her, both topical and pills, so she opted for that rather than the prescribed NSAID.

They joined Gemma and Cliff on the surprisingly comfortable chairs in the waiting room, and drank unsurprisingly disgusting coffee while they waited several hours for any information about Paul's condition.

Cliff reflected he had spent more time at Swanwick Hospital in the last three months than he had in the previous twenty years he had lived in Woodford. To his shame he had failed to be present for any of his children's births.

In the early hours of the morning a friendly nurse came to tell them they could go and see Paul for a few minutes, and she led them to a curtained cubicle where he lay. Jennifer was relieved that his face looked a lot better now all the blood and been cleaned off and swelling around his eye had reduced, although the colours of the bruising were fascinating. Paul was obviously tired but very pleased to see some familiar faces, and profusely thanked Jennifer and Cliff for coming to his rescue.

'I really thought I was going to die,' he mumbled through swollen and split lips. As well as the obviously broken leg and bruising to his face, the only other injury Paul had received from Tony and his baseball bat was a severely bruised elbow.

'Snap,' he tried to smile at Jennifer when he saw hers in a sling. 'Did he hit you too?' his face and voice as full of concern as he could manage.

'No, no,' she rushed to reassure him. 'This was all my own doing. I was admiring your oak floorboards at eye level.'

Chapter 47

Friday 26th February, 8.30am

The Woodford Tearooms had been open for an hour, and usually by this time on a Friday they would have served several takeaway breakfasts and had about ten customers sitting at the tables, with never more than four at any one time. Today the place was full, every table was occupied with only a handful of chairs to spare. Lisa and Caroline were having a competition to see if they could identify each person as belonging to one of three groups: local people hoping to find out what all the drama had been about last night; antiques dealers hoping to find out why one of their own had turned on the local auctioneer; and a table occupied by people who were clearly together but who didn't seem to fall into any obvious category. Caroline thought they may or may not have been police officers.

The bell kept ringing as more and more people came in through the door, with far fewer people leaving. Friday mornings were usually Gemma and Caroline's shift, but Gemma had phoned her sister from the hospital to ask if she minded swapping her afternoon for the morning just in case they were going to be in for a late night. But at times of peak capacity, usually during the summer lunchtimes and at weekends, they would try to have at least four people working in the tearooms, so just two was not enough. Daniel and Robert were working at their other jobs, and Nathan was away at university, so in the end Lisa reluctantly decided to phone her sister.

'Gemma, I am so sorry to wake you, but is there any chance you could come in for a couple of hours? We are absolutely inundated, Caroline and I are overwhelmed.'

'Yes, of course, I'll be with you in a minute. I was up anyway; my body clock doesn't know that when you go to bed at half past three in the morning you are allowed to sleep past half past six! I did wonder if we would be the centre for town gossip again.'

Lisa replaced the phone before picking up the next tray of orders which Caroline had set before her.

'She can come in? Oh thank goodness. Can you phone her back and ask her to pick up some more supplies on the way. I think this lot are trying to eat their own body weight in toasted sandwiches,' commented Caroline as she balanced another four plates of a breakfast order, preparing to carry them out to the waiting customers.

'Can you do it when you come back from serving those please? I need to crack on with the toasties.'

Once Gemma arrived Lisa and Caroline felt more in control of their tearooms; it is amazing the difference an extra pair of competent hands can make. By half past nine there seemed to be no reduction in the number of customers, and the three women were working very well as a team.

'Mum, isn't that your Robin sitting over there with the group we think are plain clothes officers?' Caroline pointed to the table in the far corner of the tearooms. 'I have just served them and am sure it is him, but he was blowing his nose into a tissue the whole time I was there. I thought you said he was an engineer?'

'Is it? I can't tell from here, that cap is hiding his hair and he is leaning his cheek on his hand so I can't see his face. I wouldn't have thought it was him. What would he be doing with that lot? If it is him we must have got it wrong, those men must be to do with the proposed development of the Maxwell-Lewis farm. I'll go over and take a proper look, and if it is him I'll ask, when I get a minute.'

But by the time Lisa was able to go over and talk to the man they thought might be her boyfriend, he had left. Oh well, she thought, it can't have been him. Surely he would have come over and said 'hello!'

Chapter 48

Friday 26th February, 10.30am

'Morning boss,' called Nicola, as Cliff made his way wearily down the stairs from his flat above the antiques centre.

'Hi Nicola, kettle's boiled. Would you like a drink?'

'Yes please, a mint tea would hit the spot. Are you alright? You look as though you have had a heavy night.'

'Nicola Stacey you must be the only person in Woodford who hasn't heard what happened last night!' exclaimed Cliff.

'Eh? What's happened?'

'Tony Cookson went berserk and tried to kill Paul! Jennifer Isaac and I found them before Tony could finish his task and now Paul is in hospital but at least he is alive, and Tony has done a runner.'

Nicola sat down heavily.

'So it *was* true. Paul did mess around with Tony's daughter.'

'Oh I don't think that is what it was all about. Last night wasn't the time to ask either of them for an explanation though. I know they have been having a bit of a disagreement about some stock, maybe that is what is at the bottom of it.'

'Tony's reaction seems a bit extreme doesn't it? And out of character. I wouldn't have had him down as a violent man. Are you sure it was all over a postcard or something? Paul upsetting Tony's daughter sounds like a far more likely explanation, but even then he must have done something dreadful for Tony to break into his house and go after him like that. Still, fathers and daughters can have a strong bond I suppose. Would you beat up a man for sleeping with Charlotte?'

'Well, as she is only fourteen and Paul is in his forties then, yes, I probably would kick his door in and bash him with a baseball bat!' Cliff sat down on the stairs. 'But you're right, something is off here. Paul assured me he hadn't even spoken to Lizzi, let alone broken her heart, and I believed him. He has never denied his past liaisons so I don't know why he would start now. He explained what their argument was about, but it doesn't justify such an extreme reaction from Tony. And if it was true, why has Tony disappeared? Last I heard the police were still looking for him. You haven't heard that they have caught up with him have you?'

'Cliff, I didn't even know any of this had happened! Not a soul as been in here since I opened up at ten o'clock this morning.'

At that moment the door opened and in walked Rowland Mitchell. He nodded a greeting at them and continued on his way to his stand. Cliff stood up and called out 'I'm just making some drinks. Would you like one Rowland?'

'No, thanks,' he replied and carried on checking his stock. Cliff made a face at Nicola, and started to walk back up the stairs to his kitchen, when he suddenly stopped and said 'Rebecca! Has anyone told Rebecca?'

'I'm sure someone will have phoned her Cliff, didn't you say Gemma Bartlett was there last night? She'll have told Daniel, who will have told Rebecca.'

'Gemma Isaac you mean. Yes, you are right. Gosh, can't believe I didn't think of her until now. Maybe I am finally moving on. Paul told me I needed to,' he grinned and resumed his climb up the stairs to make their tea.

'Or reverting to type,' muttered Nicola under her breath.

By the time Cliff returned with their teas a few more antiques dealers had found their way from next door into the antiques centre, and were now gathering in quite a large group around the architectural items at the back of the room.

'Cliff!' called out Andrew Dover. 'Any news on how Paul Black is? It sounds as though he received quite a beating last night.'

'Yes he did,' replied Cliff soberly. 'As far as I know he is on the mend, but he won't be running any marathons for a while. That bastard broke his leg. I'm going back up to the hospital this afternoon to see him, so I'll find out more, but when we left him in the early hours of this morning the doctors were saying he would need to be in for a few days while the swellings go down and then they can operate where they need to. Obviously they did what they could last night, but he may need a second or even third operation on his leg, and they are waiting to see how his face responds to the drugs they are giving him before they know if they need to do any reconstructive surgery.'

'Sounds nasty,' said Hazel Wilkinson. 'And it was Tony Cookson who attacked him? What on earth made him behave like that! I always thought he was a gentle man.'

'Well he does collect militaria,' Nicola had left the counter to come and join the group. 'I think you have to have some sort of violent streak in you to be interested in that sort of thing.'

This was not a popular comment, and several of the dealers shuffled their feet and looked away.

'Oh yes, the contents of his famous shed,' laughed Andrew.

'I'd love to see inside there,' someone commented.

This was much safer ground, and several of the other dealers nodded in agreement. As the discussion turned to speculation about what items of military treasure Tony Cookson had stored away in his shed at the end of his garden, Cliff and Nicola left the group to return to their places behind the counter. Rowland Mitchell joined them.

'What was it all about then Cliff?' he asked, in a direct manner.

'No idea,' replied Cliff. There was something about the man that he did not trust, and he wasn't going to divulge the secret Paul shared with him on that early frosty morning on The Green. Cliff thought that Tony's reaction to Paul's decision to contact the police about mistaking brass for bronze was peculiar, but he was even more wary of Rowland Mitchell.

Chapter 49

Friday 26th February, 8.30pm

By the evening the centre for the latest Woodford town gossip had migrated from the tearooms to the antiques centre and eventually settled in The Ship Inn. Cliff and Jennifer visited Paul in hospital together, and were now in the bar happily reporting that Paul was feeling a lot more comfortable, although was still in some pain.

'Looks like I'm in the chair,' smiled Robin as he ordered another bottle of wine from Sarah for Lisa and Gemma, a mineral water for Peter, and a fruit juice for himself. 'What can I get you two?'

'Oh that's very kind of you, I'll have a cappuccino please,' said Cliff.

'Nothing alcoholic?' asked Robin.

'No, no, I have a training run tomorrow. I am aiming for a half marathon next month so my drinking nights are few and far between at the moment. Although it does look as though I'll be going on my own, now my training partner is laid up for several months.' Cliff suddenly had an idea. 'You look like a fit guy, I don't suppose you train do you?'

Robin laughed. 'Sorry Cliff, a few lengths of a hotel pool now and then is about the limit of my fitness routine. Jennifer, would you like a drink?'

'Thank you Robin, I'll have a small glass from that bottle Gemma and Lisa are sharing,' said Jennifer, who knew she really needed to go to bed but wanted to spend a little more time in this group of friendly people.

'You'll join us for a drink won't you Sarah? Young Tom can cope running the bar now the kitchen is closed can't he? What can I get you?'

'You are absolutely right Robin!' laughed Sarah. 'But don't worry about me, I'll bring another bottle of the wine Gemma and Lisa are drinking when I bring Cliff's coffee over, and we can share that.'

'Cheap round for me then!' laughed Robin, as he collected his change and receipt.

After another three chairs had been added to the four already around the table in front of the fire and the drinks were all distributed to the right people, the group resumed their discussion about the events of the previous twenty four hours.

There was still no sign of Tony Cookson. Both Lesley and Lizzi had been at Woodford police station for much of the day, and according to the Woodford grapevine as reported by Gemma and Lisa who heard it in their tearooms, both women vehemently denied that Paul Black had made any advances of any description towards Lizzi, and neither of them had a clue as to why Tony acted in the way he did.

'So what was it all about then?' asked Sarah looking at Cliff. 'Paul and Tony have been narky with each other for several months now. I remember Mike commenting on it before...well before. Hands up, I'll admit I was as ready as anyone to believe the worst of Paul Black and totally accepted Tony's explanation for why they were knocking heads together, but even if he did try to make a move on Lizzi the whole business about banning Tony from the auction seemed a bit excessive.'

Cliff made a decision.

'For once, I don't think this had anything to do with Paul's disastrous love-life,' he said, carefully. 'Paul told me they had a disagreement about the catalogue description of an item of stock Tony wanted to put in for auction.'

'Is that all? Surely not,' Lisa looked over at her sister. 'We disagree about our menu all the time but Gemma doesn't come at me with a baseball bat!'

Everybody laughed and started making jokes about horsemeat on the menu.

'I know we are not meant to know who puts what into the auctions, but Nicola and I worked out years ago that most of those delightful little bronze figures of foxes and bears, and those evocative statues of ladies in erotic poses were put in by Tony,' Sarah said, looking at her friend for confirmation.

'Oh, is this anything to do with fake bronzes scandal?' asked Nicola.

Cliff sensed that someone in the group had tensed, but a quick glance around the faces of those present gave nothing away. Now he was faced with a dilemma: should he break his friend's confidence in order to clear his name? Or keep quiet and observe what happened next.

Jennifer said 'Dad asked Paul to check that little bronze wedding present of Dad and Gemma's, and Paul said it was really made from brass. That is the sort of thing you are talking about isn't it?' she asked Nicola.

'Yes, that's right.' Sarah joined in. She had been doing her homework. Her love of family history and portrait miniatures had stretched to include researching the factories in the nineteenth and early twentieth centuries which produced the now antique cold-painted Vienna bronzes and Art Deco nudes. 'It would be relatively easy for someone to fake one of those in brass. All they would need to do is cast from a mould in brass, and the skill would be in the painting of the detail. It would be very difficult to tell if one of those is made of brass or of bronze. Slightly larger figures, particularly art deco erotica, would be much cheaper to cast in brass than in bronze, and would be easy to do. Many of them were silvered, so all someone would need is a small plastic tank in which to dunk the figure for the silvering process, and voila, one beautiful-looking silvered brass statue masquerading as bronze. Once you start to make bigger figures with more intricate sculpting then the cost of the materials becomes irrelevant because although brass is easier to sculpt than bronze, you can create better definition out of bronze, so the skill required would outweigh the cost of the brass.'

'So why is this a big deal, if fakes were being legitimately made by the original factories in the nineteenth century?' asked Lisa.

'The fraud takes place if an auctioneer, or an antiques dealer, sells a brass figure as bronze. In the case of these small cold-painted bronzes it can mean the difference between a six centimetre high bull dog costing one hundred and twenty pounds for a brass figure compared to eight hundred and fifty for a bronze one.'

'Are you an antiques dealer as well as a landlady of a very well-run pub?' asked Robin.

Sarah laughed 'No. I do love antiques though.'

'Sarah spends hours at flea markets and auctions,' explained Lisa. 'You must have picked up a lot of knowledge over the years Sarah?'

'Oh, I know a little, but certainly not as much as the professionals like Cliff. I just know what I like, and then when I am researching something I go off at tangents and discover all sorts of useless information!'

Again Cliff felt that physical shift from someone in the group, but this time instead of tensing it was as though someone had breathed a silent sigh of relief. Who was it?

Chapter 50

Saturday 27th February, 7.28am

'Erm Mum, there's a queue of men outside the door!' Caroline called through to Lisa, who was in the kitchen of the Woodford Tearooms making the final preparations for the morning's breakfast trade. The first hour and a half on a Saturday was usually a fairly steady stream of ones and twos wanting bacon rolls and cups of tea.

'Is there? How many?'

'I can see seven.'

'Better let them in then!'

'Hi Lisa.'

'Robin! What a lovely surprise. I thought you weren't going to be back from Aberdeen until Wednesday? Don't tell me you have been there and back in a day! Sorry darling, I'm a bit busy. We seem to be very popular this morning, no idea why.'

'I know why,' he said quietly. 'Can I have a private word with you please?'

Lisa suddenly felt very cold as an unwelcome thought popped into her head.

'It will have to wait,' she said shortly. 'I have a business to run, customers to serve.' She turned her back on him.

It soon became clear, as Lisa suspected, that Robin was a part of the group of men who had been waiting for the tearoom doors to open. Between them Caroline and Lisa efficiently prepared, cooked and served a number of breakfasts consisting of bacon, eggs and toast, with tea and coffee on permanent demand.

'Lisa, Lisa, have you heard, Tony Cookson has been arrested! The police have been searching his house and taken loads of stuff away.' Gemma appeared in the kitchen, in her Woodford Tearooms uniform and ready to work even though she wasn't due in until half past eleven that morning. She washed her hands, read the order pad, saw that Lisa was cooking bacon and eggs and sausages, and started to take toast out and put bread into the toaster. 'Daniel came in and told me. The police told Paul, who phoned Rebecca, who called Daniel. Apparently he was seen by an antiques dealer over in Kent yesterday who contacted the police. He is not a popular man in the antiques community by all accounts. Hey, isn't that your Robin sitting over there with those other men? I thought you said you couldn't see him until Wednesday?'

'It is, and I did.'

'So what's...oh my god, you don't think they are police and he is one of them do you?'

'Yes, and yes.' Lisa hadn't really thought much of the mystery about the man who may or may not have been Robin sitting with a group of men she suspected were policemen a few days before, but today she was sure it had been him, and she didn't like what this suggested.

'Lisa! What is going on?'

'Other than yet again I have been deceived by a man you mean?' Lisa voice was shaking, and Gemma could see tears coursing down her face.

'Oh sis,' she said as she went over to Lisa and held her tight.

Caroline walked in with a tray of dirty plates and cutlery to find her aunt and her mum in silent embrace.

'What's happened Gem? Are you OK? Is Peter alright?'

'Yes, yes, we're all fine. Your mum has had a bit of a shock,' and Gemma nodded through the serving window in the direction of where Robin was sitting.

'Oh it *is* him!' exclaimed Caroline. 'I've only met him briefly as we passed on the doorstep. What's he doing here? I thought you said he was back on Wednesday?'

'Well now that your aunt is here I think it is time I found out the answers to some questions I have.' Lisa pulled herself away from her sister's embrace, found a tissue in her pocket and blew her nose thoroughly, before beckoning Robin in from the tearoom.

It was too cold to sit outside, so Lisa and Robin ended up standing very close together in the larder. It was a difficult conversation for both of them. Robin explained that he had been on an assignment for eighteen months, with a team of other police officers tracing and following a number of people, including Tony Cookson, who they suspected were involved in money laundering which included selling brass statues as bronze. He apologised over and over again for lying to Lisa about his true career and the reasons for his absences, and tried to assure her that his time spent with her was real. That he did like her very much, when he was with her she was with the real Robin Morton, that their love-making was genuine, and that if she could bear to trust him again he wanted to continue their relationship.

Lisa listened to him, believed him. And said no.

Chapter 51

Saturday 27th February, 9.30am

Rebecca and Cliff were having a cup of coffee upstairs in his flat above the antiques centre. Cliff was overjoyed that his wife had finally accepted his invitation to drop in any time, even if it was just so she could pass on a message from Paul Black.

'All I can tell you is what he told me, Cliff. He just said that the police have told him they raided Tony's property late last night and found a tank full of silver nitrate solution and enough brass figures and onyx clock bits and pieces to be able to add them to the case they are building against him. Why are the clocks significant?'

'The bases they are on are used to fix the brass statues onto. How on earth did he get mixed up in faking bronze figures? I can't believe the man I called a friend could have been deceiving Paul like that for years, and worse putting both Paul's liberty and business in jeopardy like that. He would have gone to prison if this had carried on.'

'So you do believe Paul is innocent?' asked Rebecca.

'Of course!' said Cliff vehemently.

'Good. So do I. He has been uncharacteristically quiet and introverted for the last few weeks. I just feel bad for believing that he and Tony had fallen out over a failed seduction attempt.'

'Oh I don't feel bad about that!' laughed Cliff. 'I do feel bad about not believing him when he first tried to explain though. I'll go up and see him again later today. Did he say if he has been given a release date yet?'

'No, but it probably won't be until the middle of next week at the earliest. He still has some swelling around his eye where Tony hit him with the baseball bat, so until that reduces significantly they can't be sure that his brain hasn't been affected. Christine is going up later today with the children, maybe she can give you a lift?'

'Good idea, I'll give her a ring. Shouldn't you be in work by now?'

'Yes, I should. The phone will probably be ringing off the hook. I'll go now, thanks for the coffee. See you later Cliff.'

Cliff washed up the cups and teaspoons and walked down the stairs to open the antiques centre, all the time with a soppy smile on his face.

'Morning Cliff, was that Rebecca I saw leaving here just now?'

'Hi Nicola, yes it was, she came to give me an update on Paul. Oh, and Tony Cookson has been arrested.'

'Yes I know, I have just been into the tearooms for breakfast where some of the police officers involved were also eating. You'll never guess who Lisa Bartlett's boyfriend has turned out to be! Only Rowland Mitchell in disguise! Or do I mean disguised as Rowland Mitchell. He was an undercover policeman.'

'No!' said Cliff, genuinely surprised. 'That smelly old dealer was Lisa's good-looking chap?'

'Yes, and that explains why he kept selling his rubbish when no one else could, doesn't it. He had to have buyers so he could keep up his stand in here. We must have been selling to undercover policemen almost every day of the week.'

'Oh, really? And I suppose that may also go some way to explaining how he knew John Robson? Although I can't see John being a grass, can you?'

Next through the door was Hazel Wilkinson.

'Goodness, what on earth is going on! The place is swarming with police. Their vehicles have been filling up Farnham Road all along the side of The Green since yesterday afternoon. Apparently Tony Cookson has been caught, at last. How is Paul Black, have you seen him?'

'It's all to do with these fake bronzes,' Nicola explained briefly.

'And Paul is feeling much more comfortable now,' Cliff reassured her. 'I am going back up to the hospital this afternoon.'

'Oh that's good. Poor man, what a shock! Please do pass on my regards to him. I just popped in to say that I am dragging Alastair away from the veterinary practice for a few days, and we are going to spend some time on the water.'

'In your barge!' exclaimed Nicola. 'Won't it be freezing on there at this time of year?'

Hazel laughed, 'no! We have a wood burner and electric heaters. The place is so toasty and cosy I swear it is warmer than our draughty old house. I'll have my mobile with me, so on the off chance anyone wants to buy my entire stall and needs a good price you can contact me,' she laughed.

'Such a nice lady,' commented Nicola after Hazel had gone.

Next through the door was Sarah Handley. 'Hello you two, I thought I would grab a few minutes to find out what is going on before the pub opens for the day and the Chinese Whispers start. What is going on?'

Nicola and Cliff looked at each other, before Cliff said 'That is what we would like to know.'

His timing was excellent, because just at that moment Robin Morton walked in through the door. 'Ah, by the look on your faces I can see the news about Rowland Mitchell has reached you already. Please let me introduce myself properly,' he said, reaching out to shake hands with Nicola and Cliff. 'My name is Robin, and yes, I am sorry for deceiving you, and for stinking the place out. I find it stops people looking too closely at me. Someone will be in early next week to clear the stand, but of course the rent will be paid until the end of next month as agreed.'

'Well I never would have recognised that you and Rowland were the same man,' exclaimed Sarah. 'But now you are here, I am sure we can all forgive you if you tell us what on earth has been going on.'

'I'll tell you what I can,' said Robin.

'Wait! Before you get started, I need another coffee,' said Cliff. 'Who else wants one?'

By the time Cliff came back down the stairs with a tray of drinks they had been joined by several other

286

people, all eager to hear from Robin why events had escalated to such a violent state. A variety of chairs had been pulled from the surrounding stands, so the predominantly jean-clad bottoms in numerous shapes and sizes were seated on a selection of Victorian upholstered insert seats, arts and crafts high backed dining chairs with William Morris reproduction material seat coverings, one person was sat on a nursing chair, and two people were sitting on a conversation seat which they had positioned sideways into the circle. Cliff reflected that this was probably the largest number of antiques dealers to be present in his antiques centre since it had opened, but none of them looked in the mood for spending any money.

Robin began to speak. 'I will tell you as much as I can. I feel I owe you all that much.

'Seventeen years ago an auctioneer in Northumberland was imprisoned for mis-describing a brass figurine as bronze. During our investigations which led successfully to his prosecution it came to light that he had probably been selling up to eight of these brass statues a year for at least three years, and cataloguing them as bronze. He tried to implicate several other people in an effort to prove his own innocence, mainly antiques dealers who were on the shady edge of the trade, but his evidence proved to be worthless and we believe he was attempting to send us in the opposite direction to those who were genuinely involved. As a direct result of his behaviour a number of those dealers he attempted to bring down with him offered to work with us on future cases.'

Robin paused as various members of his audience nodded and muttered that they remembered the case. The antiques world is tight-knit and the rogue dealers are usually well-known and remembered. In addition no one wants to be accused of something they haven't done, and everyone avoids dealing with those in the trade who are likely to make ill-founded accusations. Trouble-makers are never popular in any business.

'For a while nothing seemed to be happening. The trade in fake bronzes appeared to have come to an end, the people we suspected of being involved looked as if they were no longer interested in that business, and the investigation was put to one side. Until last year. One of our friendly dealers let us know that a number of these brass fakes were popping up here in the south-west. They were too few and being sold too far apart geographically and the time-frames were too sparse for us to pinpoint if any one person was deliberately dealing in this way. Based on our intelligence the auctioneers and antiques dealers involved were innocently describing and selling these brass items as bronze.'

Cliff looked at the faces of the people in the room. Everyone was listening with rapt attention whether their eyes were on Robin, or sightlessly looking around the room, or focused on the floor in front of them.

'We tried to keep track of all the auction catalogues available online, but the items for sale in the car boot markets, flea markets, and antiques markets were impossible to police, there are too many of them. Eight months ago another of our dealers knocked on the door and pointed in the direction of Mark Kenyon. Some of you will know him, may have even dealt with him, legitimately.'

There were a few shifting of bottoms and clearing of throats at this point, and eye contact was sparse.

'Mark was a well-established antiques dealer of militaria. He had a long history of dealing, with no anomalies that we could see, nothing remotely dodgy, a good honest reputable dealer. But our informant told us that relatives of his were selling bronze figures at their local market, in amongst old china tea sets and tomato plants and books. The quality of the figures was superb, and their explanation that they were collectors who were selling up didn't hold water for long for several reasons. Collectors who want to get rid of their collections usually sell them privately or put the whole lot into a specialist auction, for a much better return on their investment than selling them in dribs and drabs for less than they are worth at a local market. We started to take note of what they were selling, and how frequently, and once we could record the pattern of them taking orders and then producing the requested items within a month or so we knew their cover story was as fake as the 'bronzes' they were purportedly selling.'

'Surely you are not seriously standing there telling us that a load of antiques dealers have been happily trotting off to police stations around the country for years, tittle-tattling about what the chap on the stall next door is selling?' asked Sarah impatiently, and was rewarded with a general murmur of agreement by the antiques dealers present. 'And what has any of this got do with why Tony

Cookson suddenly turned from being one of the lovely Regulars in my pub to a homicidal maniac?'

'Ah, Sarah,' smiled Robin, holding his hands up in mock surrender. 'Hold on, I'm getting to him. You are very knowledgeable about the antiques business, for a member of the public. You had me worried. I thought you were going to blow the case wide open before we could completely find and record all of our evidence to make a conviction stick. For a while there I wondered if you were a part of it too.'

Aha, thought Cliff, the physical shift he sensed in the pub earlier that week must have come from Robin.

'About the people who keep us abreast of what is going on in the antiques trade,' he continued, quelling the rising sound of dissension in the room with a sweeping look. 'No, I don't want to give you the impression that we have a stream of people knocking on the door reporting on every slightly dodgy transaction. But we do have contact with people who are interested in keeping this business clean. Long gone are the days where Market Overt was not only legal but gleefully embraced by areas of the trade. The glory days of tens of thousands of pounds openly exchanging hands day after day are over. Money is tight. People are working extremely hard just to keep their heads above water.'

'I'm hanging on by my fingernails, but the trouble is they keep breaking!' laughed Chris Moses, successfully breaking the tension built up by the increasing wall of animosity which had been building up between the dealers and Robin.

'What is Market Overt?' asked Sarah.

'It used to be legal to sell stolen goods on certain markets during the hours of darkness, called Market Overt,' explained Cliff. 'Everyone in the trade knew that there were certain dealers' stands to avoid at Bermondsey market, or make a beeline for if you were that way inclined. It was only made illegal in the early 1990s.'

Robin nodded and smiled his appreciation and carried on. 'As Chris says, antiques dealing can be a daily struggle, and there are enough people who don't like to see their legally hard earned income being swamped by flash dealers who treat them with contempt, and effectively put them out of business by selling low quality, stolen, or fake goods at cheaper prices than their own quality items bought with integrity and with years of accumulated knowledge behind them. Times are hard in the antiques trade' he paused as another murmur swelled into a general chorus of agreement, and allowed himself a small smile, relieved the audience were back on his side.

'Rumour has it that the original moulds from the nineteenth century Vienna bronze factories were stolen when the factories were closed down, and that the recipe for the paint used in the cold-painting process has been lost with the dying out of the craftsmen who used it. We cannot prove it, but we believe Tony Cookson's grandfather bought those moulds a long time ago and used them for his own purposes. We think that Tony has spent all of his working life continuing the family tradition, and slowly building his business in faking cold-painted Vienna bronzes by operating on a three year programme of recruiting people to cast and paint the figures, while he concentrates on the network for retailing the finished products. From the information we have gathered we estimate he has made hundreds and thousands of pounds with each new project, each one an improvement and therefore a bigger earner than the one before. He invests almost all of the profits from the previous project into the next one, which is a big gamble. This latest project was started less than a year ago. We are still collating the evidence, but it does look as though his investment into it with his accumulated earnings would be in the region of three million pounds.'

The tension in the room was palpable as everybody silently tried to calculate how many figures Tony would have been processing in order to earn that amount of money.

'In this case Mark Kenyon's parents were casting and painting brass figures in their garage. Mark was then bringing the figures to Tony at Drayton Flea Market for him to disperse throughout the country. We believe that Mark's parents were the reason why Mark was attacked as he left his home. He was beaten up as a warning that they were drawing attention to the business Tony Cookson had been successfully running for more than thirty years, and that with all his money tied up in it so early in this latest project he could not afford for them to be careless and give the game away by being greedy.'

'Tony Cookson did that!' exclaimed Cliff. 'I don't believe you. Anyway Tony couldn't have done it, because we went to Drayton Flea Market together that day. He wouldn't have had time to drive to Shropshire and bash Mark before driving back to Woodford to collect me. I would have noticed something was wrong, surely?' All eyes were on Cliff now, and he started to waiver a little as the attention focused his thoughts. 'Well, he was a bit late, but he explained it had taken a while to defrost the van,' and then more confidently 'but there wasn't a mark on him! I saw the state Mark was in, there was blood everywhere. Tony would have got some of it on himself if he had been wielding the baseball bat, surely?'

'Oh Cliff. You know for a while we thought you were involved too, and someone was watching your movements that morning. We have CCTV footage of him on the motorway travelling in both directions, and at a service station on the way up. Would you have noticed a few blood splatters on his black coat at that time of the morning? Remember it was cold and dark. I bet you barely even looked him in the face, let alone scrutinised his clothes for cleanliness.'

Cliff was momentarily silenced by the revelation the police had been monitoring his movements, and he had to agree with Robin that Tony could have been wearing lipstick and eyeliner and Cliff probably wouldn't have noticed when he climbed into the van. Now he thought about it, the interior light wasn't working that morning for some reason. He scrabbled around for something else to defend his friend. 'But he was the one who took Mark to hospital! Mark wouldn't have let him do that if he was the one who had caused all that damage.'

'Tony Cookson,' said Robin firmly, 'didn't want Mark to know he was behind the attack because then he risked Mark and his parents pulling out completely. He wanted them to stop stealing from him but he wanted to keep them working for him because it was entirely due to their craftsmanship and skill that the quality of the brass figures could pass for bronze ones a hundred years older. We believe that Tony thought by giving Mark a fright it would be enough to stop the family from having their own business dealings in which he wasn't included. After all it was Tony's grandfather who had the original idea, and Tony who put the current operation together and invested millions of pounds into it, so he thought it was essential that he had his fingers in every aspect of the business and controlled the flow of the fakes onto the market, and of course that he received all of the money.'

Sarah interjected 'Well, in a way he was right then. If he had been successfully selling these fakes for thirty years without detection, and it wasn't until the Kenyons began to go off in their own direction that the bogus bronzes were sending off warning signals and leading you to him.'

'Yes, Tony is certainly a clever man. However the Kenyons were skilful at what they did, and Tony would not have wanted to replace them. There are not many people he could trust who also had the qualities necessary to work on these projects. He never uses the same people again, but they all continue to receive a percentage of the profits from the overall business at the end of every three year project. They are very well paid for their loyalty.

'Fortunately for us, Mark did know it was Tony because he saw his boots as he ran away, and then hours later there was Tony, pretending to be all care and concern about Mark's welfare, still wearing the same boots. They have distinctive yellow laces. When the local policeman came to take Mark's statement he named Tony without a moment's hesitation and we were able to pull all of our resources together in order to begin to build a case against him. But he didn't want Tony to know he knew, hence the confused stories which circulated. Some of you may have heard them? I did, both in here and in the tearooms next door.'

'So if all Tony was doing was selling the figures on, how do you know he is the ring-leader, and not Mark?' asked Cliff, still keen to find a reason not to believe the worst of a man he counted as a friend, even though he had witnessed him apparently trying to murder someone Cliff believed Tony thought of as a friend.

'Well, I can't tell you everything, but some things you possibly already know. We have the Kenyons' statements to that effect, which are obviously not enough on their own. Also Tony had a silvering tank in his shed, along with a number of brass figures which Mr and Mrs Kenyon admit to casting. In addition, once the auctioneer we sent to prison seventeen years ago realised no one was coming to save him he provided us with all the evidence he possibly could that Tony Cookson was the brains behind the scam. He reckoned his percentage of the profits was not adequate payment for the loss of his liberty, but as far as we know Tony was never made aware of his betrayal. Sadly, the man died six months into his sentence. Unfortunately his evidence was inadmissible for a technical reason, but thanks to him we knew who was responsible. Now that Tony has committed these two separate violent acts against two people in the antiques trade, we have informants popping up all over the country with irrefutable evidence.'

'But surely they are incriminating themselves?' Sarah was still unconvinced about Robin's account, although she sensed she was in the minority, and briefly wondered if anyone in the room was in regular contact with the police. Or maybe even involved in Tony Cookson's scam?

Robin smiled. 'Oh, we have ways of making people feel safe and confident they are doing the right thing. The antiques trade is tight; you don't like it when people mess with the authenticity of your stock, and you certainly don't like it when people bring violence to your door.'

Chapter 52

Friday 4th March, 6.30pm

Paul Black had been in hospital for over a week, and the enforced bed rest was bringing with it the chance for him to evaluate his life. Ever since Paul first became interested in the opposite sex he enjoyed flirting with women. When he was a teenager he was grateful to any girl who would sleep with him, and even when he and Christine were in a serious relationship he would still enjoy the occasional one-night stand. But once he proposed to her he no longer felt the need to bed every girl who crossed his path, and found it easy to be faithful. Until he got bored of life as a father and a husband.

His second wife Monica was the first woman he slept with since his engagement to Christine, and he would have happily stayed married to Christine and kept Monica as a mistress, but neither woman would settle for that. Paul enjoyed the thrill of the chase, the will-they-won't-they anticipation. He regretted the end of his relationship with Christine, and particularly as over the years he saw his friends celebrate their tenth, fifteenth, even twentieth wedding anniversaries he felt sad that he had never achieved such milestones with anybody. But the truth was he wasn't prepared to put the effort into nurturing and sustaining a relationship for more than a few weeks. His reputation exceeded the reality of his love life, but there was enough truth in it to keep it alive. Far from sleeping with a different woman every week, he probably only had three girlfriends a year, but he usually chose to overlap at least two if not all three, just to keep the excitement alive.

In the days he spent recovering in hospital he saw how important it was to his fellow patients for their families to come and visit them. He knew Christine only came to see him through a sense of duty so their children could come. He was grateful for Cliff and Jennifer's regular visits through friendship. It also made him reflect on why he chose not to have someone special in his life. He had been affected by the unfairness of both Gemma and Sarah's rebukes about his attitude towards women, because he didn't see himself as they did, and also because the whole story about his treatment of Lizzi Cookson had been made up by Tony as a cover for his own poor behaviour. While he lay in hospital and observed the interactions between the men and women around him he realised why Gemma and Sarah, and probably many other people in Woodford, thought so little of him.

Jennifer was on his mind. Although he had viewed her as a potential conquest when they first met back in November, he was taken by surprise at her obvious dislike for him whenever they bumped into each other around the town. Sarah's dressing down about his behaviour in particular had stung, mainly because of the injustice of it but also because he hadn't realised how pathetic his behaviour had become. He had been deeply affected a few months before when he witnessed Lisa Bartlett's distress on discovering that her boyfriend, Andrew Dover, had been two-timing her. Sarah compounded his understanding of the effect he was having on other people, and she made him face the facts that it wasn't a game; he was hurting the women he played around with. And that was how he had been viewing his relationships, as playtime. He worked hard at Black's Auctions, and enjoyed the interactions with the people he encountered there, but he liked to go home to the peace and quiet of an empty house, and his leisure time was his own. While in hospital he could see how shared histories provided foundations on which to build love, friendship and respect, which in turn provided the kind of supportive relationship he had never felt the desire to have with anyone.

As he looked around the ward and saw how the other patients were being treated by their visitors he felt sorry for himself that he had no one special, who loved him, who knew what his favourite treats were or which clothes he would have liked to have brought in for him. And in amongst the self-pity he faced the harsh reality that there was nobody in his life, other than his children, who he would be rushing to the hospital to see with carefully chosen presents or funny cards to cheer them up and aid their recovery, and be making plans with for their eventual return home.

Meanwhile Jennifer was seeing a different side to Paul. The Paul Black who was lying in the hospital bed didn't bother putting on a show of flirting with her, or make any presumptions that that was how she wanted to be treated. He was grateful for her part in rescuing him, and genuinely pleased to see her every time she arrived. Jennifer enjoyed watching the banter between him and Cliff, and it was nice to see the lighter, more humorous side of Paul rather than over-powering pathetic seduction techniques she had been previously treated too.

The fear she had felt during those minutes before the police arrived, and the sense of exhilaration at being part of the team who saved a man's life - the police were sure Tony Cookson would have killed Paul if he hadn't been interrupted - seemed to have helped Jennifer to pull herself out of the depression she was diving into. Her attitude towards her work had changed, and rather than seeing herself as a drudge at the beck and call of undeserving clients, she approached every day as a fresh new start and enjoyed the anticipation of discovering the next puzzle to solve. Her energy levels lifted, she was finally sleeping soundly at night, and at the end of every day she felt a sense of achievement at everything she had done. In a few short days her life of never-ending unwelcome demands on her time was replaced with enthusiasm and opportunities.

Chapter 53

Monday 7th March, 6.30pm

Finally, home sweet home. Paul Black was extremely pleased to walk, well hop on his crutches, through his own front door.

By the time Paul was released from hospital he and Jennifer had spent many hours comfortably chatting via email, facebook, face-to-face during hospital visits, or on the telephone. It was Jennifer who brought him back to his home, which Rebecca and Daniel had ensured was cleaned up and repaired once the police gave them the go-ahead. At her insistence, Paul gave Jennifer a shopping list for food, and she filled the fridge and larder, as well as putting the central heating on and filling the log basket for the fire ready for his return.

On that first evening Jennifer stayed with Paul while he worked out what he could and couldn't do. Fortunately he designed a relatively large downstairs cloakroom into the layout of his house when he had it built, so he at least had access to a toilet and a sink with room to manoeuvre his plastered leg.

The pair of them also prepared and cooked their first meal together. Paul's contribution was to sit on the sofa, a lap tray in front him so he could peel and chop the ingredients, despite the injuries sustained to his fingers, hands and arms, and with his plastered leg propped up on the coffee table. Jennifer did everything else.

Tony had managed to break Paul's leg but other than that everything else he had hit with the baseball bat was badly bruised but not broken, and after a week of bed rest and prescription drugs Paul was released from hospital feeling as though every part of his body was sore, but very happy to be alive.

By the end of the first evening he was feeling depressed and angry that someone who he thought was a friend could hurt him so badly that he couldn't even cook his own dinner or go upstairs so he could have a shower and sleep in his own bed. The hospital had given him a waterproof cover for his leg, and Jackie Martin gave him her shower stool which she had found invaluable while she was also coping with broken bones and plaster casts, and he would have been very happy to be able to sit in his shower for ages, in relative comfort. A bath was out of the question, he wasn't much of a bath person so he didn't mind missing out on that, but at that stage of his recovery he couldn't manage to climb the stairs using only one leg and his crutches while his hands and arms were so damaged.

Jennifer offered to stay in his spare bedroom upstairs, just in case he needed any assistance manoeuvring himself to and from the toilet during the night. There was no way Paul was going to ask for her help, but he certainly wasn't going to turn down the opportunity of sleeping in the same house with her.

Chapter 54

Tuesday 8th March, 10.00am

The following morning Paul was relieved to discover that his working life was going to be largely unaffected by the traumatic and disabling experience the previous week. He had conveniently built his house next to the auction rooms, so after Jennifer left for work, and with a huge amount of determination and courage, Paul was able to walk himself around to his office using the crutches he was rapidly finding were an essential part of him, although the damages inflicted to his arms and upper body meant his progress was very slow and he was sweating profusely by the time he had covered the distance in seven minutes which would normally take him less than forty five seconds.

Rebecca, Daniel, and the rest of the team had continued to run the business as normal while he was hospitalised, and he was grateful for their professional approach to their work. He loved the auction house, had grown up with it, learned from his father how to throw himself into it whilst managing some degree of work/life balance, and for Paul returning to a workplace which was as efficient and effective as when he left it was like winning first place in a triathlon.

Between them Rebecca and Daniel had successfully resolved most of the inevitable challenges which arose, but Rebecca put together a list of questions for Paul to answer on his return, so his first morning back was spent sitting behind his desk making telephone calls, answering emails, and sending directions to the warehouse.

He even managed to make everybody tea or coffee, although he needed someone else to carry his mug back to his desk for him.

By lunchtime he was shattered, and in danger of falling asleep at his desk. His leg was painful, his battered body was throbbing, and the thought of attempting to make it back to his house under his own steam made him want to throw-up. Daniel went round to Paul's house and collected the wheelchair Paul had refused to admit the hospital gave him but Jennifer told Rebecca where to find it when she phoned mid-morning to see if Paul had gone against doctors' orders and returned to work. He accepted Daniel's offer to push him home, and felt absolutely desolate.

When they arrived at his front door Paul was a little surprised to see a make-shift ramp was already in situ so Daniel was able to push him straight into his hallway. His mood lightened a little more when Daniel opened the door to his cloakroom and he saw that someone had rigged up a shower attachment to the sink taps, Jackie's shower stool was tucked under the sink, and a small paddling pool was standing upright along one wall. The sound of clattering on the oak floorboards in the hallway behind made him turn around and very slowly the ghost of a smile became a Cheshire Cat-style grin until finally he started to laugh. There were Suzy and Florence, the Bartlett Staffordshire Bull Terriers, standing with Lucy, Jennifer's greyhound. All three dogs were wearing back packs with various compartments filled with flasks for hot and cold drinks, and plastic boxes which Paul could see contained a variety of food items. Peering tentatively around the door to the sitting room were Christine, Sarah, Cliff and Jennifer.

'Phew! We thought you were going to have a hissy fit,' exclaimed Cliff, the relief in his voice clear to everyone listening.

'Oh guys this is wonderful! You can't have done all this in one morning?'

'No, everyone in The Ship Inn has been planning this since Monday when we knew what your injuries were and that you would be coming home,' said Jennifer as she came over and gave him a big hug and a kiss.

'But we knew what an ungrateful sod you can be so ...'

'No!' Jennifer interrupted Cliff with a mock glare. 'Remember we rehearsed this, Williamson. We know what a proud and determined man you are,' she corrected, turning back to Paul, 'so we thought it would be best for you to see what was possible, and what you think you may need help with. We have a rota of people who can pop in a couple of times during the day, and Lisa and Gemma are even donating their dogs so you can make yourself food and drink in the kitchen and they will carry it through to the sitting room where you can eat and drink comfortably. Although I wouldn't risk leaving any of that food in those back packs for longer than necessary, I'm afraid my dog is not so well-behaved as those two and she has already worked out not only how to pull the boxes from their back packs, but also how to remove the lids.'

Paul could feel his eyes welling up with tears, he didn't know whether to laugh or cry.

'Rebecca and I will both be here, present and correct, for a ten o'clock briefing every morning,' Daniel felt it was safe to contribute now that his boss was listening to his friends. He pushed Paul in his wheelchair through to the sitting room where Rebecca was setting up a temporary office on a hostess trolley.

'Is this what it means to be hot-desking?' quipped Paul, finally feeling some of his sense of humour showing up at last.

'Yes,' laughed Rebecca. 'Your phone and laptop will enable you to keep up with everything you want to, and Daniel or one of the others can bring you to the warehouse whenever you are needed. IF you are well enough.'

'These next few months are going to be really hard for you, and we all know you will want to be back on your feet and return to your previous level of fitness as soon as possible. But that won't happen if you push yourself too hard at this stage.' Paul knew that Christine was right, and that his friends only wanted to help, but it was still one of the most humiliating moments of his life. She walked around to his side and knelt down next to him. 'Paul, this is happening' she gestured to the plaster and the wheel chair and generally at his bruised and swollen face and body 'whether you want it to or not, so maybe the best thing will be to accept it, accept the help and support being offered to you, and get on with it. You have established a great team at the auction house, so maybe for the next few months you can take a back seat and enjoy reaping the benefits of the quality training you have given them.'

There was a knock on the door, and then Gemma appeared carrying a cardboard box.

'Delivery for Black!' she announced brightly.

As the rolls and cakes were distributed, and the kettle was put on to boil time and again, Paul's sitting room was filled with the noisy chatter of people relieved their efforts were received in the manner they were intended, and that even in his extremely disabled state Paul hadn't thrown them all out. Paul was feeling a little overwhelmed by the generosity of the people around him, and started to discover just how comfortable sitting on the sofa with your legs resting on a coffee table with cushions on it, and a greyhound tucked under your arm (how do they do that?) was. He sat quietly allowing the life force in the room ebb and flow around him.

Chapter 55

Wednesday 9th March, 6.30am

There had been a terrific storm during the night, and it was still raging when Cliff decided to abandon trying to sleep and reluctantly heaved himself out of bed and headed towards the shower. Today was the anniversary of the break-in to his antiques centre, and subsequent destruction of the stock, which had been the trigger for a series of life-changing events for him. Well, strictly speaking the night of the 8th/9th was the anniversary because that was when the damage had been done, and Cliff had gone to bed the night before with his mind in a turmoil over everything that had happened to him in the past year. The gales battering the windows of his flat above the antiques centre, and contributed to his restless night, and he was starting the day exhausted and mildly depressed.

By half past seven he was feeling a lot better. It is amazing how standing under a powerful stream of hot water and breathing in the soothing smells of shampoo and shower gel can boost a flagging mental attitude and tired body, and after he had eaten his porridge and drunk the first cup of coffee of the day he was in a much better frame of mind.

His mobile rang, and his mood improved even more when he saw that the caller was Rebecca.

'Hi Cliff, hope this isn't a bad time?

'No, no, of course not. Is everything alright with you? And with the kids?' he asked, suddenly concerned as to why his ex-wife would be phoning him this early in the morning.

'Yes we're all fine, thank you. I was just checking you are OK? Considering the date.'

'Oh thank you Rebecca! That is very sweet of you, but yes, I am fine. Or at least I think I am,' he laughed, 'I haven't checked everything is in order downstairs yet.'

'Oh, I think you would have heard something if anyone had been down there this time,' Rebecca was laughing too, relieved to hear that Cliff was in better spirits than she had expected him to be. 'Who is working with you today?'

'Everyone is in today. Nicola and Des will be running the centre for most of the day, and Barry is coming with me to do a couple of house calls.'

'Good, I am glad you are going to be busy. Hang on, Charlotte wants a quick word with you.'

While Cliff listened to his daughter enthusiastically telling him about her success at a swimming competition the night before, he reflected on how much he missed having somebody to check up on him in person; somebody who could have kept him company last night while his thoughts were whirling at the same speed as the wind outside. And he regretted not appreciating it when he had that someone, Rebecca, for over eighteen years.

Rebecca mentally ticked Cliff off her list of things to do that day. She knew how deeply he would be affected by the anniversary, and wanted to check he was going to have people around him all day to keep him focused on other things. Although knowing the town of Woodford as she did, and the customers of the antiques centre, she was sure the subject would be the main topic of conversation.

Once the three children were all out of the house and on their way to school she tidied away the breakfast things, checked the fridge and larder to make sure she had everything she needed to make a chicken curry for their dinner that evening, and went upstairs to shower and dress for work.

Rebecca loved the daily routine of getting ready for work. In fact, she reflected as she styled her now slightly shorter hair, she loved her life. She would never wish to relive the devastating revelations about her marriage, but out of all of that heart-break had come a new sense of peace.

She thought back to Christine's clumsy attempt at match-making a few weeks earlier and wondered why she had been so offended. She knew Christine wasn't someone who believed you could only be fulfilled if you had a man, or woman, in your life, so why did she jump down Christine's throat when she suggested meeting up with Benjamin Francis? At the time Rebecca had blamed Christine for involving herself and other people in Rebecca's private affairs, but now she wondered if asking her to join Christine and her boyfriend Dave for a drink or two with an old school friend was really such a breach of trust?

After all, it would just be for a drink. Maybe two. In public. Wouldn't it?

Chapter 56

Thursday 10th March, 7.00pm

Christine had welcomed Rebecca's tentative enquiry about whether or not she was still in contact with Benjamin Francis with kid gloves. She had been mortified by Rebecca's reaction when she first suggested a meeting, and did not want to offend her friend any more, but was keen to see her leave her peculiarly weighted relationship with Cliff Williamson behind and start to find out how good life can be when you are with someone who loves you. Not that she was expecting any great fairytale ending between Rebecca and Benjamin - that would smack of a rebound relationship - but just to see Rebecca out in a social environment which did not involve her children or responsibility on a charity committee would be wonderful.

With Rebecca's permission Christine messaged Benjamin via facebook and they agreed to meet, as a foursome, in The Ship Inn at eight o'clock that Thursday evening. With an hour to go Rebecca was in a bit of a state. She had no idea what to wear! What do you wear for a casual drink with friends? She stared hopelessly at her clothes in her dressing room, and wondered if it was too late to cancel. She could claim one of the children wasn't feeling well. Although at fourteen, sixteen and seventeen it would have to be something fairly serious to justify her staying in the house. And knowing Christine she would suggest everyone came round to keep her company!

No, that wouldn't do. There had to be something here she could wear. All her clothes were either smart work clothes or sloppy casual clothes. Come on Rebecca, she said to herself, think! Channel Christine. If Christine were here what would she say? Actually no, Rebecca quickly had second thoughts about that idea. Christine would probably bring something from her own wardrobe for Rebecca to wear, and the pair of them had rather different ideas on that subject. She thought about phoning her mum, but discarded the thought almost as soon as it had formed because that would mean telling her she was going on a date. Only she wasn't going on a date. It was just a drink. With friends. One of whom she used to date.

Rebecca suddenly had a thought: what if Benjamin was married! If he was then surely his wife would be there too, and that would take all of the pressure of her. Or maybe he was gay? Didn't Christine say he was something big in the music business? But then Michael was a very good musician and he wasn't gay. Or at least she didn't think he was. A mother would know, wouldn't she? She was surprised to find she felt a little deflated at the thought of Benjamin being married or gay. Or both.

She glanced at her watch, an Omega quartz Cliff bought her years ago, and felt a fierce flash of panic sear her gut as she saw it was half past seven. She had been standing in here for half an hour! Good grief. Right. She gave herself a little pep talk, and then chose an outfit she would wear if she was going out to a fête committee meeting. Which reminded her, there were less than three months to the next Woodford Summer Fête. No time to think about that now. Make-up done in under two minutes, hair scooped up in a pretty clip, jeans, medium-heeled brown boots, cowl-neck honey-coloured cashmere jumper, long black coat, money, car keys, phone, house keys, shut front door, go.

Chapter 57

Thursday 10th March, 8.07pm

Rebecca was pleased to spot Christine and Dave as soon as she walked through the pub door, sitting on their own at a table next to the log fire, which was burning brightly to combat the miserable drizzly rain outside even though the temperature was relatively warm.

'Oh good, I am glad I got here before him. I nearly bottled out I was getting so nervous!'

'Hi, Rebecca! You look wonderful! You haven't changed a bit!' Rebecca jumped and felt her face burn with embarrassment as a man, who had to be Benjamin, put the tray of drinks he had been collecting from the bar down on the table and enveloped her in a big hug.

'Oh, hi, you too, er, um, Benjamin,' she stumbled backwards as she tried to extricate herself from his arms, and remove her coat, and sit down, all in one movement.

Wow.

He was gorgeous. Absolutely stunning. Rebecca felt her breath had been taken away. The sweet and charming boy had turned into a tall, handsome man with a twinkle in his eye, an easy smile, and with a body he clearly worked hard to keep fit.

Rebecca suddenly realised everyone was looking at her as though waiting for her to speak. Seeing her confusion Benjamin repeated his question.

'Rebecca? Can I get you a drink? What would you like?'

'Oh yes please,' she said, aware she was gushing and smiling too wide but seemingly unable to stop. 'Um, what are you drinking Christine?'

Christine was smiling at her friend's reaction to the sight of Benjamin, and almost didn't hear her question. 'Oh, a slimline tonic. I'm driving. I can give you a lift home if you want to have a couple of drinks Rebecca? We can sort out retrieving your car from here tomorrow if you like?'

Rebecca thought this was an excellent idea. She didn't drink very much, but right at that moment a large glass of red wine would be perfect.

'Thank you Christine, that would be very kind of you, yes please.' She turned back to look up at Benjamin, who was waiting patiently for her answer. 'Thank you Benjamin, I would love a glass of red please.'

While he was up at the bar ordering her drink Rebecca took the opportunity to quickly quiz Christine about all the things she wanted to know.

'Is he married?'

'No.'

'In a relationship with anyone?'

'No.'

'Gay?'

'No.'

'Why is he single?'

'Here you are, one glass of red. I ordered you a large one, and thought we could do with some crisps too.' Damn, was the man wearing stealth shoes or something?

Rebecca tried to subtly look down at his feet, but when she saw the size of them she involuntarily started to think about the rumoured correlation between the size of a man's feet and the .... 'Have you dropped something?' he asked, looking down at the floor.

Rebecca jumped and knocked over her wine glass. It smashed and the red wine flowed across the table and onto everyone else's laps. Only she was unscathed by the staining liquid. As they all tried to leap to their feet and escape the seemingly never-ending cascade from the table Rebecca also stood and tried to pull the table away from them, succeeding in digging a large piece of broken glass into her hand as she did. She snatched her hand up to see if any of the glass had become lodged in there, but there was so much blood she couldn't see any. It was hard to tell what was blood and what was wine. Her vision blurred, and she fainted.

Tom Higston was already on his way over to the table with roll of paper towels, a damp cloth and a dustpan and brush for the glass when he saw Rebecca keel over, and he called over his shoulder for Sarah to come and help. Dave Truckell was instantly by her side, checking her airways and taking the opportunity to thoroughly peer at her hand and twisting it this way and that as he checked for glass before she regained consciousness. As a teacher his first aid training was up-to-date, although this was the first time in his life he had ever had to use it. By the time Sarah appeared with the pub's First Aid box Rebecca was coming round and trying to sit up, but Dave wouldn't let her put her right hand down and she needed it to push herself off the ground.

'No, no,' said Sarah soothingly. 'Stay where you are while we clean this wound.'

Rebecca lay still while the mess she had created was cleaned up by other people, and her hand was quickly and efficiently cleaned and a pad was placed over the wound.

'You need to go and have this checked at the hospital Rebecca,' said Dave. 'We can't fix a bandage or plaster to it in case there is some glass in there.'

'Come on,' said Christine. 'Let's get you on your feet and I'll drive you up to Swanwick. No,' she said, turning to Dave and Benjamin as they prepared to come with them. 'You two stay here and finish, er,' as she saw their drinks had also gone over when Rebecca moved the table, and Tom had cleared all of the debris away 'order yourselves more drinks, and then take yourselves home. We'll be gone for the rest of the evening. Come on Rebecca. It's your turn at Swanwick A&E tonight!'

Chapter 58

Friday 11th March, 9.30am

Rebecca awkwardly unlocked the big gothic-style front door to Black's Auctions with her left-hand. As a right-handed person this was something she had never attempted to do before, and resolved that from now on she would master the art of doing everything she could do with her right hand with her left one. She thought back to her mother's fear in the hospital about not being able to clean her teeth, and felt badly for having pooh poohed her worries. At least Rebecca used an electric toothbrush, although even that had been tricky to turn on and then manipulate around her teeth as required.

Her right hand was swathed in bandages and tucked into a scarf which was looped around her neck. It was fortunate that Dave had insisted she went to have her hand checked for glass at the accident and emergency department because the nurse had removed three broken pieces. It was well after midnight by the time she and Christine arrived back at Rebecca's home, and they stayed up talking over cups of tea and slices of buttered toast for another couple of hours.

Rebecca could not stop talking about Benjamin. Even though she had seen him for less than five minutes, and hadn't stayed long enough to hold a conversation with him, she was smitten. At first Christine had assumed it was shock which was giving Rebecca verbal diarrhoea all the way to the hospital, but after three hours when she was STILL going on about him, despite the pain she must have been in from the original accident and subsequent surgical procedures required to remove the embedded glass, Christine decided Rebecca was experiencing her first crush.

She had mentionitis.

Every subject Christine tried to steer them towards was turned back to Benjamin. By the time Christine eventually called it a night Rebecca had persuaded her to set her up with a facebook account, just so she could be 'Friends' with Benjamin. Rebecca had never felt the need to be on facebook, or any other social media platform, but once Christine created her profile Rebecca was astonished to find many of the people she interacted with on a daily or weekly basis were also on there, and she was engrossed in seeing all their updates and photographs.

But now Rebecca was regretting the lost hours of sleep, and her hand was throbbing. She had to ask her son Nicholas to drive her into work because she couldn't hold the steering wheel of her car. And now that the euphoria of being in the, albeit brief, company of a man who stimulated her senses so dramatically had worn off she was exhausted. And embarrassed. Twice he must have heard her talking about him. And then she tipped the wine he bought her all over him, and Christine, and Dave. And then she fainted at his feet. His feet. The pain shooting through her hand where she had absent-mindedly removed her arm from the fancy sling and picked up the kettle to fill it from the tap stopped that daydream in its tracks. As she blinked the automatically produced pain-response tears from her eyes she found herself smiling. There was poor Paul stuck at home with all of his broken and battered body parts, and there was her with a small cut to her hand feeling sorry for herself. There is always someone worse off than you, Rebecca Williamson, she chided.

Picking the kettle up with her left hand and then having to put it down again so she could turn the cold tap on, before picking it up and filling it, she focused her thoughts on the day ahead. With Paul out of the building, life at Black's Auctions had taken on a more professional air as his employees happily took the responsibility he usually carried on his shoulders onto theirs. Rebecca and Daniel would meet at a quarter to ten every morning and prepare themselves for a meeting with Paul in his cottage at ten o'clock, which usually lasted about twenty minutes as they checked what had been achieved the day before, what needed to be done that day, and chatted about anything else which was coming up that week and later in the month.

Daniel had started to train with Paul to take to the rostrum during some of the auctions, but he wasn't confident or competent enough to do all of them, and so they were employing a roving auctioneer who was very good at her job but didn't want to be tied to one place permanently. She had stepped in at short notice on the day after Tony's assault on Paul, and was happy to continue until Paul was able to take back the reins. They were organising a specialist Railwayana sale for Tuesday

22nd and Wednesday 23rd March by which time Paul was aiming to be back in charge, but as all of the items had been accepted and catalogued before Tony had temporarily incapacitated Paul there was no need to postpone the sale, even if Paul wasn't going to be healthy enough to run the auction.

As good as his staff were though, they didn't have his antiques expert eye, and so while Paul was more or less house-bound Rebecca was trying to organise for all of the house clearances and home visits to value stock to be booked for the middle of April onwards where possible. If someone needed their service urgently then either Cliff could step in and work with Daniel, or they would have to see that customer take their business elsewhere. When you run your own business the work still has to be done, whether you are there or not.

By the time Daniel appeared Rebecca had succeeded in making a pot of tea for them both, turned her computer on, and was checking the emails. She had sensibly decided to leave voicemails for Daniel to listen to and make handwritten notes about. He was curious when he saw her predicament, but because she told him very little about the circumstances surrounding her injury, he soon lost interest and the pair of them were able to present Paul with the usual comprehensive list of information he needed to keep the business running relatively smoothly.

Rebecca continued working hard for the rest of the day, resolutely refusing to allow her thoughts to stray towards Benjamin Francis, and only three times involuntarily cringed as unbidden memories from the night before flashed through her brain.

By four o'clock she was ready to go home. Her right hand was aching, as was her left from doing far more than it was used to. Her mum came in through the door just as Rebecca was finishing proof-reading a page in one of the upcoming auction catalogues.

'Hello darling,' Jackie said as she bent over and kissed her daughter on the top of her head. Poor you. Although it is nice for me to drive you around for a change!' she said brightly.

Rebecca laughed. Trust her mum to enjoy being the active capable one. 'Thanks for coming to collect me mum, I am nearly ready.'

Christine had fully briefed Jackie about the events of the previous night, and had made her promise not to mention anything to Rebecca until she was ready to talk about it. Jackie was used to keeping quiet about her daughter's business, but this was too exciting to keep to herself.

'So,' she said, casually, as Rebecca went around the office checking all the electric sockets were turned off, 'Christine tells me you two were meeting up with an old school-friend when all this drama took place?'

'Yes, that's right,' said Rebecca, knowing full well what was coming.

'That nice boy, Benjamin wasn't it? Who you were dating for a while?'

'That's him. I'm ready, shall we go? Come on, you go first, I'll lock up after you.' The auctions took place in the saleroom and warehouse, which had their own offices, so this part of the building was closed off to the general public, and any of the staff who needed access had their own keys.

As they walked around to where Jackie's car was parked she tried again.

'Are you going to be meeting up with him again?'

'I doubt it,' Rebecca really hoped this was not true, but she wasn't going to start discussing it with her mum.

'Oh? Why not?'

'I don't think I made a terribly good impression on him, mum.'

Jackie decided she had better leave the subject alone, because she had a nasty feeling if she continued to pursue it Rebecca would end up talking herself out of any possible future with Benjamin, whereas from what Christine had said at the moment Rebecca was very keen on seeing him again.

Chapter 59

Friday 11th March, 6.00pm

'I'll go!' Rebecca called up the stairs to let her children know they didn't need to come down and answer the door, knowing full well none of them would have stirred from their rooms anyway. She quickly glanced through the window as she passed to check who had rung the bell and stopped dead in her tracks.

Benjamin Francis was standing outside her house, with a bouquet of flowers!

Oh, god, what should she do?

What should she say? Apologise? Act as though nothing had happened? No, she could hardly do that. Throw her arms around him and give him a big snog? Yesssss, although having one arm in a sling would be a bit of a problem.

She opened the door to him.

'Benjamin! What a lovely surprise.'

'Hello Rebecca, these are for you,' he said as he stepped forward and tried to hand the bouquet over to her, but with only one free hand she couldn't take a good hold of the water-filled bag their stems were standing in, so he kept hold of them before another farce could play out. 'I'll carry them in for you, shall I?' he suggested, and Rebecca gratefully stepped aside and ushered him in through the door.

'The kitchen is this way,' she gestured. 'We can find a vase to put them in, although they do look very nice presented like this. Thank you ever so much, I don't know when was the last time anyone bought me flowers!'

'You are welcome. I came to see how you are? You didn't look terribly well when I last saw you!'

'Oh, no, I am so sorry. What a mess! Did you manage to get the red wine out of your clothes?'

'Probably,' he laughed. 'Dave and I tried to clean up in the gents, and then when I got home I just threw everything in the washing machine. It is all probably still in there. Well, it is still in there because I haven't taken it out, and mum won't do my laundry when I come home to see them.'

'I am sorry for spoiling your evening,' said Rebecca.

'Oh don't worry about that! You were very entertaining,' he said kindly. 'Dave and I stayed for a couple of pints. I haven't been out in Woodford for years, and don't really know anybody, so now I know Dave Truckell and Sarah Handley and Tom Higston, thanks to you.'

The noise of an elephant coming down the stairs made them both turn to look into the hallway, as Michael jumped down the last two steps and skidded on the tiled floor in his socks.

'Hello!' he said cheerily to Benjamin as he came into the kitchen and headed for the fridge. 'Do you want me to make dinner tonight Mum? I don't think you can do much like that,' he said nodding towards her hand.

'Yes please, thanks darling,' she said.

'Are you staying for dinner?' he asked Benjamin. 'I'm Michael, by the way.'

'Hello Michael-By-The-Way,' teased Benjamin, 'and I am Benjamin, an old school friend of your mum's. So you are the singer in the family?'

'Yes that's right, how did you know?'

'Your Aunty Christine told me all about you.'

'Oh she's not my aunt. We just call her Christine. But that was nice of her. Why did she tell you?'

'Oh, she thought I might be interested.'

By now Michael had taken various ingredients for filling tortilla wraps out of the fridge, and was arranging everything on the work surfaces. 'Are you staying for dinner?' he asked again.

Benjamin looked at Rebecca, who nodded.

'Yes, I am. Thank you.' He smiled shyly at Rebecca. He had always fancied her at school, and had been overjoyed when the opportunity finally came up to ask her out and she said yes. But he knew now he had been too reticent about keeping her attention, and it wasn't long before she had moved on. This time he felt as though he was being given a second chance, and he was damn well going to take it. 'What are you making?'

'Vegetable Tortillas!' announced Michael.

'Hmmh,' said Benjamin. 'I don't want to rain on your parade but your mother may have some difficulty getting those to her mouth.'

'Ha ha yes, I see your point!' laughed Michael. 'OK, how about vegetable curry Mum? I'll chop the veggies up so you can eat it all with a spoon or a fork in your left hand?'

'Perfect, thank you Michael,' Rebecca smiled fondly at her son, and hitched herself up onto one of the breakfast bar stools. She watched as Michael gave Benjamin various jobs to do, and the pair of them prepared the family's dinner together. Nicholas was out for the evening, but Charlotte soon appeared once cooking smells began to waft through the house. That evening Benjamin fitted into her family's way of life in a way Cliff never had. Rebecca allowed herself to enjoy it, and by the time the evening came to an end her first impressions the evening before had formed into stronger feelings.

She saw him to the door, they briefly kissed each other on the cheek, and then he was gone. But Rebecca had their next date to look forward too, and this time she was going to buy herself something new to wear.

Chapter 60

Thursday 24th March, 8.30pm

Rebecca wasn't the only woman in Woodford who was beginning to take a step out of her comfort zone and into the world of romance.

'One month ago today you were saving my life.'

Paul and Jennifer were snuggled up on his sofa, the open fire was chucking out more heat than they needed, and there was a film on the television neither of them had been watching. Their positions were extremely comfortable even though they had to take into account his leg which was hopefully healing well inside the plaster cast. Tony Cookson's actions a month before had jolted both Paul and Jennifer out of the unhealthy spirals they had both been uncomfortably living in.

As she sat, comfortably cuddled up next to Paul, with a smile on her face and love in her heart, Jennifer was thinking how much had changed in such a short space of time. Veterinary duties were still keeping her busy, but now she spent her non-working hours doing something other than worrying and fretting about her future. She and Paul were spending a lot of time together, and she marvelled at his strong spirit. He even inspired her to start exercising because she could clearly see how his core strength was helping him manoeuvre around the house in spite of his disabilities. She arranged with her father to organise their work schedules so she could join Jackie, Nicola and Sarah at their weekly Zumba sessions, and although she truly thought she would die after the first two songs, by the end of her first session she was smiling more than she had for months. Maybe even years.

With her new-found enthusiasm for life Jennifer finally started to prioritise, and one of the first things she did was to make time for horse riding, which ironically had fallen by the wayside once she started working as an equine veterinary surgeon. Her trial lesson at the local Western riding school had been thrilling, and she asked her sister Alison, a riding instructor, to be on the look out for a suitable horse to loan or buy. Over the past four months she visited a number of the local livery yards in her professional capacity, so had formed a clear idea of which one she wanted to keep her own horse in if a space became available.

Her father's plans for taking over Jackie's business were also finally exciting her with the possibilities for her own future. Instead of simply following orders and lists and keeping to appointment times and feeling as though she had no control over her working day, Jennifer realised she had an opportunity to form her own career. She could choose to be involved in an exciting new enterprise.

Almost everyone she met warned her to stay clear of Paul Black, even clients who barely knew her felt it was their duty to share their thoughts on the subject of her love-life. But for the time being she was happy to give him a chance. This was her life, and it was up to her to live it as she wanted to.

Jennifer was finally thinking that her future was very, very, bright!

Author's note

Vienna Cold Painted Bronzes

Bronze is an alloy made up of several elements, primarily copper and tin, and also aluminium, nickel and zinc. Brass is an alloy made up primarily of zinc and copper, and also similar elements to bronze, so you can see how difficult it could be to distinguish between the two.

Bronze was probably first discovered by man over six thousand years ago, and so began The Bronze Age when bronze replaced stone as the preferred material for tools and weapons. Antiques come in many shapes and sizes, and so there are plenty of bronze treasures in existence, but for the purposes of The Bronze Lady we are concentrating on nineteenth and twentieth century antique figures, mostly of European origin, cold painted, and measuring between 5cm-30cm tall. The figure which finally triggered Tony Cookson's downfall, the one bought by John Robson, was produced in the style of an Art Deco piece of erotica from brass, and this would have been perfectly legal if he had marketed it as such.

One of the most famous names associated with Vienna cold painted bronzes is Bergmann. Franz Bergmann opened a foundry in Vienna in the nineteenth century, and his son, Franz Xaver Bergmann, continued with the family business producing numerous cold painted bronzes of animals, oriental pieces, and erotic nudes which he signed B or Nam Greb. Cold painted means the figure was covered in several layers of a form of paint which didn't require firing, and this can no longer be replicated because the recipe for the paint has died out with the people who created those pieces.

Bronze is probably my favourite material for a statue or sculpture. It is such an inviting substance to touch and stroke, and I find it amazing that such a cold matter can be full of life force. Vienna cold painted bronze figures come in many different shapes, and are often in the form of people, dogs, foxes or bears, and of popular figures at the time, for example John Hoskin's The Trusty Servant. Because they are antique there is inevitable paint loss, and occasionally a missing walking stick or even foot!

Regular items seen in auctions or at antiques fairs are oriental bronzes and art deco female figures, but in my opinion nothing beats a life-size statue of a horse in bronze and you have to go to a private house or country estate to see one of those. I once went to a dinner party where there was a figure of a rolling horse, in bronze, outside the dining room window. Breath-taking. Can't remember whose house it was, though.

There are some stunning images of horses in bronze on public display, both modern and antique, including Thomas Thornycroft's bronze statue of Boadicea next to

Big Ben in London; the statue of the racehorse Best Mate, by Philip Blacker, at the Lockinge Estate in Wiltshire; Hamish Mackie's Goodman's Fields Horses, also in London; and of course the Triumphal Quadiga, otherwise known as The Horses of Saint Marks, in Venice.

Modern artists produce fantastic work in bronze, and one day these will be classed as antiques.

Devon artist Heather Jansch is particularly skilled in creating beautiful equestrian pieces. She is perhaps best known for her driftwood images, and the amount of work she puts into each piece is astounding. Her website www.heatherjansch.com details her bronze artwork and explains how they are developed.

Hamish Mackie, based in Wiltshire but travels around the globe for his research, produces stunning images of wildlife domestic animals, including horses. His website www.hamishmackie.com contains information about the process he follows to produce the bronze statues.

####

Thank you for reading The Bronze Lady, I do hope you enjoyed it! If so please leave a review on Amazon or Goodreads, or with your favourite retailer. For more information about me join us on the Kathy Morgan Facebook page and @KathyM2016 on twitter.

Thanks again,

Kathy

Made in the USA
Charleston, SC
24 June 2016